MW00427280

The HILLS of GOD

Eric Wiggin

HARVEST HOUSE PUBLISHERS
Eugene, Oregon 97402

THE HILLS OF GOD

Copyright © 1993 by Eric Wiggin
Published by Harvest House Publishers
Eugene, Oregon 97402

Library of Congress Cataloging-in-Publication Data

Wiggin, Eric E.
     The hills of God / Eric Wiggin.
         p.   cm.
     ISBN 1-56507-136-0
     1. World War, 1939–1945—Maine—Fiction.   I. Title.
PS3573.I383H55   1993
813'.54—dc20   93-10102
                                                                           CIP

Printed in the United States of America.

To

Rev. James Adams Sawyer
(1903–1986)

who, over many years, faithfully pastored Down East Maine churches of the era of The Hills of God. *As minister of the Albion Christian (Baptist) Church, in 1948 Pastor Sawyer led me to saving faith in Christ.*

Contents

The HILLS of GOD

1

September Morn

"*September morn,*" *the stranger murmured,* and his sad, sea-blue eyes seemed to lighten as he limped past. Was his voice a merry rumble or a threatening growl? Amy was uncertain.

The man's faded overalls were wet, worn through at the knees, and his flopping wading boots were streaked with muck. He was young, lanky, perhaps only ten years older than Amy. She had eyed him as he ambled directly toward her from his sudden appearance around the rocky point. He was of a kindly countenance, Amy decided, though grizzled and unshaven, with scraggly wisps of red curls dangling from under a slouch felt hat. A pronounced limp gave his gait an ogre-like aura as he struggled beneath his dripping hods of clams.

Amy's imagination suddenly caught a vision of a painting she'd once seen: a gossamer-shrouded angel rising from the sea mist on a foggy morning. It was titled "September Morn." Embarrassed at her vulnerability, she pulled her hand-knit sweater across the bodice of her nightgown and scurried off toward the path up the cliff and the safety of her new home.

❦ ❦ ❦

For at least the thousandth time that afternoon, Papa had bruised Amy's knees with the gearshift lever as the Model A coupe crawled over the interminable hills of remote coastal Maine. But the bruised knees and sticky August weather were minor hurts compared to Amy's bruised spirit at being torn from her beloved Lancaster County, with its smiling round faces, Pennsylvania-*Deutsch*-accented speech, and hex-decorated dairy barns.

"It's a lot of responsibility, but I believe you're ready for it," Lancaster County school superintendent Waarner had told her only a month earlier, when he had offered Amy a position teaching kindergarten. She would have replaced a college-educated woman who had suddenly left Comfort Primary School to take a job in a munitions factory at twice the pay. It was not often, even in 1942, that a young woman right out of high school was offered a teaching job, albeit a temporary one.

Amy had grasped at the chance greedily. "A few evening classes at the junior college, plus summer school," Papa had encouraged, "and your job will be secure. Lots of girls got into teaching that way when your mother and I were your age."

But with Papa pushed out of his Pennsylvania pastorate for opposing Roosevelt's war policies, that was all past. Amy's family needed her to help settle in to what portended to be a primitive lifestyle in Portugal, Maine, after the dozen years the family had resided in Comfort's First Baptist manse. After a trip to Portugal by train earlier that summer, Wes Andrews had reported to his family that Samoset Valley Chapel's parsonage, though spacious enough for his family of six, was heated by wood stoves, and the plumbing was limited to a hand pump by the kitchen sink. Instead of a bath, a path ran from the back porch to an outhouse by the garden, Papa had said.

Many a spring evening in 1942 Wes and Althea Andrews had discussed the events leading to his resignation. "I took my degree at a Baptist college because I believed that's where the Lord wanted me," Wes declared one evening. "For me, the die was cast when I went to that Baptist revival meeting with my cousin and dedicated my life to Christian service," he sighed.

The "clip-clop, clip-clop" of a trotting mare and the rattle of buggy wheels past the manse's open living room window that Saturday evening in June interrupted the couple's attempts to reconcile the heartache of the decision they had reached with their understanding of God's direction for the coming years. Wes had determined to resign after the evening service the next day to avoid a church split over his convictions as a conscientious objector. Wisely, he had not preached this doctrine, strange to Baptist ears, from his pulpit. Merely mentioning it in a private counseling session had aroused the zeal of half a dozen key families in his 200-member congregation. Pastor Andrews was faced with defending his position from the pulpit—or resigning. Even his appearance as a chaplain in his World War I uniform to pray at Comfort's annual Memorial Day parade had failed to assuage a suspicion that Wes was unpatriotic.

Wes chuckled as the buggy full of plain-dressed, black-bonneted ladies and gray-bearded men clattered past, suddenly sensing that even the Lord has a sense of humor. "I don't drive a buggy, but I guess in some ways I'm still rooted to my family heritage."

"That's right. Your grandfather was Amish," Althea recalled.

"To the day he died! My father rented a horse and buggy to attend his own father's funeral, so not to offend the neighbors, though they knew he'd become a Mennonite and traded his driving horse for a touring car.

"When Mother's family, all German Lutherans, came to this country, there were no German-language Lutheran churches near where they settled," Wes continued. "They quickly made friends with their German-speaking Amish neighbors—a family with the unlikely English name of Andrews. After she and my father were married, they moved to another community. They tried half a dozen churches, but finally settled on the Mennonite church, since it was closest to Father's Amish heritage."

"Did your father ever accept your studying at a Baptist college?" Althea wanted to know.

"'Ve all haf der same heritage of justification by faith, both Baptists and Mennonites. Only forget not your roots, mine son,'" Wes lightly recalled his father's advice.

"There were several other Mennonites at Pilgrim College," Althea told Amy, who had slipped quietly into the room. "They got along fine, except for the debate about neckties."

"Oh, we had our dicussions late into the night about other things..."

"Tell me about the necktie debate, Papa," Amy urged.

"Your grandfather helped me solve that one. All the men at Pilgrim were required to wear ties to classes. But as you know, most Mennonites don't wear neckties. 'You haf no right to break der rules,' Father said. 'A tie iss not evil of itself. Das iss wrong only to wear one in pride. Vere's der pride in doing vot one iss told, ja?' Well, I wore a tie after that—plain black, of course!"

Amy laughed as she scooted her chair next to Papa's and placed her head on his knee. "And vere's der pride in staying here ven you're needed in Maine?" she asked softly, picking up on Papa's imitation of Grandpa Andrews' German accent. "I phoned Superintendent Waarner yesterday and told him I won't be taking the teaching job. I had planned to wait until your resignation was official to tell you, though."

Tears came to Mama's eyes. "Amy, we had hoped you would have a career here in teaching," she said.

Papa, deep in thought, only patted his daughter's head.

To tell the truth, by moving day Wes was ready for the challenge of missionary conditions in the isolated Maine community where they were headed. In his heart he felt he had grown too comfortable in lush, prosperous Lancaster County. An old college friend from Boston had sent Wes an article from the *New England Churchman* about the desperate social and spiritual needs in eastern Maine, in which tiny Portugal was highlighted. This article had mentioned that the nondenominational Seamiest Valley Chapel was "struggling ahead without a pastor."

So though half a dozen pulpits in eastern Pennsylvania asked him to candidate, Wes took it as the Lord's leading that a small but noisome knot of parishioners had demanded his resignation on the unfounded belief that as a pacifist he was unpatriotic. When the call had come from the church in Portugal, Wes hadn't hesitated to accept.

On top of his chapel pastorate, Wes Andrews would preside as the new principal of Portugal Grammar School. His responsibilities would include teaching grades seven and eight and coaching junior-high basketball—neither one a task he looked forward to with relish. It had been fifteen years since Wes had seen the inside of a classroom. Having reached his maturity at thirty, he had expected to spend the remainder of his years preaching and leading the flocks of God wherever he would be called to minister.

Wes had taken this teaching position out of necessity. In 1942, with so many young men trained as teachers off clearing the Pacific of Japanese submarines or chasing Desert Fox Rommel's forces out of Libya, a middle-aged minister with teaching experience found a ready market for his pedagogical talents, rusty as they were. And the poverty of rural Maine parishes in those days hard on the heels of the Great Depression made a second career needful for a man with two boys to enroll in a tuition academy and a third still in grammar school.

Burdened with the Andrews family, bag and baggage, the four-cylinder '29 Ford now agonized in the high-summer afternoon heat up the backside of the mountain which made the divide between Samoset Valley and the interior plateau. Wes tuned his harried ears to the uneven bark of the exhaust. This hill was no place to clean a fouled plug, he worried. A knot of frustration tightened in his stomach as he clutched and gunned the motor and rammed the shift lever ahead. If only he could get the old flivver to the crest of the hill, he'd pull off this gravel stretch of U.S. Route One and wire brush the carbon from plug number four.

The move to seaside Portugal, a tarnished and decaying jewel of a town set in New England landscape as rugged as the north shores of Scotland, and his upcoming responsibilities as principal, teacher, and pastor—these almost fully occupied his mind. But now the car threatened to leave his family beside the dusty road. The auto had broken an oil ring in the Berkshire Hills halfway across Massachusetts the previous afternoon and every thirty miles or so since then he'd had to clean the plug in the oil-pumping cylinder and slop a quart of Oilzum 30-weight into the crankcase. If this *were* really the last hill, he thought grimly, then perhaps the car would deign to chug with his weary family into Portugal.

It was the best of times and it was the worst of times for American families like the Andrews in the summer of '42. The dozen years of grueling hardship following the crash of '29 had ended. Work was plentiful again, though wages were still pitifully meager for family men with mouths to feed. But the war which FDR had promised would "nevah" draw American sons to fight on foreign soil had rudely come to American shores with the bombing of Pearl Harbor less than a year earlier. If this were a long war, even the Andrews' underage sons might be drawn into it.

Still, Wes could hope that Hitler's storm troopers might crack as quickly as did the Kaiser's Huns in '18 when Blackjack Pershing led American doughboys out of the trenches and across the fields of France. Wes Andrews had seen that "war to end all wars" from the perspective of a chaplain praying amidst the cries of dying soldiers, the rattle of machine guns and the clatter of tanks being his benediction. He now prayed fervently and daily that his sons might be spared this new horror.

Wes should have taken his father's advice before leaving Lancaster County's rolling, open farmland four days earlier, he considered remorsefully. Had he installed in the car the four-speed transmission from their old, one-ton truck, he'd at least have had a bulldog gear to growl the aging auto over the sharply pitched, pothole-filled road around Hogback Mountain at a walk. A walk, but any motion was more progress than they would make if the three cylinders still firing were not enough to top the grade.

Althea had been adamant that the family delay their trip for a day while Wes installed the truck gearbox her father-in-law offered. Wes, though, was inclined to "Trust the Lord to get us where He's called us."

"Andy and Jack, out and push!" commanded Althea now from her seat on the passenger side. Mrs. Andrews, whose talents tended more toward earthliness than her husband's, had a knack for knowing just when the old car needed assistance.

Two lanky teens tumbled from the rumble seat and hit the ground running, each with his hand on a fender step plate. As the auto sputtered over the top, the boys fell panting under a wind-blasted ridge pine while Wes undid the hood.

"Wessie, stand in the window and push those suitcases back into place," Althea ordered Wesley, Junior, the youngest son of the Reverend and Mrs. Wesley Spurgeon Andrews. "Amy and I will retie the ropes while you hold them down. We can't have all our worldly belongings strewn across this hillside now that we're only a few miles from our new home."

"Mama, you know better than to say 'all our belongings,'" objected Amy as she stood on the driver's side running board facing her mother across the car's roof. "Papa said our furniture and stuff should have been at the freight depot in Portugal two days ago. It'll be waiting for us when we get there, Lord willing."

"I'll know it's there when I see it on the depot loading dock," Mama answered with the smallest hint of a smile. The cool salt air from the sea dashing on the rocks far, far below had lifted even Althea's practical spirit this warm, late-summer afternoon.

Amy teasingly pushed Wessie from his perch on the window-sill, then she slid into the car under the wheel to await her father's direction to start the motor. At eighteen, tall, lean, and ashen blonde with blue eyes, she had inherited both her handsome father's looks and his easy humor. Confident and sure of herself, Amy sometimes exasperated her younger brothers by taking the wheel of the old coupe on family outings, sliding through the gears as nimbly as any man. "Shall I hit the starter, Papa," Amy called as Reverend Andrews finished working on the motor and snapped the hood back into place, "or will you and the boys need to push while I hold the clutch down?"

"Try the starter," Wes sighed, stepping clear and wiping the grease from his hands on an old rag.

Amy snapped the ignition on and hit the button on the floor beside the steering column. The still-hot motor spun easily enough, but it failed to fire. "Valves'r getting weak," Papa complained. "Leave the ignition on and put it in high. Boys'n I will push. Let her roll until the speedometer reaches twenty, then let the clutch out."

"Okay, Papa!" Amy, who had never driven without Papa beside her, was not unduly impressed by the importance of her position in the chain of events leading to restarting the old auto. Except for Wessie beside her, she was now alone in the car in this trip down the mountain. A momentary feeling of freedom engulfed Amy as she pointed the flying goose radiator-cap ornament down her side of the narrow stretch of gravel, surveying the panorama far below and letting her imagination run on the future that was here to be hers.

Little Portugal Harbor at the mouth of the Samoset River, far
below the struggling family on Hogback Mountain, lay like pol-
ished pewter in the summer sun. Just outside the harbor's breakwater of granite slabs, ribbons of white foam tossed on the
breezes of the open, blue Atlantic. A cluster of gray-shingled Cape
Cod houses, with a narrow strip of business-district red brick at
the waterfront, spread from both ends of a bridge on the river's
mouth. Amy could just make out where the proud little village's
Main Street formed a chevron with a rusty, green iron-skeleton
bridge at the tip of the vee, the west end threading out among
branching side streets to become the mountain road on which
she was now driving. The east branch of the town's central street
meandered off across low hills toward New Brunswick, Canada,
further up the coast. Stately above the rooftops, even surmount-
ing the maples and elms that lined the streets, Portugal's three
churches thrust their belfries and white spires heavenward
toward Him who is invisible.

But the farms along the river road leading back into the hills
fascinated Amy even more. She had grown up among the broad
acres of Lancaster County, dotted with their black-and-white
Holsteins, brown horses, and white or red barns. The barns here
were all gray shingled, Amy observed, smaller than in Pennsylvania, with their roll doors in the end rather than in the middle.

The Samoset Valley farms which spread out below the Andrews
family were patchworks fringed by walls of loose stone and
fences of cedar, garnished here and there with stately, vine-
entwined wineglass American elms with branches which balanced up and down in the summer breezes. Apple trees filled
many a fence corner, laden with red-ripening Wolf Rivers or still-
green Northern Spies. And Concord grapevines clambered over
south-facing arbors which harbored hives of honeybees nestled
along many a pasture wall. These small farms were populated by
tidy brown English Jerseys, a breed of kine more suited to butter-
and-cream production than the milk-producing Dutch Holsteins
grazing in rolling fields around their former home.

More curious than the distant, humble valley farmsteads,
though, a once-grand set of buildings caught Amy's eye, set into
the hillside at the base of the mountain just above the highway

she now traveled with her family. The crumbling slate roof of a high-posted, multi-chimnied Georgian mansion, connected by its ell, a long, narrow wing, to a cupola-surmounted, cavernous barn, seemed to state that here once dwelled a man of means, possibly a patriarch of Portugal's better years.

Papa and the boys had quit running awhile back, Amy now realized. Checking the center mirror, she noticed with concern that they were loping after her, Mama trotting far behind. The speedometer stood just at twenty, and the road had begun to pitch more steeply downhill. Amy released the clutch, and the car lurched as the motor caught. After the engine smoothed to a steady, four-cylindered idle, Amy slowed the old car to a stop.

"I'd better back up for Mama," Amy worried as Papa clambered in the passenger side.

"Don't!" panted Papa. "If you stall it, we'd have to start this process all over again! Wessie, hop into the rumble seat with your brothers," Papa said, swinging his feet onto the running board to let Amy's youngest brother squeeze past.

Amy frowned as she peered at the side mirror while watching Mama hurry after her family in the hot sun. Worry about a probable tongue-lashing from a tired Mama over her family's inconsideration at not telling her to join Amy and Wessie in the auto *before* the coast-start mingled with Amy's anticipation over what life in Portugal in the Samoset Valley by the sea held for her in the months and years ahead. Amy adjusted her barrettes and pushed stray strands of straight blonde hair from her cheeks while holding the foot brake as Papa helped Mama squeeze into the narrow car. Papa slammed the coupe's door as Amy released the brake and let the clutch out. "Keep it back to thirty," he admonished.

❦ ❦ ❦

Amy rolled off her springless cotton mattress next morning and groped sleepily but eagerly to her uncurtained window overlooking the sea. She had already pushed her grief over abandoning a career at its very threshold and giving up her Lancaster County friends to the back of her mind. The morning sun lifted her spirits as it melted the dreary night vapors from the harbor, and she was exuberant, eager to turn what had begun in sorrow and shock into a happy adventure.

The Andrews had found that their household goods, in keeping with Papa's optimistic prediction, had arrived ahead of them. Church members had hauled their bags, boxes, and bundles to the parsonage and installed some of the more obvious pieces of furniture in their places. The bedsteads, however, had been left standing unassembled against the walls, for, explained the Ladies' Aid Society's chairwoman, who came by the evening of their arrival with a pot of yellow-eye baked beans and a loaf of moist, dark brown bread of a variety neither Amy nor her parents had ever before tasted, "We thought it'd be foolish t' put all them beds t'gether, an' then you hafta take 'em down agin when you decided who was goin' t' sleep whay-ah."

So Amy found herself sleeping on a mattress with no bed that first night in Portugal, Maine, but she did not mind. The beds would be assembled soon enough.

It was broad daylight this grand summer morning as the sun shimmered in its glory across the sea from the east. The bleating of the bass foghorn on the breakwater's lighthouse had ceased; it had kept her awake for hours, the noise coming through the screen door in the dormer leading onto the roof of the back porch. Here a wooden deck had been installed, just wide enough to hold a couple of chairs. Onto this narrow deck Amy now strolled, breathing in the sea air mingled with the fragrance of the lavender morning glories winding up the wooden downspout clear to the eaves.

Since the fall of night, the harbor scene below the parsonage had been transformed in a way Amy could not quite explain. With the lifting of the fog, the islands far out in the Bay of Fundy now appeared.

In Pennsylvania, Amy knew, lakeside boats were kept anchored at the dock; or, if small rowboats, they were turned upside down on the beach. Here, Amy could see, some indeed were turned over far from the water, high on the sand. But the beach, which stretched at places at least 200 yards to the water, was littered with boats. Rowboats, double-prowed peapods, and even a number of rough-looking cabin boats which Amy took for small fishing vessels sat tilted crazily on the sand, where surely even a team of heavy work horses could only with difficulty drag them into the water. Strange people, these New England fishermen, Amy thought.

She reentered her bedroom, startled to spy Wessie sleeping soundly on a mattress next to hers. Then she remembered. She had a choice between giving all three brothers this room with a view, she taking the small room across the hall now shared by Andy and Jack, or sharing this room with young Wessie. "You and Andy'll both be grown and gone by the time Wessie needs his own room," Mama had stoutly defended this arrangement. Amy *did* want an ocean view, and she could see it would be selfish to protest Wessie's presence, so she had willingly agreed.

She now stared at the alarm clock ticking on the windowsill, then she peered outside again. It was only 5:15, yet it was broad daylight in Down East Maine. It would be more than an hour yet before the sun rose over Lancaster County, Amy knew.

She slipped a sweater over her nightgown, then padded in bare feet downstairs. Mama and Papa's snoring from the front bedroom assured Amy that they were still deep within the Land of Nod. Into the kitchen she went and onto the back porch. She followed the footpath to a rocky precipice where steppingstones led downward perhaps thirty feet among the largest, thorniest wild rose brambles she had ever seen. Three or four scratches and a small rip in her nightgown later, Amy's bare feet touched the sand of the sea for the first time in her nearly nineteen years. The salt water was still a long ways off, but she had time enough to hurry to the water's edge and return before her parents were up and about, she decided. No one was in sight in either direction along the beach, so Amy bravely strode ahead.

Halfway to a seaweed-shrouded boulder at the water's edge, the shoreline sand abruptly became black, ankle-deep muck, and Amy was forced to retreat. But a narrow estuary flowing beyond a rocky point on the side of the parsonage away from the village caught her eye, and she decided to investigate. Amy was determined to get her feet into the salt Atlantic, or a tributary, on her first morning in Maine.

She reached the estuary easily enough. Finding the water clear and the bottom firm and sandy, Amy hiked her gown above her knees and waded in. The chill shocked her—this was not the pleasant cool which flowed in Lancaster County's muddy creeks. But as soon as her legs numbed, Amy determined she'd return in her bathing suit that very afternoon to experience the thrills of an all-over swim in the icy North Atlantic.

As Amy returned around the outcropping of rock separating the beach below the parsonage from the estuary, she was surprised, looking seaward, to discover that the weed-covered boulder, which moments earlier had stood entirely above the water line on the mud flats, now had water lapping at its base. Then it dawned on her. The tide was coming in. The large, beached fishing boats would not need to be drawn to the water by horses—these were the same ones she had seen riding at anchor the evening before. The line of driftwood and drying seaweed high on the beach, Amy realized, was the high-tide line, and most of the mud and sand would by late morning be under the water of Samoset Harbor, and the boats would again bob on their anchor ropes.

But she was startled even more by a tall, lean, red-haired man in bib overalls and tattered plaid shirt, a felt hat, rumpled and stained, perched upon the back of a shock of curly locks. His rolled hip boots flopped as he limped toward her. In each hand he carried a large, wood-slatted half-round hod filled with clams, and over his shoulder on a strap was slung a long-tined, bent fork, obviously made for digging. He had apparently been digging clams beyond the rock out of sight, and his route away from the beach took him directly past the rocky point Amy was just rounding on her return to the path up to the garden—clad only in her nightgown and a short sweater.

"September morn," the stranger murmured.

2

The Blueberry Rakers

"*People like Orin Trask* ought t' be put in an institution."

"Why do you say that?" Eddie Bessey sat facing the women from the running board of Down East Canning Co.'s field truck. He coolly eyed Sally Skillin, waiting for her to defend her opinion of Amy's red-haired neighbor. Sally only dragged laconically on a Lucky Strike atop a rock among the blueberry harvest field crew on their nooning and said nothing.

Amy stopped mid-bite on her bologna sandwich. She was about to hear Eddie's opinion about her odd, reclusive neighbor, the man who had suddenly surprised her her first morning in Portugal. Something told her that Eddie's assessment might contain some nuggets of truth.

❦ ❦ ❦

A week had not passed since Amy and her family had arrived in Portugal when it became apparent that the Andrews' slender resources would run out before Papa got his first paycheck. The fifty dollars that Samoset Valley Chapel had sent to help the family move was gone before they reached Maine, and it would be mid-September before the Portugal Public School System cut its first payroll for the fall session.

21

BLUEBERRY RAKERS WANTED—TRUCK LEAVES 7:00 A.M. read
the hand-lettered sign nailed to the community bulletin board on
the front of K.K. Ketcham's Hardware & Feeds. Amy had driven
into the village to purchase an agateware cold-pack canner and
two boxes of rubber jar rings. Alice Metcalf had that morning left
two bushels of flat-podded green beans and two dozen old-
fashioned glass-lid Mason jars on the parsonage porch. "They're
Lowe's Champion, and they're at their best," Deacon Metcalf's
wife explained. "Now't the kids are grown, Willard an' I don't eat
so much as we use t'. You kin keep the jars fer next season."

Jars and beans. Mama was too practical not to interrupt her
unpacking to can them, Amy ruefully considered. But Mama's old
canner, badly chipped and patched, had been left in Lancaster
County. A new one was $2.95—but it was an investment which
could hardly be passed over even when money was scarce.

"What's blueberry raking?" Amy asked Karl Ketcham, honestly
curious.

"Why, that's stoop work fer Micmac Injuns, wimmen, an' kids,"
Mr. Ketcham remarked. "Down East Cannery pays half a cent a
pound fer harvestin' good fields; a cent fer poor, an' y' git t' take y'
last basket of the day hum t' can."

But what are blueberries? Amy wondered. Huckleberries grew
in Pennsylvania, as well as raspberries, blackberries, and cur-
rants. Embarrassed to admit how little she knew about this Maine
fruit, she asked no more.

When she was ready to leave, Amy found the Ford blocked in
by an old, two-ton, snub-nosed Mack truck loaded with women
and teens and backed up to the store's porch. *Down East Canning Co.* was lettered in faded gold on green doors. The driver, a
tall young man probably only a year or two older than she, was
muscular, square-jawed, and black-haired. The teens jumped or
swung onto the store's porch, but the driver handed down the
half-dozen ladies, housewives all, Amy guessed, with the cour-
tesy of a Virginia cavalier of days now gone with the wind.

"Thanks, Eddie," a pert, saucy blonde of perhaps twenty-three
remarked as he helped her down. The young woman wore a
wedding band, and it occurred to Amy that she was being overly
friendly with a younger man probably not her husband.

"You the champ today, Sally?"

"Yep," the blonde smiled. "Eight bucks, a little over. My old man's hours have bin a little slack lately, and he's goin' t' be glad t' see the money!"

"First crew member t' make ten dollars in a day I'm treatin' to a lobstuh supper at Whitcombs," he chuckled.

"See ya." Sally squeezed into an ancient Overland touring car with five others, and they bounced off in a cloud of dust.

"Eddie?" Amy stopped the driver as he was about to clamber back into the cab.

"Yeah, I'm Ed Bessey," the young man smiled and tipped his cap, "all-purpose flunky for Bessey's Down East Cannery, only scion, and heir to a vast estate. Meanwhile, I'm the hauler of water and hewer of wood for a crew of desperadoes. Can I help you?"

Amy was startled by the impromptu autobiography. "Well—I guess we've been introduced!" she laughed. "I'm Amy Andrews. My father is the new minister in town. Can . . . can someone really earn eight dollars a day raking blueberries?" Amy eyed several steel-tined devices like oversized dustpans with inverted handles jammed behind a board along the side of the truck. Tiny, match-head-size blue fruit were jammed between the tines of several of these rakes.

"So yoah the new preacher's kid?" Eddie's jovial tone said he intended to be friendly rather than insulting. "You kin earn eight bucks a day if y' tough an' fast," he continued. "Strong back, weak mind—plus a dilly of a sunburn the first day out. A lot of wimmen an' kids earn cash f' school clothes at this racket."

"What can I expect to make?" Amy pressed.

"Most of our girls make five or six; kids three or four, if they don't spend too much time at the watercooler."

"Hours?"

"Be here at seven. We knock off at three-thirty."

"That girl—Sally?—she earned more than a dollar an hour. That's better'n factory wages!"

"Yep," Eddie smiled as he climbed back into the cab. "Good livin' if ennyone could keep at it year round. 'Course you'd need a back like a willow limb."

Early the next morning, Amy chose a faded housedress, pulled on an old sweater against the chill of approaching fall, then packed herself a bologna sandwich. *I'm off to seek my fortune on the blueberry (huckleberry) barrens*, she scribbled on an old envelope. She hung her note from the warming oven around the stovepipe above the wood-fired Home Atlantic kitchen range. It would be easier to explain to Mama and Papa why she had taken this job doing field work after she had experienced a day in the fields, Amy gamely decided. She slipped out the front door for the walk to the village before her parents were out of bed.

"I ache in joints I never knew I had," Amy said late that afternoon as she snapped beans for supper. "Raking blueberries is quite an experience!"

"Raking—like with a garden rake?"

"No, no. A blueberry rake has tines, like a rake, but with a short handle—more like a big dustpan."

"Your back is as red as crabapples!" Althea exclaimed. "And no wonder—you work all stooped over."

The second day on the job the crew moved to a new field, a long hillside of thirty or so acres broken only by an occasional granite boulder as it sloped upward in a sea of blue toward the forest above the valley of the Samoset River. Not a weed or clump of bushes broke this fruited expanse. "Pick the berries clean with your rakes," Eddie admonished good-naturedly as he unwound balls of string to delineate the work areas for each crew member. "Every step you take before you pick in *this* field is enough berries crushed for a piece of pie!"

By nine-thirty, however, the crew was on a sit-down strike, except for Amy, two older women, and the three Micmac Indian migrant workers from New Brunswick. The pay scale had been cut from a penny to half a penny by the move to the better field, and within minutes most work was at a standstill. Even the older workers had struck by ten.

Amy was amazed at the speed at which the virulence of the raking crew exploded into a strike. Just beneath the surface of most of these field hands, it appeared, lay the prideful, angry attitude of "us versus them" which caused many workers to cast aside even self-interest and seek conflict rather than compromise. Quietly, Amy spoke to Maddie Harding, a tanned, graying woman of compact stature and indeterminate age. "What can be done, Maddie?" she asked. "Nobody gets paid if we don't work."

"The comp'ny ain't goin' t' let 'em rot on the bush," Maddie replied. "They'll come across with an offer by tomorrow."

"What does the crew want? What's a fair price?"

"'T'aint the price. 'S the principle of the thing—t' hev our rate halved soon's we git inta good pickin'. But I'd say three-quarters of a cent would put 'em to work. Nobuddy's goin' t' tell Eddie that, though. His ol' man owns the cannery, so he's seen as a big bug, jes' like his pa."

Without another word, Amy climbed atop a rock. "Hey, everybody!"

The pickers quit grumbling and looked at the upstart at once.

"Can we work for three-quarters of a cent—split the difference?"

"Let Mr. Lloyd Bessey drive out here in his fancy LaSalle and offer it—we'll work," said one.

"Eddie kin make that decision, if he wants to. He's the boss' son," snarled another.

"You goin' t' ask him?" It was Sally Skillin speaking. She who had been happy to flirt with Eddie one day was surly and uncivil at the notion of asking his favor on another.

"Why not?" Amy was puzzled by the proud and unreasonable attitude of these people, but she pushed ahead with her determination to negotiate. She was perplexed, too, at Eddie's equally proud refusal to offer a compromise. But she jumped from the rock and hurried toward where Eddie was piling the morning's boxes of berries onto the truck. "Eddie?" Amy interrupted the shirtless man's angry labors.

"Yeah?"

"Are you in a position to make a decision on the pound rate for this field?" Amy was polite but firm in her query.

Eddie eyed her silently while he mopped his face with a bandanna. "Sure. If I can justify the rate for our bookkeeper."

"Three-quarters of a cent?"

"I'll go with that."

"Hey, everybody!" Amy raced toward where some of the crew were already gathering up their flannel shirts and sweaters to hitch a ride back to the village on the truck. "We get a raise—three-quarters!"

"That right, Eddie?" Maddie called without getting to her feet.

"That's right."

"Awright!" went up a cheer. The crew grabbed their baskets and rakes and hurried back to their rows.

❧ ❧ ❧

"Hey, Amy! Yer not an old lady ennymore! How come?" It was lunch time the day after Amy had been the ombudsman for the crew, and Sally Skillin sat atop a boulder next to the truck as Amy struggled toward the scales and winnowing machine, a rounded basket of blueberries weighing each sunburned arm.

"The jeans, you mean?" It was Amy's third day with the blueberry raking crew, and she had switched to denim trousers in conformity with the rest of the under-thirty women.

"Yeah—your dungarees. In that old dress you looked like you were born in the last century." Sally jerked her thumb toward Maddie and another fifty-something lady who *had* been born in the nineteenth century.

"'When in Rome, do as the Romans do,'" quipped Amy.

"I guess the Aimish down where you're from wear black dresses an' drive buggies," Sally observed. "Must be tough on their kids."

"It's Amish," Amy corrected pleasantly. "And they wear blue as well as black—but no dungarees, except on the men."

"Men!" Sally huffed. "They kin git away with ennything. Why, I got rigged out in a fancy full skirt and my only pair o' silk hose to go t' the dance las' Satiddy night. I ast my ol' man, Harry, when he was gettin' ready. Know what? He refused to wear a tie. I was lucky to get him into the wool slacks I'd jest pressed fer him!"

"Harry's the casual kind, eh?"

"Yeah." Sally took a drag on her cigarette. "Speaking o' men, aren't you nervous—living across the ruhd from that Trask guy, the cripple with the short leg that people say is crazy?" Sally tried to varnish her remarks about Orin Trask by prefixing "people say" to her criticism. "*I* think he's probably only feebleminded—and feebleminded people can't be held responsible for their actions."

"That's a rather negative assessment of my neighbor," Amy replied, suppressing her rising indignation. Orin had not seemed dangerous that morning on the beach, though their meeting had been brief and embarrassing, Amy considered. "He certainly is handicapped—anyone with eyes in his head can see that. But why do you call him feebleminded?"

"Well...he only went through fourth grade," Sally began to sound defensive.

"So did my grandmother—and she reads both English and German. Taught me how to speak the language. And she ran a coffee shop for fifteen years after my grandfather sold his milk cows. Kept her own books, too!"

"They say his grandfather was the richest man in Samoset County," Sally changed the subject. "Left a couple of million, but Orin's father couldn't hang onto it. When his grandmother dies, I suppose the court will appoint a guardian for him. Probably they'll move him out and tear that old place down. It's getting to be an eyesore, and old lady Trask won't part with a nickel f' paint an' shingles."

"Maybe she can't afford the repairs," Amy demurred.

"Maybe she can, maybe she can't," Sally sniffed. "They say Orin's old man usta spend money like he had Fort Knox under that mountain. Spent his last years loafin' all wintuh, then he'd try to make a year's pay all at once takin' tourists deep sea fishin'. He owned the best boat east o' Bar Harbor—a solid mahogany Chris Craft. My mom says he could o' had a good business iffen a few more tourists would only drive this far Down East. Giles Trask could sell iceboxes to Eskimos."

"What happened to his boat?" Amy asked, remembering having seen the ruined, roofless Trask boathouse from the Route One bridge across Sabbathday Brook, the mountain rivulet which divided the Trask beachfront from the waterfront along the parsonage backyard.

"Old man Bessey's got it."

"Eddie's father, Lloyd?" Amy shot a glance at Eddie on the truck's running board.

"Yep. Giles III lost it in a sour business deal." Sally seemed to relish telling about the Trasks' financial downfall. "Trask was in the cannery business with Bessey—Down East Canning was then Bessey & Trask Packing—but they say that Trask kept sellin'

Bessey interest in his share to pay for failed ventures until there warn't nuthin' left but IOU's. Then the boat went, just before he died. I've heard the boat was Bessey's years earlier, but he didn't claim possession 'cause it was the Trasks' only source of income."

"What . . . what are Orin and his grandmother living on now?" Amy couldn't help feeling for the old woman and her crippled grandson.

"Orin digs clams to sell to tourists. Keeps hens an' sells a few eggs. Then there's his so-called art."

"He's an artist?"

"Thinks he is," Sally laughed sarcastically. "Glues shells and rocks and moss onto driftwood. Paints on a few gulls, terns, or sandpipers. It fools the tourists. Guess they think stuff made by a looney is rilly swell!"

Amy took a bite from her sandwich and chewed awhile, trying to come up with a reply appropriate for Sally's narrow-minded rancor. In the three days Amy had known Sally, she had watched her continually shift between venomous spite and teasing flirtation.

Hearing no response, Sally continued. "People like Orin Trask ought t' be put in an institution," she asserted with seeming conviction.

Who'd care for his grandmother? was the unspoken question on Amy's tongue.

Eddie Bessey, listening with amused interest from his seat on the truck's running board, decided to enter the conversation. "Why do you say that?" Not receiving a reply, Eddie continued, "My mother hired Orin to tutor me in algebra when I was in high school. That seems to put him a few percentage points above the loons. I don't recall you gettin' straight A's at the academy, Sally."

🐦 🐦 🐦

"*You* ought t' be paying for this meal," Eddie joked. "I get paid eight dollars a day for teaming that ol' truck around and taking all the guff the field crew can dish out. Sally Skillin was shoah steamed when she learned she'd earned only nine dollars and sixty-five cents to your ten, fifteen."

"What's fifty cents between friends?" giggled Amy. "As for the lobster, a dollar fifty-nine makes it the costliest meal on the menu. I'd have been happy to settle for steak—it's only seventy-nine cents."

"Actually, it comes out of the company's petty cash," Eddie admitted.

"'Company,' as in Lloyd Bessey & Son?"

"Whatever." Eddie shrugged. "Bet you've never had lobster before."

"I've heard it's much like crab," Amy said. "I bought a can of crabmeat once for sandwiches, and I loved it. But on a bologna income, I can't splurge like that very often."

"Want t' know something?" A sly grin spread across Eddie's face. "I pretty much had my mind made up that if you tied with Sally in the race to break ten dollars, I'd weigh my thumb with your last basket of blueberries!"

"You wouldn't!"

Eddie shrugged. "Two wimmen at once is more'n I could take."

"I had you pegged for at least two—three or four, if you had enough arms to hang onto," Amy teased.

"*One* Sally Skillin is more'n I can take." Eddie rolled his eyes. "Actually I was relieved that you won. Sally's married, and it'd be like her t' use a dinnuh with me t' make Harry jealous."

Amy flushed, and she bit her tongue to keep from repeating one of the coquettish remarks she had heard pass Sally's pretty, sometimes profane lips. "How much of what Sally said about Orin Trask is true?" she turned to less personal matters.

"Let's see now—he's crazy, he's feebleminded, and if his father hadn't left him a farm, he and his grandmother would have starved, or at least be town paupers," Eddie counted off the facts about Orin on his fingers. "And another thing, he even spent a night in jail once, when the sheriff arrested him for digging clams at low tide in the light of the moon. Somebody called the law and said they feared he was diggin' a grave out theyuh, plannin' to murder Old Cora."

"You can't be serious," Amy sputtered. "It's not true!"

"Shoah is," Eddie chuckled. "And the sheriff now believes Orin's crazy."

"He's crazy for digging clams at night?" Amy was incredulous. "Even I know that one has to dig when the tide is out, whatever the time of day or night."

"Oh, not for digging. The sheriff locked him up pretty much t' please the neighbors." Eddie's eyes began to twinkle as he shared the now-famous story from Portugal's past. "But after takin' Orin home next mornin', he chewed 'em out good fer gettin' him outta bed." Eddie turned to the waitress, who just then arrived with two lobster dinners on a tray.

"Suppah's ready," she said, setting the tray on the table to unload it.

"That's one wicked good lobstuh," Eddie exulted, pointing at the larger one. "Give it to the pretty lady, here," he said.

"I like your style, Eddie," Amy remarked as the waitress left. "But you haven't finished telling me about Orin's arrest."

"Well, it seems that Orin and his grandmother are both pretty religious, though they've never gone to church since their congregation joined the Federated Union. I guess if I was a church goin' man, I'd hate t' see my church d'vided an' watered down like that. Folks say that at the Federated church you kin b'lieve most ennything an' still join up.

"Ennyways, the sheriff heard Orin prayin' in his cell for the Father to forgive the sheriff and the neighbor who complained, 'for they know not what they do'—the sort of thing Jesus said on Good Friday." Eddie paused to take a bite of lobster. "So the sheriff has jined those that think Orin's crazy. But I dunno. I think if I was religious, I might be inclined t' pray for people who threw me in jail for night clammin'," Eddie chuckled.

"I see." Amy joined in the laughter. "Tell me about the algebra. Did you make that up to squelch Sally?"

"Oh, I told it to shut 'er up. But it's true, all the same."

"But Sally said Orin quit after grade four."

"He did that! He came down with infantile paralysis, like President Franklin Roosevelt. But as soon as he could sit up, his father bought him school books, and they studied together. Orin even learned college-level advanced math—calculus, trigonometry, and a lot of theoretical stuff." Quietly he continued, "I have reason to know how smart Orin really is. My mother hired him for two full school years t' tutor me in algebra and geometry, so I got to see him twice a week.

"Giles III, Orin's father, was a mechanical engineer—an honor graduate of MIT," Eddie went on. "You see, he brought more into his partnership with my father than the Trask fortune."

"Then Sally Skillin *was* tellin' the truth about how Orin's father lost his money." The snide remarks Sally and the others had made about the Bessey wealth flitted through Amy's mind. She thought of the fancy boat that had once belonged to Giles Trask, Mr. Bessey's expensive LaSalle, and the red '39 Mercury which she and Eddie had driven to Whitcombs. "The Trask wealth has become the Bessey wealth?" Suddenly the huge lobster claw Amy had just split with a nutcracker didn't smell so sweet.

"Whoa, back!" protested Eddie. "No hasty conclusions, please!"

Amy felt her indignation rising, but she managed to restrain herself to a polite, "Go on."

"The Besseys are, as some folks put it, 'well off.' I guess that's nothing to be ashamed of." Eddie shifted in his chair. "Giles Trask was a brilliant engineer. He designed the hydroelectric dams on the Samoset River which have made what little industry this town has left possible—profitable, even."

"With the Besseys owning it!" Amy exclaimed.

"That's true, but..." Eddie searched for the right words. "The difference between my father and Giles is that Dad is a business-man, Giles was a gambler. If Dad hadn't stepped in and had an outside comptroller manage the books, the cannery and the sawmill would be in the hands of the Boston bankers. The bankers would have had the Trask estate, too. My father had Giles sign his house and land over to his mother and son—Cora and Orin—to protect the property from creditors who wanted to bleed him for money to pay for losses in joint ventures."

"Ventures?" Amy questioned. "I thought your father and Giles Trask were business partners."

"They were. And had Giles kept his money invested in the businesses they owned together, Dad and Orin would today both be wealthy." Eddie sighed. "But every six months or so Giles would sell a piece of his interest to Dad for cash to buy into a Colorado silver mine, an Alaska gold mine, or a ranch in Argen-tina. By 'n' by the only thing Giles had t' offer the business was his gee whiz as an engineer. And he drank so much that Dad often had to hire outside firms to finish what Giles had begun. Dad had to keep the deeds to Hogback Mountain and the Captain's mansion locked in his private safe until Giles died, else he'd 'a sold that, too."

"Who has the deeds now?"

"Cora Trask. Dad took them to her personally the day after her son's funeral. The estate is hern, free an' clear, just the way her husband would have wanted it."

"And while the Besseys were busy protecting the Trasks from their financial follies, they were spending their profits on nice autos!" As soon as the words were out, Amy realized, to her embarrassment, how accusatory they sounded.

"That Merc'," Eddie's good nature seemed undaunted by Amy's tone, "it cost me $1,400 this spring, $200 more'n it was sold fer new three years ago—wartime prices. And I earned every penny at fifty cents an hour—a dollar since I finished high school. Been saving fer it sence I was fifteen."

Amy's earlier indignation over the Besseys' prosperity while the Trasks lost their fortune was now assuaged as she recalled the unfair jealousy of the blueberry field hands. It occurred to her then that she shared some of the prejudices of the blueberry rakers against wealthy folks, even those who had earned their riches honestly by hard labor. "I guess...I guess it's sort o' like what a philosopher wrote about the burden a farmer's son bears who inherits his father's farm. Perhaps wealth drove Giles III to his drinking," she said softly.

"That's one quote I remember," chuckled Eddie. "It's one of Dad's favorites—from Henry David Thoreau. That's why my father made me earn my own wheels!"

"Well," Amy mused as she turned again to her lobster, "how little we know when we first form our opinions. I...I guess those rakers put you in a tight spot with their strike—right?"

"Hey, you got it. I couldn't fire 'em or we'd 'a' had no crew. Iffen I hadn't come up with a compromise t' satisfy the bookkeeper by nex' day, my ol' man'd bin on my case somethin' wicked."

3

Yankee School Marm

"*Hows 'bout puttin' yoah dottah* in t' r'place Miz Crommett."

Even Mama, ordinarily all-business, laughed at Papa's imitation of the Portugal School Board chairman's suggestion that Amy be hired as the fifth- and sixth-grade teacher to replace the elderly Mrs. Sadie Crommett, stricken with a stroke days before Portugal Grammar School opened in mid-September. According to Papa, Hezekiah "Hezzy" Willoughby had continued, "She's bin t' high school, ain't she? Time was, we hired district school teachuhs that'd only bin through grade eight."

"There's Amy's chance!" Althea hung up her dish towel and sat down with Wes and Amy. It was after ten in the evening, and Wes had just returned from an emergency school board meeting. Amy, who had stayed on Down East Company's crew to work as a factory hand in the cannery when the corn harvest replaced blueberries, had moments earlier come home from a fourteen-hour stretch standing at a moving belt picking over kernels.

"I *was* offered a teaching job before we left Pennsylvania," Amy agreed.

"I'm for it," Papa nodded his assent. "But you're going to have a tough row to hoe."

"Tougher than in Lancaster County?"

"For openers, you've got two grades to prepare for—and only three days to get ready. Mrs. Crommett is seventy-three, and she *did* begin teaching right after grade eight. That was—let's see—1887."

"Wow!" Amy remarked. "I'll bet she's an institution around here. That means..."

"That means that anyone born in Portugal since about 1877 has been her scholar!" Papa chuckled.

❦ ❦ ❦

"If she's kept under close supervision of a teacher with full credentials, we can grant her a one-year emergency permit," the certification officer in Augusta told Papa the next day on the phone. "You wouldn't believe how many of our teachers have joined 'Rosie the Riveter' building battleships at Bath Iron Works—pays better than a four-year teaching degree," moaned the man on the telephone. "We've got a batch of temporary certificates going out this afternoon. I'll add your daughter's to the pile."

"I'm leaving," Amy explained to the plant foreman that afternoon. "I've been offered a teaching job. The belt supervisor says she expects the work to be slack after supper, so if it's all right with you, I won't be returning for the night shift," she added, handing the surprised man her time card.

"You're...you're our best girl in the corn processing room," he stammered. "Can you come in Sattidays an' two or three nights a week? It's only till the middle o' October."

"I'm sorry. Thanks." Amy ducked past the boss and headed out into the afternoon shadows.

"Not so fast, lady!" Strong fingers grasped the sleeve of Amy's sweater. "You're ours fer the season!" The man relaxed his grip, and the grin told her he was teasing. It was Eddie. "Can I help you celebrate your new job over suppah at Whitcombs—steak, this time?"

In the chill of the fast-approaching fall, Eddie had put the top up on his convertible, and he and Amy wound among the pines and elms, following River Road from the cannery above the hydroelectric dam on the Samoset into the village. For some moments, Amy simply enjoyed the comfort and coziness of the closed car. Then in surprise, she said, "You've got a radio? I guess I didn't notice it the other evening."

"Ayuh! Nice one, too."

"My folks have never had a car with a radio. We're lucky even to have one in the living room," Amy wistfully admitted.

"See how it sounds." Eddie turned an ivory knob, and WABI, the powerful Bangor station which blanketed eastern Maine with its AM waves, came on. "Don't sit under the apple tree with anyone else but me" came in loud and clear without static, and for a few moments Amy was enthralled with the romance of being by herself in the sharpest car in Samoset Valley with the handsome son of Portugal's wealthy first citizen.

"This one's for the old soldiers who fought in the trenches of France in '18," the disk jockey chattered. "Over There," the tune that helped put Americans a quarter century earlier in a mood to fight Kaiser's army, switched Amy's mood from romantic to melancholy. "Was your dad in the First World War?" she asked at last.

"Yep. Yours?"

"Yes. Papa was a chaplain."

"So he didn't have to go where the bullets were flying?"

Amy sighed and bit her lip. It irritated her to have to point out that chaplains, who went into the trenches, were in just as much danger as the infantry men who carried guns. Not a few of Papa's fellow chaplains, she knew, awaited the resurrection beneath their white crosses in Flanders Fields. "Papa shot and killed a German soldier," she answered defensively. "Then he had to conduct the fellow's funeral because they couldn't find a German army chaplain."

"You're kidding!"

Why did I tell him that? Amy angrily asked herself. Papa, during his heart searching over being pushed out of his pastoral position at the First Baptist Church, had wrestled with his convictions as a conscientious objector. "Would it make any difference if I told these people that I once shot and killed a Hun?" he had asked Mama in anguish.

When Amy had heard those words from Papa, she had come within a hair's breadth of dropping the china gravy boat she was drying. Mama, reared a Baptist and not a conscientious objector, had replied evenly and firmly: "Wes, you have to answer to the Lord, not to these narrow-minded people. Do what's right. God puts even our lives' most shattered Humpty Dumpties back together when we follow our consciences and His Word—and He makes 'em stronger, too."

Eddie pulled the red Mercury up to the curb in front of Whitcombs just then. Thankful that he did not press for details, Amy climbed out without waiting for him to open her door.

Amy was finishing the last of her apple pie when the soft strains of the "Tennessee Waltz" floated on the evening air from several speakers wired to the jukebox. "C'mon, Amy—let's cut a few circles on the flagstones outside," Eddie suggested.

Amy looked long through the bay window behind their table. The couple who had fed the jukebox was dancing slow and close beneath the gnarled sweet apple tree at the edge of the harbor-side patio. A loudspeaker, protected from rain by an inverted galvanized bucket, did its tinny best to reproduce the violins and muted trombones of a Nashville orchestra.

The tide was high, and the roar of the rapids where the river met the harbor was now silent, the salt water having pushed back up into the fresh mountain current to stifle the sound. Far out, in the gathering dusk, the lighthouse had begun its incessant blinking: white-red-white-red-white-red. . . . Here and there a west-facing cottage window on a Bay of Fundy island glowed golden in the last rays of the sun setting over Hogback Mountain.

"I can't," Amy said at last, patting his sleeve. "I've been on my feet since seven this morning."

"You must be tired," Eddie agreed, not pressing the matter further. "Some other time?"

Amy's only reply was a smile.

Amy rode in silence most of the way home. Why did I lead him to believe that I was too tired to dance? Amy now asked herself. Andrews girls did not dance with boys—period. Not Amy, not her cousins in Pennsylvania, not most of the girls from her church in Portugal or the one she had left in Lancaster County. Amy's parents had taught her that many dances were a form of sexual temptation, public dance halls were seedy places where coarse people gathered, and drinking, necking—and worse—often went on in cars right in the parking lots of such places. Yet when faced with a powerful urge to please, sorting out what seemed innocent fun from the sordid and sullied had left Amy in consternation.

Amy knew that she *could* dance, of course. Many a time in the upper elementary grades she had held hands with a girl her age and twirled and whirled to "Way Down in Columbus, Georgia," or "Beer-Barrel Polka" from a scratchy record on the hand-cranked Victrola in her schoolroom after lunch.

But now there was Eddie Bessey. And now Amy was a woman. She must make her own choices. Papa and Mama trusted her to do so. Somehow Papa's decision to kill an enemy soldier came into sharper focus. Papa had had to violate his conscience in one matter to avoid violating his conscience in an even greater matter: His decision to kill the German had saved the life of a helpless friend. She found her mind aswirl with conflicting values and confusing choices; small, yes, but real conflicts all the same.

❦ ❦ ❦

"Miz Andrews," inquired fifth-grader Mayo Parmenter the second day of school, "why do you talk so funny?" Amy had finally got her nine sixth-graders settled down to work on fractions. Even though she had the aid of Maxine Chalmers, a brilliant, efficient eighth-grader who had been in high school math since last year, Amy was nervous about letting the older class work without her supervision. So Mayo's seemingly impudent question nearly evoked a sharp reply. Instead, a quick prayer resulted in brilliant illumination.

"That's a good question to begin our geography lesson on, Mayo. Class, open your books to the map of the Middle Atlantic States, on page thirty-seven," Amy pleasantly responded. "One of the interesting things about geography is that people *do* sound funny to folks from other regions of the country. I'm from southern Pennsylvania, and people from my section of Pennsylvania speak much differently than those only a few miles east in Philadelphia, who sound to us like New Yorkers—though Phillies would be insulted to be told this. And in the southwestern corner of my home state live folks who sound much like Southern mountaineers."

"Everybuddy in Maine sounds the same," Mayo stoutly asserted. "It's folks frum away that sound diff'runt."

"You might be surprised to learn that folks from up north in Maine's largest county, Aroostook, actually sound more like me than they do like you." Amy knew she was taking a chance on this assertion, since her experience with folks from "up-country" had been a brief acquaintance with two families in the blueberry field who had traveled to Samoset County to rake blueberries in the weeks before they were needed for the Aroostook County potato harvest.

"Naw. Yer makin' that up," Mayo protested.

"Miss Andrews is *right*!" stated Lyle Abbott. "I use t' live in Caribou, up in The County. When I go back to visit my grandparents, seems like I'm in another state."

"You see," Amy gently concluded, "speech patterns across America were set largely when this country was first settled, hundreds of years ago, by people from England and Scotland who brought various ways of speaking with them. Our speech has been modified by accents added over the years by Germans, Italians, and other immigrants, especially in New York. In the state of Mississippi, more than a thousand miles away, there are speakers who sound more like Samoset County than folks from Aroostook County, practically next door."

"But why?" Mayo was amazed and incredulous.

"What do you think, class?"

"Teacher!" It was Lyle. "Is it because people from the same part of England settled in Maine and Mississippi?"

"It's more complicated than that," Amy admitted. "But that's pretty close to what happened."

❦ ❦ ❦

"Wessie, what's this?" It was the Monday before Christmas, and Mama lifted a round, wooden object, newly painted black, from the mantel above the old, bricked-shut fireplace behind the wood-fired kitchen range in the parsonage kitchen. The disk, which Wessie had cut from a piece of maple stovewood the evening before, left behind a ring of paint the diameter of a baking powder can.

"That's m' puck, Ma."

"But you bought a new one at Ketcham's Hardware just last week."

"I know. Mayo Parmenter knocked it through the ice yesterday."

"But you said the ice on the millpond is two feet thick! Where were you boys playing hockey Saturday that you could lose a puck?" Althea was worried and indignant.

"Let me explain," interrupted Jack, looking up from lacing his boots beside the stove's firebox. "Wessie's right. The pond is safe. But the puck got away from the kids and went into the water where Bessey's crew is cutting ice to fill his icehouse."

"Icehouse?" Icehouses and iceboxes had been replaced by electric refrigerators in Lancaster County by the time she and Wes married. There, only the Amish used pond ice, and there were no Amish in Samoset Valley.

"You're still learning about Down-East ways, Mama," chuckled Amy, who was clearing the breakfast dishes. "First our wood range and outhouse, and now icehouses! Eddie says his father puts ice up in sawdust to supply several dozen farmers on back roads beyond the electric lines. He even supplies ice to Jake Milliken, who's got a route and a horse-drawn delivery wagon."

"Why... why, I've *seen* that ice wagon," Mama was incredulous, "if it's the one parked in a shed behind Bessey's sawmill. I saw it when I went over there last fall to buy your father some pine boards for new bookshelves. But that's an *antique!*"

"It *is* an antique," agreed Andy, who was struggling into his mackinaw. "But it's a working antique, all the same. Lloyd Bessey has hired Jack and me to help cut ice for a few days during Christmas vacation. When that's done, there are several village folks who need their woodpiles split. We've lined up enough work to keep us going Saturdays until spring."

Christmas vacation was bringing a welcome respite from the school routine for the entire Andrews family. Papa was glad to use his days off from teaching to visit parishioners in outlying farms before the snows of January made travel with his old car nearly impossible beyond the village. Amy had sent her fifth- and sixth-graders racing off to their skating or sledding a week before

Christmas. Andy and Jack had both found jobs with Lloyd Bessey, since several of the young men who usually worked on his ice crew had gone off to the South Pacific or North Africa, where the climate was warm and the war hot. Wessie, warned by newfound friends that by Christmas—New Year's at the latest—the mill-pond would be blanketed with snow too deep to shovel off for skating, spent his mornings with his pals knocking homemade pucks across the glassy surface. In the afternoons he split the family woodpile at a penny a junk—already he had learned, Maine fashion, to refer to a bolt of wood as a "junk."

And Amy, though like Papa she was relieved of teaching responsibilities, now took it on herself to help Mama make their century-old parsonage a home. There were still curtains to sew on the treadle-powered New Home sewing machine left behind by the previous minister's wife. The sitting room wanted papering ("needed" was the verb she'd have used in Pennsylvania). And several burlap bags of down plucked from the bellies of three dozen Barred Rock roosters hung from the woodshed rafters waiting to be stuffed into ticking for pillows. The Ladies' Aid Society had slaughtered and canned these cockerels in the fall to ensure that their new pastor and family would not suffer a meatless winter.

❧ ❧ ❧

"Give me a hand with this cylinder head, Jack." It was the day after New Year's 1943, and, having helped Papa rick the wood in the shed to make room for the Model A coupe, Jack and Andy—done with the ice-cutting crew for the season—stood ready to help Reverend Andrews get "up to his elbows in grease," as Mama tartly put it. Papa thumped along the edge of the Ford head with a hammer and wooden wedge, and the cast-iron engine head popped loose. Father and sons lifted the head clear of the radiator and sat it on the chopping block.

"Phew," Papa grunted, peering inside the engine with a flashlight, "not much to work with there." The cylinder walls, which had seen 180,000 miles, were worn oval. "All I can do is grind the valves and slap 'er back together. She'll burn oil like a pig, but at least we won't have to push-start her every morning."

By February, Papa had found himself with a problem more frustrating than a recalcitrant car. His eighth-graders had begun pre-algebra when school reconvened the second week of January. Within three weeks, Wes, who knew verb declensions and the wars of the Caesars, was stuck. He hadn't seen an algebra book in twenty-five years. Amy and Jack, like their father, were inclined more to the arts than to the sciences, and so they were of little help. Andy, however, had managed straight A's in math. He and Wes pored over the pre-algebra lessons evening after evening, and for several days Papa made enough progress to point out the nuances of "$X=5$; $Y=2$. Find the value of XY^2" to his eighth-graders.

The impasse was reached on St. Valentine's Day. Andy's talents were more practical than pedagogic, and he could only with difficulty understand why his father found algebra so incomprehensible. "You might as well be trying to explain why $E=MC^2$," Wes groused one evening, slapping the book shut in disgust.

"Papa," Amy interjected, "I think I know who can help. He's right across the road."

"Orin Trask?"

"He tutored Edward Bessey in high school algebra. Orin's father was an engineer."

"Well!" Papa was stunned. "I have heard that Giles Trask III was an MIT graduate. But I've been given the impression that Orin is...uh, slow."

"You haven't met him?" Amy was between teasing and pleading.

"Well...I've called on his grandmother a couple of times," Papa said. "She's a professing Christian, and I think she'd come to church, except that the Trask reputation—thanks to her son, Giles—has left her feeling that folks gossip about her and Orin. But Orin—he's been up on the mountain each time I've called, hauling firewood with his ox team. 'Twitchin' logs,' Cora Trask calls it."

"I hear he's very smart," Amy insisted.

"Well," Papa sighed, "perhaps I should ask for his assistance then."

The February evening when Amy heard Orin Trask's uneven tread on the porch steps, she quickly snatched up her briefcase full of uncorrected school papers and fled toward the stairs. She had been about to spread her work on the kitchen table, Papa having already occupied the other side with his. *Why am I running?* Amy asked herself, her heart pounding as the antique, worn stair treads creaked loudly beneath her feet. Several perfectly logical answers came to mind: With Orin and Papa discussing algebraic equations, she couldn't possibly get any work done. Orin, used to the company of only Grandmother Trask, would surely be uncomfortable in the presence of a young woman—wouldn't he? And the heft of her bag of papers urgently called her to get off by herself, light the oil stove, and grade papers like the furies!

Orin *had* given Amy a fright that August morn when they had suddenly and briefly encountered on the beach below the parsonage. Was it fright? Or some more subtle, not-fully-recognized emotion? She wasn't sure. Alone in her room, Amy found herself analyzing these feelings of six months earlier. She resisted the thoughts which crept into her mind yet she toyed with them, all the same.

Amy exchanged her sweater and wool skirt for flannel pajamas and a corduroy bathrobe. She peered at herself for some moments in the mirror on her dresser. *Pretty.* How often she'd heard that as a little girl. She straightened the lashes outlining her pale blue eyes, laughing at her own vanity. Were it not for mascara, I'd have no eyelashes at all, Amy mused, noting that the delicate, ash-blonde of her German-English heritage gave her hair a gossamer texture so light that, as a child, strangers had embarrassed her with comparisons to ethereal beings of the heavenlies. Suddenly disgusted at her own silly waste of time, Amy left off preening and turned to correcting papers.

❦ ❦ ❦

Reverend Andrews' ongoing acquaintance with Orin Trask solved not only his troubles with algebra, but the mystery of why folks round about Portugal thought Orin feebleminded. "That boy's his own worst enemy," Wes declared one evening in April. "Folks think he's slow, so he makes no attempt to prove otherwise."

"Papa," Amy objected, "doesn't the Bible say that 'Man looketh on the outward appearance'?"

"I wonder what implications that verse has for social conformity—or the lack thereof," Papa mused.

The ice had finally left the streams and brooks of the Valley of the Samoset on April Fools' Day. Along the edge of the millpond, among last year's cattails and this year's pussy willows, the peepers each evening sent their chorus down the valley, announcing to the Andrews family that spring, a full month behind Lancaster County, was indeed sprung.

Springing also was the sap in the veins of valley youth, and to Althea Andrews' consternation, her own teen boys joined as gleefully in local rites of spring as if they had been born in Portugal. "You boys fell in?" she exclaimed one Friday evening, when instead of hiking straight up the hill from their ride from Samoset Valley Classical Institute in East Portugal, they arrived late, soaking wet, and shivering beneath their jackets.

"Nah," Andy explained. "We dove in. It's part of the celebration kickoff." Andy's jovial manner made him Mama's favorite, and when he and Jack were in the soup kettle together, he would take the heat for both of them, usually waylaying Mama's wrath before the damage was made worse.

"*Dove* in? You went swimming in April! To celebrate what?" Mama's exasperation was clear.

"Sure," Andy smiled at his mother's reaction. "Half the high school was up to the millpond. We peeled down to our dungarees, jumped off the springboard, and swam out to the ice and back. Some of the girls, too. Redbeard the Pirate Week begins Monday."

"And I suppose you'll be flying the Jolly Roger from the town flagpole! You boys get into dry clothes before you catch cold."

"Aw, Ma, colds are caused by germs—or didn't they teach the germ theory of disease when you were in school?" Andy teased as he and Jack ran up to their room.

Amy had decided to use Redbeard the Pirate Week as an opportunity to impress upon her pupils the importance of their town's place in early America's history, but she was hardly prepared for what happened. "What's this? And who are you?" Lyle Abbott and Mayo Parmenter traipsed into Amy's classroom the Monday after

Amy's brothers had joined their high school friends in a Friday spring swim.

"I'm Redbeard, and I'm gonna be hung for makin' the men o' Portugal walk the plank." Lyle, Amy thought, appeared inordinately cheerful for a victim of an impending execution.

"And you're the hangman?" Mayo was dressed in white, except for a black, tricornered Colonial hat. Even his shoes had been plastered with ceiling whitewash.

"Nah. I'm the ghost of Captain Trask," Mayo exclaimed. "The same ghost that walks with his telescope in the cupola on top of the old Trask barn durin' Redbeard Week."

Though Lyle was hanged in paper nooses at every opportunity all day, Amy was unable to elicit one iota of sense from her class as to the connection between Redbeard and Captain Trask. She did, however, impart a fair amount of knowledge about regional history.

Amy had learned during a trip to the Portugal Public Library that in Colonial days, not only Indian raids but pirate raids were a menace to isolated villages along the North Atlantic coast. But in 1759, a group of English adventurers had settled on the mouth of the Samoset to engage in cod fishing and beaver fur trading.

Francis Magwitch, known in folklore as Redbeard, decided about that time that he needed a kingdom on Samoset Harbor as a land base for his tyrannical naval operations. His game was raiding coastal villages for women and supplies, and robbing hapless privateer merchant vessels. Redbeard moved against the two dozen fragile huts, quickly dispatching the men of Samoset by walking them off a plank into the harbor. He did the same with those wives and daughters who refused the amorous overtures of himself or his sailors. Those who cooperated were forced into fearful concubinage, and the Jolly Roger replaced the Union Jack atop a tall pine on Hogback Mountain.

But two girls escaped to Boston with their tales of terror. The British man-of-war *Somerset*, carrying more than 100 Redcoats, arrived next spring as soon as the harbor was clear of ice, and the soldiers rounded up Redbeard and as many of his renegades as they could catch in a nighttime raid. The legendary pirate and most of his men were hanged together on a single hawser, strung

across the Samoset River between two hemlocks, and their
bodies were left to feed the crows and gulls.

Amy's research also uncovered the next chapter in Portugal's
history. In 1787, Captain Giles Trask I arrived to take possession
of one square mile on Hogback Mountain as pay for services his
vessel had rendered General Washington in the Revolutionary
War. The good captain found a small, wretched, and wicked
settlement at the river's mouth, consisting primarily of the
descendants of three pirates who had escaped the wrath of the
Redcoats twenty-six years earlier by fleeing into the woods
behind the mountain with their reluctant wives.

Captain Trask put Portugal in order, not with musket and the
hangman's noose of the garrote, but with morality and the holy
news of the gospel. The Captain put several of the men of the
village to work on his clipper ship in the Far East trade. Then in
1807, at the hale age of sixty, Giles Trask the Elder took as his
bride a widow from the Adams family of Boston. He built for her
the mansion which now stands on the side of Hogback Mountain,
and a year afterward, sired the second Giles Trask.

Giles II obtained a commission to West Point. He served his
country in the Mexican War, and later as a minor general in the
War Between the States. In his father's footsteps, Giles II remained a bachelor until his retirement in modest fame. Then he
married Cora Chamberlain, daughter of Maine's Civil War hero,
General Joshua Chamberlain, and he returned to Portugal to
settle down as a gentleman farmer.

Fascinated with the reference to General Chamberlain as the
father of her neighbor, the aged Grandmother Trask, Amy fished
Maine Folks and Facts from the library shelf. Its index quickly
took her to several references to "Chamberlain, Joshua L." Next
to a photo of a handsome, handlebar-mustachioed, Roman-nosed
gentleman, it was written that Chamberlain had been governor
of Maine and president of Bowdoin College. As an officer he had
distinguished himself at Gettysburg as commander of Maine's
famous 20th Infantry.

Amy was startled to discover that this maternal great-grand-
sire of Orin Trask, General U.S. Grant's aide at the time, had
received the sword of surrender from Robert E. Lee at Appomatox

Court House! The implications of these facts took Amy's breath away. Orin, the reclusive young man ridiculed by the community and handicapped by polio, was actually the distillation of his state's greatest heritage.

The greatest chapter, perhaps, in the Trask history, though, concerned Captain Giles Trask I, and it was written after he had married and built his home, with its barn and cupola overlooking Fundy Bay, from which with a spyglass he could peer into Canadian waters and see almost to Nova Scotia. Amy found this only hinted at in a brief sketch of the old Captain's life, which referred to him as "Maine's Naval Hero of the War of 1812."

The librarian told Amy that for more information about the good Captain she would need to consult the archives of Portugal's waterfront seafaring museum, The China Tavern. "However," the librarian politely informed her, "this time o' yeah the Tavern is open by appointment only."

With a smile Amy thanked the librarian for her help. Wearied of her research, she trudged for home.

4

Jack Renounces Pacifism

"*You people will be juniors* and seniors next year," growled Harvey Ayers. "Paragraph juncture, spelling—what did you learn in ninth-grade English anyway?"

Ayers was one of the least-liked instructors at Samoset Valley Classical Institute. The papers he was returning to Jack Andrews' U.S. History I class in April had been turned in on Washington's Birthday. He had marked the assignments with a vengeance— red ink all the way. "If Ayers hadn't waited so long to grade our papers, he wouldn't need t' bury his embarrassment by takin' it out on us." Jack ignored the whispered comment by Cecil Tuttle in the seat behind him. Maybe Mr. Ayers was lax, Jack thought as he perused his A paper. But if Cec had given it an honest try, he wouldn't be beefing.

"One A," snarled Mr. Ayers. "Our Pennsylvania Dutch Boy did it again *without* the benefit of Portugal's fine schools." Jack's square German features and blue eyes inherited from his mother, and his straw-blond hair that had skipped a generation—Grandma Andrews had been a Dietrich born in the Old Country, and in her youth as blonde as the actress whose last name she shared—had earned him an unfair comparison with the boy on the paint can. That the "Dutch" in Lancaster County are actually *Deutsch* was an explanation lost on the Anglo-French sons of farmers, woodcutters, fishermen, and mill hands in Samoset Valley.

"The Dutch Boy gets the A, an' Ayers couldn't bring himself to give me even a C-minus if his life depended on it." Pierre "Pete" Pellitier crumpled his F paper into a wad and arced it into the wastebasket from across the room.

"If you'd been hittin' like that the other night, Pellitier, we'd 'a' beat Calais," chortled Myron "Moose" MacFarland. Moose was Pete's admirer and understudy in petty pranks. Skinny and mean, he was usually seen in Pete's shadow, even imitating his swagger.

Though surly when crossed, Pete Pellitier had learned that he didn't need to knock others around to get his way. Muscular from afternoons and weekends spent working a crosscut saw or stacking pulpwood, Pete didn't need to make a point with his fists to maintain his status as bull-of-the-school-corridors, and he knew it.

But Moose, though tough for his thin build, needed a strong leader to follow and a weakling (in his eyes) to slap around. What better target than the Dutch Boy? And since Jack's A had made Moose's hero look stupid, Moose found his own ego bruised, as well. But he'd take care of that later.

"I've talked with Miss Mitchell about this class," Ayers went on, bringing his students' attention back to the subject at hand. The elderly Miss Mitchell taught English, and though she was personally well-liked, her subject matter was politely despised by MacFarland, Pellitier, and pals.

"She and I will jointly grade the next assignment," Mr. Ayers continued. "Miss Mitchell will grade you closely on grammar and composition, and I shall grade on content. To sweeten the pot, Miss Mitchell has agreed to record your grade as a composition paper for this quarter—two grades for one paper. Several of you sorely need to bring your English grade up."

"Two more chances at an F," muttered Pete.

"Here's your topic." *Important Mariners of Maine Before the Civil War,* he wrote on the board. "Five to eight pages, typed or written in ink in a neat, legible hand."

Jack took up the challenge with his usual fervor, determined to get an A in both subjects. Getting *two* credits for one paper was an opportunity he would not miss.

Only a week earlier, Amy had run into a stone wall in her attempts to glean information about Portugal's most famous—

but all-but-forgotten—pre-Civil War mariner. "Why don't we go see the China Tavern Museum's curator?" Amy suggested when Jack told her about his assignment. "I'd like to see what they have in their files about Captain Trask, myself. Perhaps we can persuade Miss Wolcott to ride over with us and open the place up on Saturday morning."

After hours of research, Jack laboriously typed his paper on Papa's old L.C. Smith with its worn ribbon. "Here," he handed the paper to Amy. "See what you think. I kind of dramatized it to make it a little more interesting." He smiled.

"You did, eh?" Amy raised her eyebrows, then began to read.

Jack Andrews
U.S. History I
English Composition II

Giles Trask I,
Portugal's Hero of The War of 1812

"It's not our war, sir." Jack Haskell of Boston was polite but adamant. Captain Giles Trask sighed and wiped his mouth. The tall clock at the end of the dining room struck three, and the smoky whale oil lamp on the table of the Trask mansion's dining room sputtered on its last bit of fuel.

"Well, matey, you may be right," replied the older man at last. "But the sun will be up within the hour, and the tide turns at ten past four. The *Acadian* sails for Brazil with me as her skipper at first light, even if it's still foggy. Unless I miss my guess, the cannon we heard last night were from a British man-o'-war sending some hapless American schooner to the bottom of Fundy Bay. When I was your age, I fought many an English frigate to the finish in the War for Independence, and I shan't back down now!"

"Massachusetts is sending a delegation to the capitol in Washington asking that we sue the English Crown for peace." Frustration edged Jack Haskell's voice. "Let Napoleon and his French Empire have their little fight with England without us!"

"To think that our own revolution began in Massachusetts! What's happened to today's young people?" huffed Captain Trask. "I met the General Marquis de LaFayette when he came from France to aid General Washington. We needed France, then, in 1777, and they need us today. We're sailing through that blockade! If you want out of a fight, it's a long walk back to Boston. This tabby-padding around has got a lot of our Maine men talking about seceding from the Bay State!"

Captain Giles Trask was nearly 70 in 1813, but he was as tough as ever. More than this, he had experience in sea battles, and he was determined beyond persuasion. Trask had bought the sloop, *Acadian*, a packet vessel in the South American trade, after her owner, lacking nerve to brave the British blockade, had converted her to cod fishing. The old captain managed to salvage eight cannon from a derelict British man-of-war wrecked off Cape Ann, Massachusetts, and mounted them on the open main deck of the *Acadian*. Eight former U.S. Navy sailors, along with Lieutenant Jack Haskell, all seasoned under Captain Stephen Decatur in subduing the Barbary pirates off the coast of Africa, answered Trask's advertisement in the *Boston Post* for sailors who also could fight. Captain Trask gave them weeks of practice until his gunnery crew was among the most accomplished in the North Atlantic. But Lieutenant Haskell, though willing enough to fight Moorish pirates in the Mediterranean, was having second thoughts about battling King George's Royal Navy in the Gulf of Maine.

"Eight guns'll take thirty-eight any day or night in the hands of practiced gunners," the Captain had boasted over coffee one evening in the China Tavern. And every soul in Portugal knew that Giles Trask was no idle braggart.

Since the blockade, the price of foreign merchandise in the young nation had doubled, then tripled. Yankee farmers and manufacturers found their products rotting or gathering dust in barns and warehouses, while their families languished for want of necessary goods. New England's mills sent workers home unpaid for want of spare parts from Europe to keep the looms clattering and spinning jennys whirling. To Captain Trask, this situation had become not merely a chance for a lucrative venture. To run the British blockade in the War of 1812 was his patriotic duty.

The *Acadian* weighed anchor in Portugal Harbor at exactly 4 A.M., July 4, 1813. The coast was still under heavy fog, but the channel between the shoals was marked with a red-painted bobber every 100 yards, so that a sailor leaning across the bow could make them out in the light of early dawn. Once in the open sea, the *Acadian* could sail by compass until the sun burst through the fog.

By half past four, the sloop had cleared the harbor, and she was tacking in a westerly breeze for the open Atlantic. Captain Trask had a sense of the imminent, so he had ordered his gunners to load and prepare for battle, though he could not account for his uneasiness. A greater danger, most sober sailors would have agreed, was collision with another vessel in the fog.

But Trask had ordered First Mate Haskell to put on all the sail the sloop's single mast would carry; and pleased with his mate's skill at sailing, the captain paced the deck, now and again stopping to peer into the haze through his spyglass. For some moments he had been trying to make out the coast, lest the *Acadian* run onto one of the many shoals running out from the rocky Maine coast.

"Captain!" Haskell grasped Trask's arm. "Nearly dead ahead—we'll just miss her to the right!" It was a frigate, riding high in the water, twice the size of the *Acadian*. She had two decks of guns below board, and several more mounted on the open main deck—at least two dozen to a side.

"Aye, she's British! I see the Union Jack."

"Shall I tell the men to fire if fired on, sir?"

"We'll fire on her first, the moment we are broadside."

"But sir," Haskell was astonished at the Captain's orders, "one volley from her guns point-blank, and our sloop will be kindling wood!"

"What time is it, matey?"

"Why, it's quarter to five, sir."

"Good." Captain Trask lowered his spyglass and calmly turned toward the Lieutenant. "We'll pass her on the right in about ten minutes. Tell the helmsman to bring our sloop close enough so that they can wash our deck with their slop buckets, if they choose! Most of their sailors are still in their hammocks—their gunners certainly are. Tell our starboard gunners to bring their guns around across our deck, and we'll give 'em a broadside from port with all eight cannons at once. We can load again as we tack and get a second volley through her at the waterline before these limeys are out of bed!"

"We'll fire first, then?" Lieutenant Haskell wanted to be sure there was no misunderstanding of this brash order.

"Aye, matey, aye. Congress declared war a year, June. 'Twould be a fool's game to let them fire first. Our only chance against a frigate is to poke holes enough at her waterline to swamp her bilge pumps before they can bring her about and get our range. Then we'll stand off out of range until they lower the lifeboats. We'll pick up their survivors and give 'em a pretty ride to the Boston jail!"

"I've seen the bulldog do the bull in before—or should I say the Maine lobster grab John Bull by the big toe. It's done, sir!"

It was Haskell who took charge of the starboard guns while Trask directed those on the larboard side, and the *Lionheart* had eight holes at the waterline before her morning watch could cry, "Ship ahoy!" Seconds later, at Jack Haskell's direction, the guns were reloaded and refired. Yet a third volley split the fog as the vessels parted in the morning mists.

The *Lionheart* did manage a single, lucky shot from a gun on her fantail, which passed harmlessly through the *Acadian's* sail. As Captain Trask had predicted, the fog lifted within the half hour, and by nightfall he landed his sloop in Boston with more than a hundred British sailors huddled under guard on deck as captives.

Captain Trask, a prudent man, attributed his conquest of the *Lionheart* at an hour when most of her gunners were still asleep in their hammocks more to an act of a merciful God (amazingly, there were no casualties on either ship) than to the skill and bravery of his crew. He made annual trips to Brazil without further incident until 1815, when the Battle of New Orleans set the British running with General Andrew Jackson on their heels.

Trask died in 1837, after seeing his son, Giles II, grow to manhood. His son's widow, Cora, still lives in the old Trask mansion on Hogback Mountain with her grandson, Orin, a bachelor of about 30.

🐞 🐞 🐞

Senior Alice Perkins, the student librarian at the academy, looked up from her desk and frowned. The Dutch Boy's books had landed on the floor twice in ten minutes, and she knew it was not his fault. Moose MacFarland was looping about the room, apparently with nothing in particular to do. "Moose, do you have something to study? If not, I'll have to ask you to leave." Moose was a junior, and because he had failed a grade, older than she. But Alice was unimpressed with his sulking and skulking.

"Awright awreddy," Moose muttered around an obscene wad of bubble gum. "I'm goin' t' my seat." He sat down, and Alice returned to her homework.

Crash! Alice came alert with a start. The Dutch Boy stood beside his toppled chair, his books on the floor. A glob of pink bubble gum was plastered in his hair. Moose stood an arm's length away, smirking. Alice thought she had never seen the Dutch Boy look so calm.

There was an inscrutable peace on Jack Andrews' face, a resolute earnestness that said he was ready to tackle an unpleasant task no matter what it cost him. His eyes did not narrow in hate, nor were they wide in fear. Had Alice the maturity to read such an expression, she'd have gone for help at once.

"Yer books'r on the floor, Dutchy. Whyn't y' pick 'em up?" Moose taunted.

Alice guessed Moose might be ready for a fight, and she guessed Jack would back down, as he had on past occasions. *Should I go for a teacher?* she wondered. She decided to stay.

Jack pushed the books aside with his foot while keeping his eyes on Myron. "You're afraid of me." His words were emotionless, flat.

"I knocked y' books off. Does that look like I'm afraid?" Moose chortled.

"Would you have done it with me watching—unless you had Pete to hold your hand?"

This is going to be war, Alice changed her mind. Jack's words, not his manner, were provocative. But now the excitement kept her riveted to her seat. Three girls who had been using encyclopedias had caught the spirit of the occasion and watched in hushed awe.

"I'm not afraid of you." But Moose sounded more like Mouse.

"Why don't you come over to our place on Shore Road after school? Andy and I have boxing gloves. You can show me what you're made of then." By now, Jack had become almost cordial. Slowly, he sat his chair upright. "Well?"

"You wan' t' fight? Les' fight now!" Moose clenched his fists. "Hit me, Dutchy!"

"Your move." Jack's voice had gone cold again and he pointed to his raised chin.

"I hit you awreddy when I put that gum in y' hair."

"I can't believe that, because I didn't see you, and you don't tell the truth. It could've been anyone in the library." Jack turned his head to look at Alice, but she evidently was not about to call for help. He held that pose for half a second.

"Smack!" Myron caught Jack across the cheek with the back of his hand.

Jack feinted with his left, and when Myron ducked he hit him in the face with a right haymaker. Muscles hardened from handling baled hay, stacking boxes of canned blueberries, wrestling cakes of ice, and splitting wood had uncoiled in that single swing, sparing no mercy. Jack's left came up, but there was nothing to strike. Moose was on the oiled maple floor, blood pouring from both nostrils and a split lip, tears streaming from both eyes.

"You should go to the basement and wash your face." Jack was compassionate now, but his sincerity was lost on Myron MacFarland.

"I'll get you yet, you ..."

"Please! Ladies are present." There was just a touch of teasing in Jack's voice now. Myron ran for the door.

"What's going on here?" It was Mr. Ayers, whom Alice had called after Myron had fallen.

"I'm picking these books up for Moose MacFarland, sir. He knocked 'em off and he wasn't able to stay around to pick them up." Jack was polite, even pleasant, but he had begun to shake.

Ayers eyed the blood drops trailing from the end of the library table and out the hall door. "We haven't had a fight in this building for years, Dutch Boy!"

"My name is Jack, sir," Jack said evenly. "I'd appreciate it if you'd use it."

"You're to wait in Mr. Stackpole's office. He'll see you and MacFarland when he's through his last class ... Mr. Jack Andrews!"

❦ ❦ ❦

"Don't take it so hard, Reverend," Russell Stackpole, the academy principal, comforted Wes Andrews that evening on the phone. "I'm phoning you because I think it's unfair to parents to be left hanging when their child is being disciplined. And, as I'm sure Jack has told you, he's not getting expelled, nor losing academic privileges. I'm sure he'll do a good job on the essay on school deportment which I assigned."

"Do you think I should ground him for a while?" Wes was unused to asking strangers for advice about child rearing.

"If he were my son, I wouldn't." Mr. Stackpole's voice was kind. "And I'm adding this as one educator to another; I trust you'll keep it under your hat. Young Mr. MacFarland has been pretty much of a bully around here for nearly three years. I'm rather glad it was your Jack he chose to pick on this year. And by the way, I don't think Mr. Ayers will be calling Jack 'Dutch Boy' again."

❦ ❦ ❦

"I thought I'd feel terribly guilty after slugging Myron, Pa. But it's more like a burden I've carried for months has suddenly fallen off." Jack passed his father a wheel wrench as Wes changed a flat tire in their driveway. "Myron was even joking with me in Mr. Stackpole's office while we were waiting for him to come and chew us out. We may even manage to be friends from now on."

"Sooner or later each man has to meet his Goliath—and choose to fight or run." Wes sighed. "I only wish I could've slain mine without a bolt-action rifle."

"In France, you mean?" Jack was awed by his father's candid reference to killing the German soldier.

"Yes. And there are times when I still must fight Goliath's ghost."

"I'd 'a' strewn MacFarland the length of the library, so's Mr. Ayers would o' needed a manure shovel to scrape him off the floor," admitted Andy, who had been quietly listening to his younger brother recount his conquest.

Papa silently stepped back with the flat tire. He admired his eldest son's bulging biceps as Andy hoisted the spare wheel onto the bare hub.

Hearing no reply, Andy continued, "You should have punched his lights out months ago, the first time he messed with you, Jack." Andy was his mother's son all the way: direct, take-the-bull-by-the-horns.

"What do you think Jesus would have done?" There was no trace of false piety in Reverend Andrews' question. His sincerity was respected by the scion who, independent thinker that Andy was, sometimes disagreed with his sire.

"You mentioned Goliath. David didn't sing psalms to him," Andy pointed out. "And he didn't throw paper wads—he used a rock on the first throw! When Jesus said we should 'turn the other cheek,' wasn't He referring to persecution for His sake? MacFarland is a common bully. Now't Jack's slapped him down, a lot of kids at the academy will thank him!"

"Honest men do differ on the application of that passage," affirmed Papa.

5

"Ask the Man Who Owns One"

"*Afternoon, Rev'rund.*" Merchant Charlie Farrington was an enigma to Amy. Though he had acknowledged Papa, Charlie had taken no note of her beyond a brief glance. Often gruff, seldom cheerful, but never obviously cross, the proprietor of Farrington's Groceries & Dry Goods seemed to Amy to fit Thoreau's image of a man who lives a "life of quiet desperation."

Farrington's store was a comfortable living, Amy guessed. But storekeeping apparently offered little challenge in an out-of-the-way community of settled habits and slow competition. It was hardly an occupation to inspire a man to consider his purpose in life, Papa had once remarked. Amy peered down the long aisles where walls and shelves hadn't seen paint since the last century, and nickel-plated antique oil chandeliers had been left in place when they were supplanted by bare electric bulbs just after the First World War. Dismal dilapidation? New England frugality? She was unsure how to assess it.

"Good afternoon, Charlie," Wes greeted the poker-faced grocer with the Basset eyes. "Hi, Mr. Farrington," Amy chimed in. Two days of April showers had given way to sunshine, and it was Friday. Amy and Papa had left their weekly cares at Portugal Grammar School, and they were happily anticipating an evening at home.

Amy briefly checked the shopping list Mama had handed her on the way out in the morning: *25 lbs. Pillsbury's Best, lb. split peas, and lb. bak. pwdr.* was scribbled on the back of an envelope. She went for the flour and soon plunked the sack on the counter next to the cash register. As they waited for Charlie Farrington to fetch the smaller items from a high shelf with his long-handled grabber, Papa reached inside the jacket of his rumpled corduroy suit coat for his checkbook. Papa was out of cash, and he needed to get a couple of dollars over for gas at Ed Norton's Flying A Gasoline. Ed didn't trust checks, even from preachers.

"I seem to have left my checkbook in my other suit, Amy. Do you have any money?"

"A quarter, Papa." Amy shook her head.

Their purchases totaled three dollars, all told. Wes eyed the green metal cabinet where Charlie kept dozens of receipt books of accounts, then he glanced at Amy. "Can you set it down, Charlie? I'll settle with you Monday."

"I've got a five-dollar limit on new accounts, and they must be paid off weekly," Charlie explained, going on to tell them how his wholesale suppliers had to be paid on time, and that he had an electric bill, heat, taxes, and repairs to pay for before he could even claim a profit.

Why is he giving us the whole rigamarole about credit buying, for Pete's sake? Amy asked herself, amazed at the merchant's insistence on rattling off such a ridiculously long speech as a prelude to granting Papa seventy-two hours to pay a three-dollar charge.

"An' I know this's no business o' yourn, or per'aps it is, sence yoah the new ministuh at the chapel," Charlie added. "I got an unpaid account left by y' pree-decessuh. Ast yoah deacon, Mistuh Metcalf, about it, en he said t'warn't the church's bill. Preachus are independent and self-employed n' responsible fer theyah own debts, he sez."

"How much is it?" Papa asked.

"Thirty-seven dolluhs an' seventy-three cents. Las' payment was, lessee, April 23, 1942—jes' 'bout a yeah ago. Las' chawg was May 30—two loaves of sandwich bread and a jar of Grandee Olive Butter, day before he left town."

Amy felt her ears begin to burn as Papa asked, "Please make me a copy of that, showing those two dates and the final balance. Can you copy it onto a page of a receipt book?"

"Ayuh."

"What will you do with Pastor Small's old account, Papa?" Amy asked as they drove home on the gallon of gas she bought with her quarter.

"We've got his address in the church files. It'll only cost a three-cent stamp to mail it. Perhaps I'd better find out who else he may owe, if it can be done discreetly."

Wes paid off his own charge at Farrington's right after school on Monday. At Ketcham's Hardware he and Amy learned that a bill for new stove grates and several gallons of paint for the parsonage had gone unpaid for six months, then Mr. Ketcham had sent it to the church. The account had then been promptly paid, and Ketcham seemed satisfied. But what kind of financial relationships did Mr. Small have with the church to need to charge parsonage repairs in his own name? Amy wondered, listening to Papa and Karl Ketcham discuss the account.

At Norton's Flying A, they found a $5.70 charge left unpaid by Reverend Small. Papa paid it at once out of his own pocket. "Showah nice t' see how you Christians take cayah o' one another," Ed Norton remarked, nodding at Amy.

"I'm glad that one local businessman, at least, has a positive view of our church," Papa said as they drove away.

Doctor Abbott's office was a different story altogether. The doctor's receptionist confirmed that Pastor Small had left a substantial bill. "His kids were sick all the time, seems like. I'll haf t' ask the doctuh," she said, when Papa inquired about making arrangements to pay the bill off.

Doctor Abbott, friendly enough when the Andrews family had required his medical attention, was virtually livid at what he termed, "An audacious request to examine another person's account."

"I'm sorry, Doctor, I thought . . . ." Amy had never seen Papa lose his composure so.

"I wrote it off as a bad debt at tax time," he snarled. "Now I have a waiting room full of patients!"

"Well, thank you for your time." Amy managed to smile at the doctor as Papa put his hat on.

Portugal's road repair crew had just graded the spring pot-holes and washboards smooth along Route One, they discovered as Papa pointed the Model A's flying goose radiator ornament down the straight, level mile southward from the village before the road began to climb Hogback Mountain toward the par-sonage and the Trask mansion. Thirty-five—the speed limit! Papa hadn't driven so fast all winter. To tell the truth, he not only was grieved that his predecessor's, and the church's, financial dealings had hurt the testimony of God's people in Portugal, but Wes was boiling over Doctor Abbott's having treated them so rudely as well.

They soon overtook a truckload of hay lumbering along. "Last year's hay—moldy stuff, hardly worth the gas to haul it home," was Papa's curt appraisal as he waited for a car coming the other way. He floored the throttle, and the Ford's four pistons pumped with unaccustomed power.

"That valve job you and Jack gave the motor after Christmas has given this car quite a kick, Papa!" Amy hoped a cheerful comment would take his mind off their dismaying dealings with the creditors of Reverend Small.

The Model A shot ahead, and quickly they were clear of the truck. Papa wheeled their vehicle back to the right side of the road, and at the same time he took his foot off the gas. The Model A backfired, sputtered, and stalled. Papa kicked the clutch down, then hit the starter with his toe. The engine spun, but it would not fire. "Dear Lord," he cried, as they coasted onto the shoulder.

Was Papa swearing or praying? Amy hoped it was the latter.

❦ ❦ ❦

"She's jumped 'er timin'" was Ed Norton's assessment of the Model A coupe, after his Flying A wrecker had pulled the Ford in on its hook on Monday.

"Worth fixing?" Papa inquired. He and Amy had walked over from the grammar school after classes.

Ed shrugged. "'S an old car. But with the war on, most enny-thing's worth fixin' if it'll get y' there an' back."

"How much?"

"Thirty-five dollars if I kin buy the pahts right. If I kin hev a new timin' chain sent outta Bangor on the Thursday train, we'll hev y' fixed up by suppah time Friday." Ed looked at his watch. "I kin send the order off Western Union telegram today, yet, ef you say."

"I'll talk with my wife."

"Papa, I've got enough in my savings," Amy volunteered.

"That's your college fund," Papa objected. "Besides, we've got to decide if the car is worth it. The rings are bad, and when I looked into the engine to do the valves, I could see it needed reboring."

"Ayuh," Ed nodded. "Suit yourself. Just help me push 'er off t' one side."

For the next two days, which thankfully were fair weather, the Andrews family walked back and forth to the village, except when given rides by helpful neighbors. By Wednesday afternoon, Wes had all but decided to add five dollars a week to their already overburdened budget, if Mr. Norton would agree to carry him on the books until the bill was paid off. The Ford hadn't been worth more than thirty-five dollars in 1941, but since Pearl Harbor, it was worth whatever a motorist was willing to pay. And Norton was right: There were no used cars to be had in Portugal, and though one *might* be found in Bangor, the price would be exorbitant.

❦ ❦ ❦

"Our family needs the Lord's direction about a car," Amy told the ladies in her prayer group simply at prayer meeting Wednesday evening. She knew that neither Mama nor Papa would say anything that might sound like asking the church for help.

A temporary answer came at once. "My Allen won't be using his truck much until hayin', but he's kept it licensed t' haul wood this wintuh," Gladys Keay remarked after they had prayed. "If Mr. Andrews wants t' ride home with us, he kin bring it back tonight."

The truck, which Amy and Papa had both assumed to be a pickup, turned out to be a two-ton '34 Reo with a flatbed body. It had not been run since January, and the battery was stored in the Keay's cellar. "I could hook m' batt'ry chahg-uh up, but you don't want t' wait all night," Allen Keay observed. Amy and Papa silently agreed. The battery in place, the men managed to tow the truck onto the road with Mr. Keay's car and a chain. To their relief, the truck started easily.

A two-ton farm truck has wheels. So does an auto. Beyond that, it takes a good deal of imagination to see any further resemblance, Papa and Amy quickly discovered. They bounced into the village to school on Thursday morning. That afternoon, they bounced back, with Amy gamely learning to double-clutch and speed shift to keep "The Beast," as the family quickly named it, moving over the highway.

"Ask the Man Who Owns One," chuckled Papa, reading the slogan in an auto ad out loud. He reclined in his swivel chair in the principal's office Friday afternoon, and for Amy to see he held up a September 1936 edition of *National Geographic,* which he had been perusing for background for a history lesson. A shiny, black, '37 Packard Clipper straight-eight was spread the length of a full page, and "the man who owns one," in homburg and dapper three-piece suit, gold watch fob hanging from a vest pocket, was about to embark on a business trip. "Who do we know in Portugal who owns a Packard, Amy?"

"There are no Packards in Samoset Valley, Papa. Wessie has memorized make, year, and model of every car for miles around, and he was rattling off his list just the other evening. Quite a feat!"

"Not for a boy who'll soon be a man," Papa chuckled.

"The nearest thing to luxury in Portugal is Mr. Bessey's La-Salle," Amy affirmed.

"Late model car and old Chris Craft boat—solid mahogany," Papa mused.

"The motor boat used to belong to Giles Trask III," Amy reminded her father.

"I know. How fortunes do change." Papa sighed. "Let's go home. There's a lot of clutching and shifting between here and there."

"Maybe I can get a job driving a truck when I get tired of teaching school," Amy laughed.

❦ ❦ ❦

"It's for you, Wes," Mama called when the parsonage phone rang that evening. "It's Mrs. Foss."

"I hope she's all right." Papa did not anticipate making a nighttime pastoral call in the old truck.

"Sounds chipper enough to me!"

"Kin you come around about eight tomorrow mawnin'—bring y' family f' breakfast?" cackled the voice on the line.

"All of them?" Mrs. Foss was eighty-three, and Papa was concerned about the burden of cooking for a family of six, especially on a lady who'd had a stroke a year earlier.

"Oh, my yes," Mrs. Foss chuckled. "I've got a kettle of potatoes already boiled, an' a good junk o' cawned beef in a crock in the cellar. We'll have cawn beef hash. Tell Althea if she's got a jar o' mild chili sauce in her pantry t' bring it along t' go on the hash, though."

Breakfast over on Saturday morning, Mrs. Foss led Amy's family out the kitchen door, through the ell—which housed her woodshed and laying hens—and past the outhouse attached to the ell's back wall.

"Roll this door aside, please, young man." Mrs. Foss designated Andy, as she herself bent to remove a steel pin which prevented the door leading from the ell to the barn from being opened from inside the barn. Andy obliged, pushing the heavy plank door aside on its track. Morning sunlight streamed through the barn's high south windows as the family crowded through the door after Mrs. Foss. In the open space between the haylofts, a mound of chaff and barn swallow droppings splattered over a swaddling of old sheets which disguised an auto-sized lump.

"Remove the cloth, please, boys."

Jack and Andy hauled away.

"It's yours, if you kin use it."

The entire family was awestruck. Shiny and black, identical to the one in the photo in the *National Geographic* illustration, an immaculate '37 Packard Clipper straight-eight four-door sedan appeared before them.

Deacon John Foss had died only weeks after buying the Packard new, it turned out, which accounted for its having only 5,000
miles on the odometer, though it was six years old. Mrs. Foss had
gotten a driver's license right after her husband's death, and she
had driven the car to church and local shopping during the years
before her stroke, but only in warm weather. "I had the belts an'
hoses replaced in the summer of '42," she explained. "Mr. Norton
at the garage told me that the ones that came on the car were
rotten with age. Oh yes—the tires are new, too."

The battery, however, had died in Mrs. Foss' cellar, the acid
having eaten the plates after it had lost its charge. "I have a
battery in the Ford that will work just fine," Papa told her. "If it's
all right with you, I'll take my family home, and I'll be back with
the battery."

Amy's brothers rode home on the open truck body, while she
squeezed into the Reo's cab with Mama and Papa. "Wes, how are
you going to put the battery from that old Model A coupe into a
big Packard sedan?" Mama worried.

"Fords and Packards both use six volts," Papa explained. "The
battery will work with either car."

"Well," Mama agreed hesitantly, "if you say so."

"Ed Norton can have the Model A for fifteen dollars, after we
take the battery." Big-hearted Papa.

"He cannot!" Mama was adamant.

"What?"

"He wanted thirty-five dollars to fix it. Tell him you'll sell it to
him for thirty-five." Sensible Mama.

Ed Norton unfolded three tens and a five from a greasy wallet
without a quibble when Papa offered to sell him the Ford. A week
later, the Model A, having new piston rings and a timing chain,
and freshly enameled with a brush, appeared beside Norton's
Flying A with "For Sale—$200" in the window. The young man
who paid $175 for it felt he got a bargain, Amy learned later.

🐚 🐚 🐚

"I'm taking a day off next week and going to Bangor to do some
car trading," Papa announced.

Amy was sitting by a slow fire in the parlor stove, where she
had been preparing a lesson for her class of junior girls at

Samoset Valley Chapel. She put her Bible down. How would Mama answer Papa's anxiety over his becoming "A prophet in ermine and silk," as he had termed it, when he and Amy had gone together to Mrs. Foss' place late that morning to drive home with the Packard and return the Reo to Allen Keay. "I'm a simple country preacher, Amy," he had said. "I can't be seen around Portugal in an expensive automobile with whitewall tires!"

"Is it the Packard or the whitewalls?" Amy had teased, remembering that Papa wore a necktie only because Baptist preachers were expected to wear ties. Mennonite men from Papa's heritage in his youth wore no ties. "The car *is* ecclesiastical black, not two-tone, like the Ford. And you could paint the tires black," Amy had giggled. She fiercely wanted Papa to keep the Packard, a reward he richly deserved. But she was out of her league countering his philosophical arguments, so she said no more.

Amy now listened to Mama and Papa's quiet drone coming through the kitchen archway. She peered for a moment past the lace curtains which framed the double colonial windows facing the drive. The Packard gleamed black beneath the spring moon, its chrome and whitewalls silhouetting the grand, coffin-nosed auto so that all passersby could see that the Andrews had a new car.

"You've wanted a Dodge six for years, I know, Wes," Mama quietly responded. Amy's ears again tuned to her parents' discussion.

"That's not the point. I like Packards, too. But what business does a preacher have riding around in the poshest set of wheels in town?"

"The Lord gave you that car—remember?"

"It's a gas hog." That remark sounded to Amy like Papa was trying to sidetrack the main point of his own argument. Papa had more education, but Mama's wits were every bit as sharp as his. He sometimes resorted to these tactics when he was tired and overwrought.

"You can buy a lot of gas for the money you'd have to spend to trade for a Dodge—money we don't have." Mama was the voice of reason. "And with three licensed drivers now, we already get more gasoline ration stamps than we need."

"But what will it do to our testimony to keep the Packard?"

"There's not a soul in the valley but who knows where you got that car!"

"And some of them will say 'Just like a preachuh, t' rob widders.'" Papa laughed at his own imitation, then he sighed. "John the Baptist wore camel hair and ate wild honey and locusts, and they said he was demon possessed. Christ wore a robe of good wool and ate good food when offered it, and they accused Him of hobnobbing with tax collectors and sinners. I guess people who'd accuse me of robbing widows wouldn't be happy if I wore burlap and went barefoot!"

"I think," Mama summarized, "the problem may be that you're trying to make perfect by the flesh what you began in the Spirit. Isn't that what you preached last Sunday? A Dodge may seem more pious and self-denying than a Packard to folks who try to please God by their own efforts and who criticize those not as self-righteous as they. Can't we take the Packard as from the Lord, and just be thankful?"

"You know," Papa remarked, "there is something I can do which might help our church's testimony in this community."

"Oh?"

"If Reverend Small hasn't paid that old bill at Farrington's in thirty days from the date I mailed it off, I shall pay it myself, at five dollars a week."

That Saturday evening Amy found herself with fresh insight for teaching her class of girls.

❦ ❦ ❦

Fifty on a fine Saturday—fifteen miles over the limit—seemed to Amy barely moving in the heavy Packard now that Route One had had its potholes graded smooth. Amy usually honored Papa's caution to "stick to thirty-five for testimony's sake." But once in a while it seemed almost a crime not to give the mighty straight-eight some rein.

A lone, red-haired figure pulling a child's wagon, its extended-slat sides burdened with hods of clams and boxes of eggs, trudged downhill toward the village. Amy politely touched the brakes and swung wide to give her handicapped neighbor an ample berth.

Many a time she had passed Orin Trask, leaving him in a cloud of dust as she clattered past in Papa's Model A coupe. The Ford had no backseat; to pile Orin's gear into the rumble seat would have required a good bit of bother. *I can't use that excuse now, can I?* Amy mused, as she sailed along toward East Portugal on an errand for Mama.

On the return trip, Amy dutifully maintained thirty-five. To her astonishment, Orin Trask was walking along the road again. The man now labored uphill on uneven legs ahead of a wagon-load of groceries, the hundred-pound sack of chicken feed he had stashed in the rear causing the wheels to cut into the soft earth of the shoulder. Amy sighed and cranked the window down, braking the Packard to a stop. "Goin' far with that load?" Amy was tense, but she managed to sound casual.

"Only up the mountain."

"Let me give you a lift."

"You can haul these groceries, but I need the exercise," Orin chuckled.

"Plenty of room for both." Amy opened the door to the empty passenger seat. Glad that Mama had covered the rear seat with an old blanket, she added, "The wagon will ride just fine in back." How easily the words slipped out! Amy amazed herself. The auto coasted backward, its front door catching Orin in the chest just as Amy bore down on the brakes. He sat down suddenly in the road, but he was unharmed.

"I'm sorry!" Amy felt her ears redden as she frantically groped for the emergency brake lever.

Orin just smiled and looked at her evenly. He loaded his groceries and climbed in. "Your father's not much of a warmonger," he remarked when at last they were underway.

Startled at Orin's direct approach, Amy merely murmured, "No—that's true."

"How do *you* feel about the war?"

"Why...I..." Amy was only used to small talk with casual acquaintances. She was unready to deal with a man who bore directly in on a delicate topic with little introduction.

"I guess that's a little unfair," Orin chuckled. "We've just met." After a pause, he added, his eyes a-twinkle, "Perhaps we *did* meet before. I told Grandmother about spyin' a siren at Sabbathday Cove just at dawn last fall. Can you guess what she said?"

"I'd love to hear."

"'If...iffen her voice's as silky as you say her hair is, I'll haf t' chain ye to a porch pillar frum now on.'"

At this point, Amy downshifted to climb the steep Trask drive. She clutched too quickly and stalled the motor.

6

Fannie's Secret

"*Your grandfather brought you* this morning, Fannie?" Amy watched through the school window as a heavy, canvas-top DeSoto touring car with wood-spoke wheels clattered off in the spring rain and mud. The small, gray-haired male driver clung to the steering wheel as the auto bounced crazily over potholes. "Note, please." Amy held out her hand for the obligatory note, since Fannie Wellington had arrived an hour late for school.

"I must've left it in my coat . . . oh, I have it somewhere." Fannie hesitated between the door and Amy's desk.

"Go get it, then," Amy said almost gleefully. Whenever Fannie arrived, Amy's day brightened. Serious gray eyes, a thick shock of strawberry blonde curls, expressive mouth a little too wide for her face—fifth-grader Fannie, an early bloomer, combined a childish beauty which already showed the markings of maturing womanhood with her charm as a chatterbox. The hall door banged as Fannie returned with the note, scribbled with a blunt lead pencil on the back of a cardboard tag from a chicken feed sack.

"Frances overslept," read the brief epistle. It was signed, "Wilfred Wellington." Amy looked up from the note and shot a glance around the schoolroom. The fifth-graders were locating state capitals on maps they had traced, and the sixth-graders were busily working at fractions. Penny Meader, two chapters ahead of her class in arithmetic, was huddled with Nancy Dowe and Billy Blaisdell, showing them how to invert and cross-multiply.

"Frances?" Amy queried, returning to her tardy scholar.

"That's m' real name, Miss Andrews."

"How little we know," Amy murmured, realizing that she ought earlier to have checked Fannie's records in Papa's office files. Fannie, though often tardy, absorbed knowledge as a sponge soaks up water. Even when her assignments were incomplete, as if by osmosis she seemed to learn enough to manage at least a B-plus on tests and quizzes.

But there had been inexplicable mysteries about Fannie. She had disappeared for more than a week in January, and the truant officer was neither able to find her nor get her mother to say where she had gone. When Fannie returned, besides her usual unwashed odor, her clothes smelled rankly of pipe tobacco and burning green fir boughs, an aroma Amy had learned to identify from Andy, who worked Saturdays on a logging crew and came home smelling of the fire the men built to warm themselves with at lunch time. "I was with Father in his camp in the woods," was the only explanation Amy was able to get Fannie to divulge.

"Wilfred Wellington is your grandfather?" Amy asked pleasantly.

"He's my *father*," Fannie insisted.

"Who is Donald Wellington?" Donald had signed most excuse notes for Fannie that school year. Amy had met him briefly on one occasion when he had come to the classroom to get Fannie before school let out. He was a lank, balding man in his early thirties with a chain-smoker's breath. He was grizzled from woods work, bashful in Amy's presence (a shyness which Amy had at the time modestly imagined had more to do with her position as a well-dressed school marm than with her being female), but he had become defensive and evasive at the simplest question about Fannie's home life.

"Brother Donnie's enlisted. Father says he'll stay home an' not live in the camp now't he don't have t' fight with Donnie. Mother'd rather have Donnie, though." Fannie had revealed more about her family in this statement than Amy had learned all year.

"Mothers can be very fond of their older boys," Amy agreed. She had learned shortly after coming to Portugal that large families born over perhaps a quarter of a century were not unusual in rural Maine.

"Oh, Donnie ain't Mother's boy. He's Father's oldest. Donnie's ma's dead. He and Mother are the same age, and they sleep in the same bed," Fannie stated matter-of-factly.

Amy caught her breath at this revelation. Should she draw the curtain of decency across Fannie's report on the doings of her mother and half-brother, or let her continue? "How do you know this?" Perhaps Fannie had been mistaken, or she had misunderstood.

"We all sleep in the same room. I sleep with Willie." This did not shock Amy; little Willie, whom she now guessed might be Wilfred, Jr., was in the third grade. "Sometimes I usta crawl in with Mother, but I didn't stay all night. Donnie tickled me, and I had to get out."

Amy did not like this report. "Let's go out into the hall." Fannie followed her teacher outside the classroom. "Fannie, why are you telling me . . . these things?"

"'Cause I hate Donnie, an' I hope he gits hisself kilt in the army. I hope an ol' Jap shoots him right 'tween the eyes." Her lower lip curled down, and she trembled, fighting back tears.

Amy caught her breath. Dreading the answer, she asked, "Why do you hate him so much?"

"'Cause . . ." Fannie's voice grew sober, old, drained of all emotion, "'cause sometimes when Mother warn't home, Donnie usta slap me hard for not cookin' his beans t' suit him, er not gettin' his beer fast enough. Onct he let me down the well on a rope for dumpin' his bottle o' beer in the well, an' I didn't know he'd left it in the water bucket t' cool. I was scared he wouldn't pull me back up." Fannie shuddered visibly at the recollection.

"When . . . when did Donnie last hit you?"

"Couple o' days ago. He came home on leave, jest 'fore he shipped out fer Okinawa. Father says he may kill Donnie, if the Japs don't."

"Please go back in the classroom and take your seat." As soon as Fannie disappeared through the door, Amy sat on the floor in the hallway and wept.

After a quick trip to the restroom to straighten her appearance, Amy returned to her classroom to find Papa there, walking quietly from desk to desk, pointing out to one student that though Augusta is the capital of Maine, Atlanta rather than Augusta is the capital of Georgia; to another that though Springfield is the capital of Illinois, the Springfields in Missouri and Massachusetts are merely major cities. "You're not feeling well?" he eyed his daughter.

"I'm all right now." Amy forced a smile.

"I put my volunteer in charge of the seventh and eighth grade when I heard things getting out of hand over here," Papa explained. "Are you sure you don't want me to call a substitute?"

"No . . . really." Amy turned her back on Papa and went directly to work with her fifth-graders, careful to give Fannie Wellington more than the usual portion of individual help. Papa watched her a moment, then he slipped out quietly.

Amy's mind ran again and again that day to the incidents of the seven months since Fannie had been her pupil. Only one stood out as unusual—her disappearance to stay at Wilfred's camp. Fannie's unwashed odor after this hiatus had begun to cause objection in the classroom, even from girls who ordinarily jumped rope with her. Most of the homes outside the village, Amy knew, had no bathrooms, but a galvanized or oaken tub, hauled in on Saturday evening beside the kitchen range's hot water reservoir, satisfied social propriety as to odor abatement.

The boy's half of Portugal Grammar School's basement had a hot shower, heated by a coal stove, which Papa fired up twice weekly before basketball practice at the Samoset Grange. Amy kept a cake of soap and a couple of towels at the school, since the parsonage's hot water supply, like that of most of Reverend Andrews' parishioners, was dependent on the kitchen range's reservoir, and it would scarcely supply two baths an evening for their family of six. She found she could lock the door to the boys' basement and shower luxuriously while the junior high ball team was at practice, and the efficient coal heater would bring the water back to near boiling for Papa's six sweaty preteens by the time they came racing down the street.

So, on several occasions, Amy had selected boys from her fifth- and sixth-grade classroom whose intimate acquaintance with a cow tie-up or horse stable had made them unpalatable to their village-dwelling schoolmates by midweek. Downstairs they would run with soap and towels to scrub until they shone, to return pleased that they had been thus initiated into a masculine activity—showering—ordinarily reserved for the seventh grade.

It had not seemed a serious matter to Amy, therefore, to send smelly Fannie to the shower in the boys' basement during lunch hour, bolt the door, and show her how to use the bar of white Ivory to work the grime out of her pink-hued locks once they had been unbraided. Fannie went home that afternoon with her hair not quite dry, but combed neatly and pinned back with extra barrettes Amy carried in her purse. A pleased and prettified Fannie had at three o'clock scrambled aboard the old panel truck which served as a school bus, waving gaily at Amy in the schoolhouse door.

On that occasion, Amy now recalled, there were marks on Fannie, though there had been no welts or fresh bruises. Several yellowed, bluish stripes, of the kind Amy had seen once or twice on an elderly aunt who bruised easily, had been barely discernible on Fannie's thighs.

It had been a sullen, unsmiling Fannie who handed Amy a note the morning after her shower, scrawled—more legibly than the notes written by Donald—on a sheet of arithmetic paper Fannie had taken home in her math book. *Dear Miss Prissy Quaker Teacher from Pennsylvania: Please keep yor* (obscenity written over) *meddling hands off the Wellingtons. We send our children to schol to learn ther branes, NOT ther bodys. Love* (Amy had found herself smiling at the closing), *Mrs. Ruth Wellington.*

Donald Wellington was out of the home now, Amy thankfully considered. And the adultery Fannie had reported, evil as it was, was not Amy's major concern. What Donald Wellington had done to his not-yet-eleven half-sister was vile enough to cause a feud resulting in his joining the army, perhaps to "git hisself kilt." How frequently had he hit her? And did Fannie's mother know what was going on but chose to ignore it because of her involvement with Donald? Amy did not even wish to consider this. She knew, however, that sooner or later she must allow the love of Christ to overcome her loathing for Fannie's mother, if the Lord were to work through Amy to reach the Wellington home.

❦ ❦ ❦

"Those five school-age Wellington kids are in Sunday school almost every week. I'm sure there are at least two younger ones at home," Mama remarked that evening, when Amy told how Fannie had been treated. "I've told Wes that he ought to make a house call, but he's not been able to get around to see all of our regular church members yet. If only he could be free of school responsibilities. Maybe in the summer..."

Amy had heard Mama's "if onlys" before. Papa *was* overworked, but with prayer and a bit of sanctified consideration, solutions always arrived for every impasse. And this one seemed too obvious. "Let's you and I go over there." As soon as she suggested it, though, the fear of facing Mrs. Wellington tied her stomach in knots. But having committed herself, Amy was not about to turn back.

A ruined barn, its rafters and purlins naked as the ribs of a long-dead horse, rose above the hill as Amy and Mama turned the Packard into the wheel ruts past the rusty Wellington mailbox. The barn's lower story, protected by rotting hay piled in an earlier generation into the now-open mow, housed a skinny, one-horned cow and two cross-breed heifers which wandered in and out without a pasture fence. A pile of weathered clapboards and shingles, collapsed in an enormous heap behind an untamed clump of lilacs, appeared where once had been a house. Only the ell, stretched between the rubble of the house and the roofless barn, was fully upright. From a teetering chimney on the end of the ell next to the ruins of the house came a curl of smoke.

Amy pulled the Packard up beside a well box, on which an inverted galvanized bucket showed that the family could not afford a pump. Donald's beer is not cooling in the well today, Amy grimly told herself. The wheel tracks stopped by the well, and a walk of loose boards, some with protruding rusty nails, led along the muddy path to the door. She was thankful, at least, that the ancient DeSoto touring car was not to be seen.

"Come in!" was the husky, monotone greeting in response to Amy's knock. She pushed the door open, raising it by its old-fashioned iron thumb latch from where its scraping had over the years worn a groove in the floor, and she adjusted her eyes to the grimy interior. Suddenly pummeled by seven dancing, dirty bodies, Amy caught her breath, then she picked the children up one at a time, except for Fannie, whom she only hugged, then kissed her forehead.

"This's my teachuh—an' this's the minister's wife, Mrs. Andrews," Fannie introduced them.

"Hullo. Well, Fannie, git the ladies a chair!" Amy took this momentary distraction for an opportunity to size up her hostess. Florid of face, rotund of girth, fleshy and muscular of arm and leg, Ruth Wellington, at nearly six feet and, Amy guessed, nearly 300 pounds, was a woman to be reckoned with.

"Mrs. Wellington—may I call you Ruth?" Amy began as soon as she and Mama were seated.

"Yeah—shoah. I bin called worse names." She picked up a cigarette smoldering on the edge of the wood-burning kitchen range, dragged on it at length, and blew the smoke toward the ceiling.

"It's a pleasure to have Fannie in my fifth-grade class and in Sunday school," Amy remarked.

"She's a bright one—takes after Wilfred. Wilfred was a fireman on the Bangor & Aroostook. Could 'a' been an engineer, but his back give out, an' they laid him off. Got his license, though." Ruth gestured with her hand toward a yellowed document nailed to the wall. "If it weren't fer a streak o' bad luck, we wouldn't be livin' in this dump. I warn't raised this way!"

Mrs. Wellington, though wary, seemed loquacious, friendly even, Amy considered. Perhaps Amy and Mama had opened a door through which they and Papa might one day step to minister.

Amy's eyes took in "this dump" as Ruth Wellington spoke. Just as Fannie had described it, the home was all one room, though once it had been two. A large country kitchen, which in past years must have amply served the collapsed house beyond the plastered wall, was the main portion of this shack. It had a tight floor of matched maple boards, she noticed. Worn and cupped, they nonetheless furnished an adequate support for the furnishings and feet—most of them bare—which trod on it.

Two-thirds of the way across this room a wall had been removed—or it had collapsed—which once had separated the kitchen from the woodshed. Here, the floor stopped at a drop of perhaps two feet, beyond which was a pit littered with moldy hay and tattered quilts tossed helter-skelter where the children had crawled out of them in the morning. Next to the outside wall in this pit stood an antique double bedstead with a feather tick, bereft of sheets, and a couple of patchwork quilts which had patches upon patches. The walls themselves were protected from the winter's drafts only by cardboard held in place by weathered shingles and rusty nails, evidently salvaged from the ruins. A rickety ladder ascended from this bedroom pit to an open storage loft above the kitchen ceiling.

Amy's head swam with the needs of the Wellington children and toddlers as she fought the Packard's steering wheel, trying to keep the wheels in the ruts as she and Mama motored toward home that Saturday morning in early spring. Food? They seemed to have enough. As Mrs. Wellington had acknowledged bitterly, they kept an account at Farrington's Grocery, paid by Portugal's selectmen out of the town pauper fund. Clothing? "I'm sure I can get our Ladies' Aid Society at the church to put together a box of clean clothes and even get the children some new shoes," Mama had said. Medical attention? Abscessed ears and runny noses seemed to be epidemic in this home. Amy determined to check with the county health nurse and make sure the children had had all their shots. Dr. Abbott, like the grocer, served indigent patients, Amy knew, and he sent the bill to the selectmen for the town to pay.

But what could Amy do about Fannie's special emotional needs? At least Donald was out of the house now. "She'll be a teenager able to defend herself better by the time his hitch with Uncle Sam is up," Papa pointed out as the three conferred on the Wellingtons' family problems in quiet tones at the kitchen table after the boys had gone to bed. "In the meantime, love her," he said. "And I need to see if I can help Wilfred be a proper father to Fannie and her brothers and sisters," Papa added, talking more to himself than to Amy or Althea.

"You're right, Wes," Mama quietly agreed. "Unless I'm mistaken, Ruth Wellington runs the household." Tears came to Althea's eyes as she observed, "The Wellingtons have a marital mix which seems to be much like ours ..."

"Except…" Wes finished Mama's sentence, "except that their relationship is out of control and out of balance."

"What…what do you mean?" Amy was concerned, shocked almost.

"Just this…" Mama was smiling now, "like Ruth Wellington, I have a tendency to push—to ram my will through. Sometimes the Lord uses some rather dramatic lessons to teach us to become godly examples of Christian womanhood."

"I'm beginning to see the picture," Amy said at last. "I'm the one woman in her life Fannie can trust—and I'm to be *her* example."

"And see that you don't betray that trust. Meantime," Papa said, "we'll take it to the Lord. His solutions will come out in such an obvious fashion that we'll wonder why we didn't see them all along." Papa had his stubborn thorns in the flesh, but when it came to the most difficult needs of others, his faith never wavered that the Lord would see them through.

❦ ❦ ❦

"This is the third day you've had a headache, Fannie." A little more than a week had passed since Amy and Mama had visited in the Wellington home, and Amy had found opportunity to show special love for Fannie every day since. Now Fannie had headaches and, thinking perhaps she needed to unburden her soul once more, Amy let her stay at her desk during recess.

"I'm sick, Miss Andrews," Fannie moaned.

"Where do you hurt?"

Amy had expected a complaint of general ill feeling. "My head hurts, and the whole side of my face is achin'," Fannie groaned instead.

Amy felt Fannie's forehead. "You *are* hot." She touched the girl's cheek, but Fannie quickly pulled away. "Face hurt?"

"Yes. Don't want to talk."

Why is Fannie avoiding me? Has there been another episode? Are her parents abusive, also? Amy studied the beautiful face dozing as she rested her head on her arm at her desk, its womanly features just beginning to overshadow the infant roundness of childhood. Amy touched the cheek again.

"Ouch!"

That the pain was physical was obvious, at least. "Can you sit up and look at me, Fannie?" Fannie sat up. "Why, Fannie, I believe you've got the mumps!" The right side of her face was beginning to puff out, and the inflammation had swollen her jaw. Fannie's right eye was open only a slit, and Amy pulled the eyelid up for a better look. Her eye was bloodshot. "Let's get you to bed." There was a cot in Papa's office where Fannie could at least lie down. "C'mon." Amy bent to help Fannie struggle to her feet, then she felt the dead weight of the girl as she collapsed into her arms.

"Hurt herself on the playground?" Papa was concerned, and he swung the office door wide as Amy carried Fannie past.

"Fannie's sick, Papa! Look at her face." Fannie's head was thrown back over Amy's arm, and they both got a look into her mouth in the light of the window of Wes Andrews' office. "Why— her upper jaw!" Amy exclaimed.

"That's one abscessed tooth, if I ever saw one!" Papa fished in the First Aid cabinet for a clinical thermometer as Amy laid her burden gently on the cot. The semi-comatose Fannie fought her efforts, but Amy managed to get her mouth open for another look. An upper tooth had rotted off at the gum, and the infected flesh had swollen so that it hid the stump.

Amy decided not to try putting a glass thermometer under the child's tongue. An armpit would have to do. "Papa, it's 104°," Amy exclaimed moments later. "Can't we get the county health nurse?"

"Mrs. Knollett's at Eastern Maine General Hospital in Bangor for a conference today." Papa shook his head. He cranked a long ring on the oak box screwed to the end of his desk, then took the receiver from the cradle of the candlestick desk phone. "Central? Principal Andrews, here. Get me Doctor Abbott, please. It's an emergency!" A moment later Papa slammed the receiver down in disgust. "Doc's making house calls. Secretary says he'll call in *if* he stops at a home that has a telephone!" Papa rubbed his chin. Amy prayed. This was beyond her capabilities.

"Let's do this. You stay here with Fannie and keep her comfortable," Papa instructed. "Give her all the water she'll drink, and keep a damp cloth on her head. Get her to take an aspirin or two, if she can swallow. When Doctor Abbott phones, explain the situation, and arrange to meet him at once. If we can't reach the doctor by noon, I'll have to drive over to the Wellingtons'—they have no phone. I'll call a substitute for your class."

Twenty minutes later the office phone rang. Doctor Abbott was on Hardscrabble Road back of the mountain, only a mile from the Wellington place. He agreed to meet Amy there with Fannie in an hour. "I've been in that hovel," he growled. "I think it's time someone got on the selectmen's case about finding that family a decent place to live."

"Take Route One back over the mountain and catch Hardscrabble Road's south end," Amy remained calm in spite of the life-threatening situation. "If you try to get through from River Road this time of year, you'll likely need Ed Norton's wrecker. And since you're going that way, take Mama along. I'll phone her and tell her you're on your way."

Wilfred Wellington sulked and smoked his pipe in a rocker beside the kitchen range as Doctor Abbott checked Fannie's pulse, listening to her breathing with his stethoscope until Amy wondered if he had found a child with more than the usual two lungs. "Penicillin is what she needs," he stated at last, with no obvious emotion. "But the Armed Forces have the penicillin supply tied up in the war effort, and I can't get the pharmacist in Bangor to ship me any. She's *got* to go to Bangor. They'll give her a shot of penicillin and put her to bed for a day or two. Then a dentist can get the tooth out—what's left of it."

"Can't go t' Bang-gaw. M' cah wun't make it," Wilfred drawled from his rocker by the stove. He was a small man, Amy observed, bearded and elfin, hunkered into an old mackinaw like a shrouded monk.

"I'll tend her right here t' hum," declared Ruth Wellington.

"We can take her," offered Amy, looking at Mama for approval. Mama nodded assent. It was three hours over rough roads to the Queen City of Maine's Northland, but a girl's life was at stake.

"She's not leaving me!" Mrs. Wellington was adamant.

"Then you go to Bangor with Amy and Fannie. Take her there in your arms—you're her mother. I'll stay here and get supper for Wilfred and your children!" Mama had surprised Amy before, but this was the biggest surprise yet. But Mama had a heart for children, and the sacrifice weighed nothing in contrast with Fannie's need.

"I'll git my ol' man his suppah myself, an' I'll nuhss my dottah without no help frum ennybuddy!" Fannie's mother declared.

Doctor Abbott had packed his stethoscope away, and he strode for the door, pausing where Wilfred still sat smoking. "You, sir, are a gutless coward, if you let that woman talk you out of taking that child to the hospital." Doctor Abbott swore, and Wilfred Wellington returned the profanity, partly obliterated by the door slamming as the doctor went out.

"We want to take her, you know," Amy pleaded with Mrs. Wellington through her tears, but to no avail. Had the doctor's temper fit solidified the Wellingtons' determination to keep Fannie home? Only God could know.

❦ ❦ ❦

"She had been gone for at least an hour before I got there," Nurse Maxine Knollett told Amy the next morning in Papa's office. "I think the autopsy will show that Fannie died of a blood clot caused by the infected tooth."

"Did she . . . ?" Amy could not get the words out.

"In such cases, the patient goes to sleep as the brain shuts down. Consciousness of pain is lost. I'm sure Fannie died peacefully," Mrs. Knollett said softly.

Amy did not respond, so Mrs. Knollett continued, "If anything like this happens again, and I'm anywhere in the valley, call me, even if it's the middle of the night. *I'd get help*," she added fiercely.

"Who . . . who would you call?" Amy felt the tears trickle down her cheeks.

"The Maine State Police. They'd have taken her to Bangor for treatment."

"But Doctor Abbott—why couldn't he?"

"The Doc's got his practice to think about," Mrs. Knollett stated honestly. "After twenty years, he's still 'from away,' in a lot of people's minds. And if he leaves, who then will minister to the children of the valley?"

Amy could not answer this assessment of Samoset County mind-set.

The day of Fannie's funeral had come bright and sunny, but by the time Wes Andrews had ministered to the living in the presence of the dead, and the four sixth-grade boys chosen for pallbearers had slid the small wooden casket into the back of Hansen's hearse, the April skies had turned leaden. Amy huddled with Papa under his old black umbrella, father and daughter weeping together quietly beside the new grave cut into the Wellington lot in Maple Grove Cemetery. The hearse had driven off, and relatives and friends from school were gone. A whiff of pipe tobacco caught Amy's attention, and she and Papa raised their heads together. The Wellingtons' old touring DeSoto stood nearby, its tattered black canvas top leaking onto the seats. But the car was empty. A cough behind them caused Amy and Papa to turn.

"Wilfred?" Papa said. The man stood alone, his rumpled fedora dripping onto an ill-fitting suit coat.

"It's Bill," the man replied flatly. "Folks who know me call me Bill."

"Has your family left?" Papa asked.

"Gone with Ruth's mother. May not see 'em for a while."

Papa took Wilfred's hand. "What can we do to help?"

"I'm okay. I'll manage." The man broke into tears. "I didn't mean to hurt her. She'd had achy teeth b'fore, and allus she'd got better, soon's Doc Abbott yanked 'em out."

Amy had never seen Papa hug a man before; of all the men she knew, Wilfred Wellington was the least likely person for him to hug. "We've all done things we can't take back, but God gives us the strength to go on," he told Wilfred. "In Jesus, we can be forgiven and accept forgivness."

"Thanks." Mr. Wellington turned and shuffled toward his car.

"Bill," Papa called.

"Yeah?"

"C'mon home with me for the evening. Althea will be glad to put another plate on."

Mr. Wellington hesitated.

"I *mean* it, Bill!"

7

The Hidden Path

"*Your father certainly is proud* of you," Mama insisted one Saturday morning late in May.

"I know, Mama." The hiss of Mama's new pressure canner on the wood-fired kitchen range filled the silence of the lull in the strained conversation. Amy tipped the heavy, wide-armed oak rocker back an inch too far as she watched Mama pack dandelion greens into just-scalded quart canning jars. The board Amy had placed across the chair's arms as a desk slipped, and a pile of just-corrected fifth- and sixth-grade theme papers skittered sideways like winged maple seeds across the worn linoleum.

Sighing, Amy set the board, still laden with books and uncorrected papers, across the corner of the breakfast table and slipped to the floor. When finally her papers were in hand, she rose, this time sending the board flying, cracking her head in the process. Books, red-and-blue pencils, and ungraded papers scattered clear to the sink where Mama stood amongst puddles of water and snippets of dandelion leaves, as the board hit the floor with a hollow clatter.

"Perhaps Somebody's trying to tell you something," Mama archly remarked.

"Perhaps," sighed Amy. "I'm going to the beach for a swim. I can sometimes hear the Lord better when I'm alone."

"But it's…" Althea caught herself in mid-sentence. She and Amy had been sparring with words most of the morning, and Mama knew she could not let her daughter leave the house on a sour note.

"…too early in the season to swim," Amy finished her mother's sentence for her. Her sigh turned to a merry laugh as she chirped, "I'll take my dungarees and a sweater along to put on over my bathing suit so I won't get chilled when I walk home."

Things had been tense between mother and daughter for two weeks—since the afternoon Amy had driven over to get Jack and Andy at Samoset Valley Classical Institute. Jack had said something about an "army recruiter" when he phoned Amy to say why he and his older brother had missed the school bus. Though Jack, at sixteen, was as interested in the recruiter's talk on patriotism and a world safe for democracy as Andy, he was agitated at himself for having decided to wait for his brother, who had joined a small knot of young men asking questions.

Jack shared his father's sensitive nature, and though curious about what this living, khaki-uniformed extension of Uncle Sam had to say, he became indignant when the man seemed to pressure Jack's school friends to enlist as soon as they turned eighteen.

But to Amy, who listened quietly from a seat in the back, it was not a question of whether she should enlist in the newly formed Woman's Army Corps—the WACS. It was merely a matter of *when*. And for her, whether she held Papa's conscientious objector convictions was hardly an issue. A WAC did not bear arms, and the recruiter had assured her she could be assigned to a medical unit if she requested. She could decide the issue of objection after she had seen war firsthand, Amy concluded.

Then there was the matter of parental permission. The recruiter said it wasn't necessary if she were eighteen, which she found strange, since a driver's license or a legal contract— voting, even—required one to be twenty-one. But Papa had stated his position times enough. Christians were to save lives, not to take them. So, intoxicated with the thrill of helping "our boys over there" drive Hitler and his evil Nazis out of Europe, consoled with the belief that she would be saving lives as a

nurse's aid or an ambulance driver, Amy put the dripping fountain pen to the enlistment document. "Amy Elizabeth Andrews"
she wrote with the flair she had taken on for her signature since
becoming a schoolteacher. Under "D.O.B" she carefully noted,
"November 21, 1923." Dating the form, "May 10, 1943," she passed
it back to the recruiter.

"Nineteen-and-a-half," he exclaimed warmly. "We get a lot of
girls your age. You're certainly ready to know your own mind!"

Amy turned to leave, goose bumps crawling up her spine,
speechless at her adult decision. "Miss Andrews," the recruiter
stopped her, "we'll see you at the Bangor Armory in two weeks for
your physical and formal induction. You'll get a notice in the mail.
Basic training is in New Jersey at Fort Dix right after the Fourth of
July."

Amy numbly grasped the big steering wheel of the heavy
Packard as she guided the speeding sedan toward home. Only a
bad skid, caused when she tried to brake down from fifty on the
loose gravel of the highway, brought her back to reality. Ernie
Sylvester, a senior like Andy, had called out, "I get off here," just as
they shot past the Sylvester farmstead on a downgrade.

🌱 🌱 🌱

Amy, in her red maillot and clutching her blue jeans and a pink
sweatshirt wrapped in a tattered towel reserved for beach use,
hurried past the garden toward the bluff overlooking the sea. She
was glad to be out of the stifling kitchen, where Mama, canning
greens over the hot stove, had repeatedly tried to suggest without actually saying so that Amy ought not to have enlisted without
both parents' express approval. Amy's spirit was wounded, and
she now struggled with Mama's implication that Amy had be-
trayed parental authority.

Amy angrily flung her bundle of clothes out beyond the rocky
precipice toward the sand and seashells thirty feet below. The
dungarees, weighted with the belt and copper rivets, dropped
straight downward, and the sweatshirt fluttered after. But the
towel, unrolled with the force of her thrust, sailed into the cruel
thorns of a spreading wild rosebush perhaps fifteen feet beneath
her feet.

Lithe as any acrobat, Amy grabbed the rope which last summer, to ease the descent to the beach, she and Andy had installed in the wind-blasted old hemlock which leaned over the cliff. Shinnying slowly to avoid rope burns on her hands and bare legs, she began to let herself down. Finding herself atop a granite boulder protruding from the clay embankment, Amy abandoned caution. She sprung off, arced out, and caught the towel easily enough. But the return swing, arcing closer, dragged Amy straight though the middle of the rosebush.

She dropped the towel again, this time getting it onto the beach. Then kicking against the clay cliff, Amy hurried down to survey her smarting, bleeding scratches. "Perhaps Someone *is* trying to tell me something," she said half-aloud, examining the damage.

The tide was out. Undaunted, Amy left her clothes by the climbing rope and, clutching the towel, hurried to the mouth of Sabbathday Brook which tumbled off Hogback Mountain from across the highway, above the parsonage, then flowed into a marshy estuary beside a strip of sand along Sabbathday Cove. Her towel now became a shawl on her shoulders, and she splashed upstream under low-hanging hemlocks from the ruins of the old boathouse, seeking a pool of fresh water where she might plunge in all over. Though Amy certainly would have found the water deep enough for swimming oceanward, the prospect of wading directly into the black muck of the estuary repulsed her.

Here, though, the streambed was sand and small pebbles. Too, a flagstone path meandered along the stream just above the low tide line at the far side. The brook bent in the underbrush ahead, and beyond the bend it flowed deeper, forming a chest-high pool beneath the highway bridge. Past the bridge, Amy could see, the stream tumbled over ledges as it rushed down the mountain.

Past the bridge, also, the flag walk began to mount the streambank in a series of level stretches interspersed with granite steps, two, three, or five in a row. Then the walk ended at the foot of high, iron stairs which climbed steeply to a landing far above, then mounted dizzily to where it disappeared through a tangle of wild roses.

Amy considered briefly that she might merely cross the stream where it flowed, fresh and cold, out of the pool, then walk without getting wet above her shins to the mysterious staircase. Instead, she did the adventurous thing: throwing her towel onto the flagstones across the narrow brook, she plunged headfirst into the mountain-cold water of May, chilled by the snows still melting from the forested slopes far above. The shock of the swim erased from Amy's spirit the last rancorous traces of the strained morning chat with Mama. In a few moments she had swum beyond the bridge, and here she found iron rungs set into the sheer granite wall, leading straight up to the foot of the stairs.

Once out of the water, Amy found herself attacked by near-microscopic black flies—midges, millions of them, the bane of Maine woods in May. Slapping frantically, Amy raced back to her towel, and shivering in the shade, she snapped it around her head to hold her tormentors at bay.

But having gone that far, Amy was intent on seeing where the stairs led. She climbed up, and the flies left her alone once she got beyond the chill of the bridge's shade into the sunlight. The rosebushes, she was pleased to discover, had been pruned and wired back to make an arch through which she slipped without further injury. The stairs finally ended in another flagstone path, this time leading out through overhanging lilac bushes, the perfume of their lavender blooms a happy contrast with the moldy decay from the hidden path below. Heedless of what might lie ahead, Amy stepped through the lilacs onto a walled patio of flagstones, rife with a riot of spring flowers. The aged Cora Trask was there alone, bent over her peony bed.

Amy turned to hurry off, but Mrs. Trask spotted her before she could get out of sight. "Ayuh! If it ain't the minister's dottuh! I've told Orin more'n once effen he didn't put a gate on that walk we'd have pirates or smugglers or who knows what sneakin' in our back way."

"Mrs. Trask, I . . ."

"Now, think nothing of it, dearie," Mrs. Trask waved her garden trowel as if dismissing Amy's trespassing. "You were explorin' like enny kid. Last minister lived in that pahs-nidge hed a couple o' rascals usta sneak up he-ah an' help themselves t' my best peonies. Well, I fixed them, I did!"

Amy was beginning to feel like Gretel just before the witch closed the oven door. "I . . . I'm sorry. I'll be going."

"Oh my, no! You jest set yourself down," Mrs. Trask cackled, pointing with her trowel to a stone bench. "I've got a batch o' doughnuts made fresh this mawnin', an' milk. I'll be right back."

Amy was more than a little nervous as she waited. Suppose Mrs. Trask tried to "fix" her? But Mama, who had several times visited the aged dame of the manse, had indicated no sinister forebodings about Mrs. Trask, so she forced herself to wait.

Presently the old woman popped through the kitchen door, tray with doughnuts and pewter mugs of milk held before her, the screen door clattering shut with a nerve-rattling bang behind. She set their food on a white-enameled wrought-iron stool in front of Amy. "Now would you say grace before we eat, dearie? I know you're a Baptist and we're Congregationalists, but we pray to the same God, don't we?"

As Amy mumbled a prayer, she felt like she was blessing an execution rather than a meal. But the doughnuts *were* delicious, she soon discovered. And the milk was rich and creamy, not thin like the bottled milk from the store.

"My extravagant son bought a refrigerator before his wife died, an' now he's not with us to enjoy it, either," Mrs. Trask sadly explained at Amy's evident surprise at finding cold milk in her mug. "Now let me fix them legs o' yourn."

The word "fix" got Amy's attention, and she quickly stood, though she felt silly about running from an apparently harmless old lady.

"That's right, stand up, so's I can get at ye better." Mrs. Trask bent toward Amy's bare knees as she slipped a small brown bottle from her apron pocket. It was iodine. Relieved that the fix was to be nonfatal, Amy stood quietly while Mrs. Trask painted her rose-thorn scratches and fly bites with the bottle's dauber. "There—I can't send you home with wounds from beach bushes that may get infected, can I?" she chuckled. "Young girls nowadays go 'round as bare-legged as infants," she added with a touch of indignation.

"Well, I shall surely put my dungarees on before anybody sees my war paint," Amy assured her. She considered explaining that she never went out in public without a skirt or jeans, but decided not to press the matter.

"I took a course in practical nursing after my husband died, and I was in France during the First War as a nurse for the military," Mrs. Trask said, explaining her knowledge of hygiene.

"You...you were in the war!" Amy blurted out. "So was my papa. He was a chaplain."

"Oh, yes. I was sixty-three at the time. If I'd 'a' bin two years olduh, they wouldn't 'a' taken me. But my boy was grown—he was too old to fight, they said—and I thought someone in the Trask family should do somethin' for their country."

The old lady's mention of nursing in France during the First World War left Amy nearly speechless. "I've joined the WACS," she said at last. "I leave for training camp next week."

"The Women's Army Corps? I've read about it in the papers. Good for you!" Mrs. Trask's sincere smile warmed Amy's heart. "There now. That's bettah." She slipped the iodine back in her pocket.

"What..." Amy began hesitantly as she sat down again, "what did your family say when you enlisted?"

"Well, I didn't enlist, exactly. They didn't hev the WACS back then." Mrs. Trask paused a moment and smiled at her recollection. "I wuz an American Red Cross volunteer—paid my own way, too," she said proudly. "My son, he didn't mind. I warn't needed to mother little Orin, sence his mother was still with us then. An' my parents were both gone, though my daddy a-bin proud o' me iffen he'd lived a few more ye-ahs. But my sister frum Baws-tun, she wrote me one hot lettuh. Sed iffen I wanted t' help the cause o' liberty, I should volunteer t' roll bandages an' pack vict'ry boxes here on the home front, not go gallivanting off to Europe with girls less 'n half my age!"

Amy paused, then pressed further. "Is...is it hard in the war, being a woman?"

It was Mrs. Trask's turn to be sober. "I've held boys in my arms in the trenches as they died crying for their mothers, while machine guns rattled over our heads."

Amy caught her breath.

"Most dyin' is done with a woman nearby, I figguh. 'S natcherly a woman's place t' tend the ill an' dyin'. You know..." She stopped, measuring her words carefully. "You know, some of the young girls who went with the Red Cross grew up in a hurry on the front lines in France. They went there thinkin' they'd be patchin' flesh wounds, then foxtrottin' with lieutenants in Paris cabarets every weekend. You forget the dancin' an' partyin' when you're shooting morphine into a young boy's veins so he kin die without screaming after his vitals have bin torn apart by a land mine."

A stillness fell between the two women and a cool ocean breeze raised goose bumps on Amy's skin. "I really must go," she said softly. "I've got to help Mama can and clean the house." She rose and took several steps along the slate flags toward the lilacs, then turned back. "Mrs. Trask, what *did* you do to stop the other minister's kids from sneaking up your back way?"

"Oh, I didn't try to stop 'em," Mrs. Trask grinned broadly. "I jest made sure their mama knew where they'd bin. I fed 'em blueberry pie. Did you ever see an eight- or nine-year-old after he's bin eatin' blueberry pie?" Amy joined Mrs. Trask in her laugh.

Grandma Trask, Amy considered as she made her way home, was a lady of special graces, rather than the woman of dark mystery the villagers believed her to be. Someday, Amy knew, she'd tell Mama about their conversation. Just now, though, she felt that the old lady's war experiences were from a past as precious as an alabaster box of expensive spikenard, too sacred to share, a tale not meant to be retold by lips as unaccustomed to reality as her own.

And though Amy had not spoken with Orin Trask that day, she now felt even more strongly that the strange rumors she'd heard about him in Portugal were certainly untrue; or if in any sense true, seen through bias so bent that the beholder could not comprehend the view.

As the afternoon sun made its unimpeded march through the Maine sky, Amy scurried home just ahead of the rising tide.

8

The Corn Borers' Ball

Amy caught herself giggling like one of her fifth-graders when Eddie Bessey gallantly lifted his baseball cap. "Let me touch it," she heard herself brashly request, pointing at his butch haircut.

"Touch it all you want." Eddie scooched his lanky, six-foot-three frame so that Amy could pat his crew cut as he stood in the parsonage living room that October evening in 1943.

"It feels like a just-clipped poodle," giggled Amy again. "But you didn't sign up?"

"Naw," Eddie admitted, his usual brash demeanor melting under Amy's fawning behavior and direct questioning. "Tried to. They said I have flat feet. Couldn't march. But I suppose you got to pat a lot of butch haircuts at Fort Dix?"

"No, silly. The women are kept separate from the men. We were lucky to see them drill from a distance!" She paused to take a closer look at Eddie's hair. "Thought you'd avoid the guff by getting it cut beforehand, did you?"

"You got it. Now I've got to live with being called 'soldier,' even though I didn't get drafted." Eddie grinned broadly, then he paused.

"And?"

"And since I'm not a soldier, I thought I'd like to take one out before she ships out for Europe."

"Meaning?"

"Meaning will you be my guest at the corn borers' ball? It's Friday at eight. We're finishin' our last run o' sweet cawn at the cannery Tuesday, an' I'm in charge of settin' up the warehouse for a ballroom."

"Well...I..." Amy detected a hurt frown which quickly changed to a boyish grin.

"Hey, I know your folks don't approve of you goin' t' dances," he said, knowing full well that Althea Andrews was in the kitchen and in earshot as he spoke. Amy admired Eddie for his grit. When Eddie Bessey had something on his mind he spoke his piece, no matter who was around to hear. "But this ain't a dance hall," he went on. "It's 'auld lang syne' for the season. And they'll all be happy to see you agin. I'll bet you kin git a couple o' the girls to enlist," he chuckled. "We kin allus leave early, if things get rough."

"Promise?" Amy was torn between her family's long-standing rule against attendance at dances and her desire to please Eddie and meet old friends at the cannery.

Should she ask Mama? At once Amy knew better. Mama had pretty much left Amy to her own decisions for several years now. She had been hurt, though, when Amy had enlisted in the WACS without discussing it with her parents first. Hurt, Amy discovered, not so much because she had not asked for their permission but because she had not sought their advice.

"I'll check with Mama and see if we've got anything planned for Friday evening," Amy murmured. Without offering Eddie a chair, she hurried self-consciously into the kitchen.

"The church's party for you is on Saturday," Mama said quickly without looking up from the potatoes she was paring. She paused and sighed, but instead of suggesting that Amy invite Eddie to church, added, "And we don't have anything planned for Friday."

❦ ❦ ❦

Friday was one of those rare October evenings when the weather is warm under a clear sky. Eddie had the top down on his '39 Mercury convertible. "I'll put it right up if you think you'll be cold," he remarked.

"Cold? With you? Come on!" Amy teased.

The moon rose orange over Portugal Harbor as the couple rolled down Route One into the village. Portugal's half-mile of shops and stores lined a red brick street, outlined by gray granite curbing and strips of grass still green in spite of fall's sharp frosts. One business, Whitcombs Cafe, by the bridge where at low tide Samoset River tumbled over a ledgy rapids into the foaming brine, was open on this end of the village.

On the far side of this modest downtown, Eddie slowed to make a left turn onto the narrow country lane leading upriver past the cannery, sawmill, and into the coastal hills. He stopped for an aged Ford coupe turning onto the same road from the other direction. The establishment at the intersection was still lighted, and the cigar smoke which wafted out on the light sea breeze with the muffled clack of billiard balls left Amy pleased with herself that she had chosen more wholesome evening entertainment.

Of the Andrews family, only Papa ventured into Morais' Barber Shop & Pool Parlour, and he never went after dark. Though the fifty cents Rudy Morais charged for cutting hair would pay for two gallons of milk for their table, right after their pilgrimage to Maine from Lancaster County, Reverend Andrews had determined to patronize Portugal's only barber. "It's a matter of testimony," Papa remarked one day right after his family had settled in. As the grammar school principal and minister of one of only two churches holding regular weekly services, he had found himself quite unintentionally a prominent citizen of Samoset Valley. So, for the sake of being seen spending his money locally, and because, "I need to look my best in the pulpit," Papa paid a twice-monthly visit to Morais'.

Eddie popped the clutch and kicked gravel as he turned the corner behind the dilapidated coupe, which Amy guessed might be the reincarnation of Papa's old Model A. Two cigarette-smoking young women jounced along in the rumble seat, and a lanky youth in bib overalls stood on the bumper, hanging onto the spare tire with one hand, his other occupied with a long-necked bottle. In the Mercury's headlights Amy could see four more heads silhouetted within the coupe as she and Eddie idled along behind.

The car bounced roughly across the Samoset & Down East Railway's uneven double-track grade crossing, and the bumper passenger celebrated having survived nearly being thrown into the path of Eddie's convertible by waving his brown bottle at the moon and yodeling at the top of his lungs. "Let's get around 'em," chortled Eddie. He slipped the gearshift into second, and as soon as they cleared the tracks, he bore down on the gas. Amy settled happily into the leatherette seats, listening to the resonant bark of the big Merc's straight-through mufflers beneath them. This was a night to savor, a night to remember.

Samoset Valley Cannery had undergone a metamorphosis since Amy had worked there a year earlier, though most of the change, she realized, had been made at Eddie's direction in the two days since the plant closed its seasonal operation. The conveyor belts which had daily carried endless rows of tinned beans, corn, and blueberries from seven o'clock in the morning until well after midnight had been disassembled and stacked against a wall. The plank floor, worn rough by the constant traffic of hand trucks, had had its broken boards replaced. It had been painted and waxed, and it was so slick with spangles that Amy found she had to coast to a stop like a skater. Paper Japanese lanterns shrouded dim electric bulbs, giving the dance-floor-nee-work-area an illumination scarcely brighter than the moonlight outside.

Shocked field corn stood in one corner, and around this were pumpkins and squashes. Apples and pears were available by the bushel for the munching of the merrymakers. Two barrels of fresh, sweet cider dripped their wooden spigots into boxes of sawdust, and ample stacks of paper cups gave evidence that no dancer was expected to go home thirsty. A plank bench was spread with homemade doughnuts, cupcakes, and pies of mince, pumpkin, apple, blueberry, and custard.

Eddie drew a cup of cider, passed it to Amy, then bent to draw one for himself. She tasted it; it was mellow and smooth, not the sour stuff made from windfalls and wormy apples found at most cider mills. "This is swell!" she exclaimed.

"Wolf Rivers," Eddie chuckled through his grin. "My ol' man gets these apples from Babkirk's orchard up on Quaker Hill Road.

They make cider that's pink and clear—not the murky brown stuff that commercial mills turn out."

"It's okay if you like cider'" remarked a fat man in cowboy boots and a ten-gallon hat, who waddled up at that moment. "Needs a few fifths o' gin to liven it up."

"Remember our deal, Al?" Eddie inquired pleasantly. "No booze. We're payin' you guys twenty bucks for the evening."

"Aw, my boys play far better after a few beers," Big Al argued good-naturedly.

"And we *pay* better without the beer," Eddie answered. "Your band can get lubricated all they want at the dance hall tomorrow night. We're runnin' a clean ship here."

Amy was taken aback by this exchange, but she took it in stride, pleased that Eddie and his father evidently took a stand against inebriated partying. Big Al slung his saxophone across his fat belly and began to play the "Tennessee Waltz." This was followed by the lively "Arkansas Traveler," then "The Blue Danube," as fast numbers alternated with slow in the early evening hours.

For Amy, the element of fun began to wane as the evening waxed late. The romance of swirling with cannery workers in a smoke-filled, dimly lighted room lost its glow. She refused to dance with anyone but Eddie, which meant she spent a lot of time chatting with several older women who sat around on cases of canned goods while their husbands kicked their heels up with girls half their age.

A couple of times Eddie purposely had to shield her from men who, smelling strongly of beer and tobacco, asked to "Cut in and cut the mustard with the preachuh's dottah."

"C'mon—that's our song," Eddie called as a tune Amy hadn't heard since her long-ago grammar school days in Pennsylvania began to play. Big Al's Dance Band struck up a foxtrot, and "I wonder who's kissing her now; I wonder if she ever tells him of me..." raced through Amy's memory. Eddie danced her onto the open platform by the millpond where during canning season the hot, pressure-canning retorts, fed by live steam from the boiler house, needed plenty of cool air to make the work bearable for the sweating men who in late summer and fall had hoisted great tubs of canned goods for fourteen-hour shifts. They danced toward the railing, and the moon, now high over the factory roof, had faded from its moonrise orange to the pallor of oatmeal, reflecting its dim rays into the black water which lapped the foundation beneath their dancing feet.

The coughing of a young woman in dungarees, whom Amy had earlier seen return on unsteady feet from the darkness of the warehouse, broke whatever spell Venus still had on Amy's soul. The girl now bent over the rail and retched violently.

"Too much of Bessey's apple cider?" her male companion snickered with a glance at Eddie. Amy recognized the fellow as the wild rider on the Model A's bumper.

"Too much of your rum, Zeke," she moaned with a curse.

"Let's go back inside," Amy suggested. Even the smoke-filled room seemed preferable to sharing the girl's drunken humiliation, she decided. Still, there was a pity in Amy's soul that made her want to reach out to this girl, to hold her, to take her home and clean her up.

"Why don't we cut out of here? I've already paid Al," Eddie suggested. "Whitcombs is still open. We can duck through the packing room."

Amy followed him toward a side door as he weaved around several machines next to invisible in the dark. They paused on the shipping platform to listen momentarily to the band and foot shuffling coming from the main entrance down the way. Tobacco smoke curled from the open door, glowing white in the glare of the parking lot floodlight. Eddie perused the lot for a moment. "Look what happens when you don't let 'em bring their booze inside," he growled. Beer and liquor bottles littered the drive between the cars. A couple sat on the tailgate of a dilapidated pickup in the shadows, alternately kissing and sipping from a bottle of whiskey. "Here's the keys. Turn the car around. I'll toss enough of these bottles out of the way so's we kin git out o' here without cuttin' the tires. I've a good mind t' call the constable an' have him set up a breath checkpoint when this hog rassle breaks up at midnight!"

The bark of Eddie's V-8 drowned his indignant complaints as Amy touched the starter button. She followed him to the end of the drive, set the hand brake, then slid over to the passenger side.

Suddenly an uncomfortable wetness on the seat of her uniform
skirt caused Amy to raise up, feeling under herself. Her fingers
came out dripping. "Beer!" Empty bottles clinked together on the
floor in the darkness as she swung her feet past the gearshift
lever.

"Toss 'em out! A few more won't make much difference."
Eddie gunned the big car, and they roared off in a shower of
gravel.

"Aren't we going t' stop at Whitcombs?" Amy asked in surprise
as they shot down Main toward the bridge at twice the twenty-
five mile per hour limit.

"Ya wanna—after this?"

"Sure. I could use a Coke an' a dog," she chirped, trying to
brighten his spirits. "I'll have t' sit on a pile of napkins, but I don't
mind."

"Things were gettin' kind o' seamy at that dance," Eddie volunteered as they ate. "Some of my father's employees can get out o'
hand when they decide t' have a little fun."

"What . . . what was it like in past years? You've had corn borers'
balls as an annual event each season, haven't you?" Amy did not
wish to believe Eddie would knowingly take her into such a
sordid bash as this had been.

"As long's I can remember Pa's had the high school band from
Samoset Valley Classical Institute," he said. "They play for free,
but he sends the school a hundred dollars for their extracur-
ricular fund."

"Why the switch?"

"Some o' the guys at the corn shop had heard Big Al's band over
at the Bey-ah Trap Pavilion. They pestered me. Said it would draw
a crowd."

"Well, his band *is* good," Amy agreed.

"And what a crowd," sulked Eddie.

"Don't worry about it, Eddie." Amy patted his sleeve empathet-
ically. In spite of the unpleasant turn of events, Amy knew she'd
always remember this evening with a warm fondness.

Mama was stirring in the kitchen already as Amy sat on the
edge of her bed Saturday morning, her feet on the register feeling

the warmth rising from the wood-burning cookstove which Mama had fired up to fry a pan of breakfast corned beef hash. Just beyond the backyard, Amy could see a pair of sugar maples, scarlet in their full autumn glory, the early rays of the eastern sun pouring through their leaves illuminating them in such grandeur that Amy felt even Eden would be jealous.

Further east, just at the horizon of the sea, the sun lighted also the columns of smoke and steam from a freighter moving down the Bay of Fundy. Hitler's U-Boats, Amy had heard, sometimes prowled the North Atlantic within striking distance of cargo vessels in the mouth of Fundy. American and Canadian ships too often went down from Nazi torpedoes, as young men like Eddie Bessey and her brothers died in burning oil slicks. Into this sinister milieu, Amy knew, she would herself trespass inside a week; and if she survived the passing through, she would land in war-stricken Europe where men killed each other over human freedoms, land, and hate.

But with the glories of God in the sunrise highlighting the fall colors, the petty quarrels of men with submarines and machine guns faded from her imaginations as Amy considered with dismay the mess Eddie and his cleanup crew would face this morning. Then she reached for her Bible on the nightstand. She found Psalm 51, which she felt the need of just then. "Purge me with hyssop, and I shall be clean: wash me, and I shall be whiter than snow," Amy read from verse seven. While the events of the previous evening had left her feeling somewhat soiled, Eddie had been the perfect gentleman, her protector, and he had seemed to prove himself above the sordid behavior of the rabble which Big Al's band had attracted. As for Eddie himself, he was fun to be with, to chat with, to laugh with. They had talked long at Whitcombs, talked of life in little Portugal, of her new, larger life in the WACS, until the last light in the cottages at the harbor's mouth winked out and the manager, after midnight, had done with sweeping the floor.

Amy's romantic feelings had returned by the time Eddie brought her home and walked her up the steep steps of the parsonage's front porch. Gallant and courteous, he made no attempt to press a passionate kiss, but satisfied himself with a peck on her cheek as she blushed rosy in the light of the moon.

But was this love? Amy could not be sure.

"Make me to hear joy and gladness," Amy read from verse eight. How I need that, she pondered. "That the bones which Thou hast broken may rejoice." In the glory of an autumn morning, she had almost begun to rejoice.

Then came Mama's sharp rap at the bedroom door. "Amy," she said softly but persistently, "I've started a wash load of white clothes. Do you have anything you wish to toss in?"

"Come in, Mama." Amy laid her Bible aside and fished in her clothes hamper.

"Did you fall in the millpond?" Mama inquired, noting Amy's military skirt and underwear hanging from a chair on the porch roof.

"No...I..." How *would* she explain this?

Mama hurried onto the roof to gather the soiled slip and underpants before Amy could stop her. "I'll put them in the washer," she said with no further comment. But Mama's wrinkled nose told Amy she recognized the odor of stale beer.

"I'll wash the skirt myself with Woolite," Amy remarked helplessly as Mama went downstairs.

Thankfully, all three of Amy's brothers had left for Saturday jobs before she joined her parents for a leisurely late breakfast in the kitchen. Amy explained frankly to Mama and Papa the events of the evening before, and how she had slid into the spilled beer in Eddie's open convertible without knowing it was there. Mama's response was only stony silence. "It's not *fair* for you to act like that," Amy protested. "Besides, how do *you* know what beer smells like?"

"That *is* an interesting question," Papa mildly observed. "And Althea, the stain *was* on her backside. Hardly the place one would spill it if they were drinking it."

"All the same..." Althea Andrews began. She caught herself. "I'm sure it must have been very uncomfortable for you—and Eddie," she added. Amy thought Mama sounded just a wee bit sympathetic, and she hugged her, then kissed Mama's forehead.

"There are greater issues for a father to discuss with his daughter about to leave home than spilled beer or even corn-shop dances," Papa remarked, a look of love and concern mixing in his eyes. "You're a grown-up girl, and grown-ups must make grown-up decisions. Up to now, your choices have been pretty much confined to what involved your family." He hesitated, carefully weighing the words he was about to say. "When you decided, last spring, to join the WACS, I was hurt that you didn't consult us first, I admit. But I was proud that you joined the WACS. Mama and I had some pretty long talks about that while you were in basic training."

Papa and Mama were both crying now. Amy had seen Mama cry; she had cried the morning Papa placed the key to the Baptist manse under the doormat and the Model A coupe chugged off for Maine with the Andrews family. Amy had seen Papa in tears only once or twice over her nineteen years. But now appallingly, unashamedly he let the tears flow.

"I ... I thought you were mad at me," Amy said. "Mama and I argued about it that day I went under the bridge and met Mrs. Trask."

"Mama told me about that." Papa wiped his eyes and blew his nose while Amy and Mama waited in silence. "She said you looked as though you'd been worked over by the torturers of the Inquisition—what with the mosquito bites and the thorn scratches on your legs." Papa was smiling now, and he chuckled as he spoke.

"It was not fair to you that I didn't ask." For the first time Amy herself realized the full impact her choice would have on the two people she loved most. "I'm sorry."

"What Papa means to say is, his answer would have been, 'yes,'" Mama put in.

"With no reservations, Papa?"

"None," Papa said emphatically. "You're going overseas to save lives. That is something I can be proud of. I went to France in '17 to save lives—and souls."

Amy thought Papa sounded less than convincing. "There *is* a question, isn't there?" she asked.

"Were you ... were you given weapons training at Fort Dix, like the men?"

"Papa, you know Jack taught me to hunt rabbits and squirrels on the mountain with his shotgun." Why did Papa have to ask?

"Yes," Amy said at last. "They taught me to shoot a .45 pistol. I may have to carry one, if I'm in a combat zone."

"Would you use it, Amy?" Mama asked the question that Papa feared to put into words. To Mama, war until now had been an academic issue, personified only by the likes of Gary Cooper's silverscreen version. But Papa knew firsthand that guns killed more than rabbits and squirrels.

"I would defend the boys in my ambulance with my life, even if it meant killing an enemy with my pistol. Would that be murder, Papa?"

Wes's blue eyes captured for a millisecond a scene on a body-strewn French battlefield exactly a quarter of a century earlier when a young, sandy-haired theology student was faced with the same question his girl-cum-woman now posed. Wes now focused on the deadly serious pair of pale-blue eyes across the table, eyes which reflected his own. He saw for a moment in those eyes his mother's eyes, framed like Amy's in ash-blonde hair. "*Ach!* Ve left the old country because there ist war, always war," his mother had once explained. Now the granddaughter would return to "the old country" because of war. "No," Papa said at last. "No, I don't think so. But someday the Prince of Peace will come, and these decisions won't have to be made."

Papa's argument seemed convoluted to Amy, but satisfied that he was on her side in her choice, she slid to the floor beside him and placed her head in his lap. "Remember, Papa—long ago in Pennsylvania when you used to read the story Bible to me and the boys? I would sit at your knees, like this."

To Papa, this was only yesterday. He could not reply as he patted her head.

"I think," said Mama at last, "we need a family portrait. Do you have a clean uniform?"

"Yes!"

Amy was surprised to find Orin Trask waiting in the parsonage kitchen when she returned from dressing upstairs. He held Mama's black box Kodak as he sat, obviously embarrassed, in the rocker by the window. "The boys are away, and we needed a photographer," Mama explained. "Orin is somewhat of an artist, you know."

Orin's sheepish grin was now covered with a modest blush which spread across his freckled face from the roots of his red hair. He rose and stood stiffly, eyeing Amy's khaki jacket, pleated, calf-length khaki wool skirt, and plain brown shoes. She had pinned her military cap jauntily on the side of her head with bobby pins. "Well, general, do I need to salute?" he asked with a twinkle in his eyes.

Amy's only reply was a stifled giggle.

At Mama's direction, Orin shot three poses of Amy with both her parents, one each with Papa and Mama, and one with Amy standing on the porch steps. Orin then suggested a modestly dramatic pose, having Amy sit on the Packard's fender, an arm draped across the auto's long nose. "One frame left," Orin remarked, handing Papa the camera.

"Why don't you two kids sit in the porch swing?" Mama suggested. "Papa can take a snapshot of you together."

Amy was giddy with delight at the picture taking, and her former reticence at being neighborly around Orin melted in her glee. They sat together. "Let me hold your hand," she teased.

"Don't get fresh," Orin laughed, reaching for her hand anyway.

"No—that's too intimate." Amy suddenly felt shy and pulled her hand away. "We'll just link arms."

The picture taken, Amy gave Orin's arm a friendly squeeze. "Wait here a moment," she said, and ran inside. Amy returned with a sheet of typing paper and a pair of scissors. "My APO military address," she explained. "I've typed up a few dozen to give out at church tomorrow, but I hadn't yet cut them apart," she apologized to Orin as she began to snip.

9
The Road to Rome

Naples, Italy
November 10, 1943

Dearest Mama and Papa, Andy, Jack, and Wessie,

I tasted the bitterness of war two days ago, just before *The City of Chicago* sailed into the Mediterranean. I went out on deck at dawn, as usual, to get away from the stifling heat of the quarters I share with thirty-eight nurses and WACS, and to read my Bible and pray. I was surprised to see the coast of Europe straight ahead, with Morocco, in Africa, across the straits to the south. North of the straits, lighted by the sun rising behind it, was a sight so like a life insurance ad that I thought it should have "Prudential" written on it. Then it dawned on me—I was looking at the Rock of Gibraltar, on the south coast of Spain.

But my pleasure was soon interrupted. Perhaps 200 yards ahead of us and slightly to starboard (I've learned a few sailing terms from the merchant marines sailing on this old freighter), a submarine broke the surface, and a sailor with binoculars climbed out of a hatch. This didn't surprise me, since our convoy of ships was escorted by American subs, and they do ride the surface quite a bit. But instead of the serial numbers I've seen painted on our subs, this sub had a black and white iron cross painted on its bridge. "This is not Uncle Sam's Navy," I told myself. "Not German, either," I thought. I expected to see a swastika painted on a German boat, but I have since learned that the swastika is the symbol of the Nazi party, and that both symbols are used by the German Reich.

I looked up at our ship's pilothouse to see if our men had noticed the strange sub. Sure enough, the captain had his binoculars on it, and the men had aimed our single navy gun toward the sub. They didn't fire, I suppose, because they didn't want to provoke an attack.

Then it happened. A torpedo came streaking toward us, and it looked like it would hit just below my feet! I dove behind a lifeboat, but the explosion just made a low "boom" and sent up a geyser. It didn't even rock our ship. I was too excited to be scared.

By the time I stood up, the sub was nearly underwater, but I was surprised to see their sailor bobbing on the water in his life jacket. Their sub (it really was a German U-boat!) was sinking with a black oil slick spreading around it. An American sub surfaced a little farther off, and I was glad to know that one of our boats had sunk theirs.

The sailors were talking in the mess hall at breakfast, and they said the U-boat had probably been following us for several hours before dawn, hiding behind a freighter as protection from the American submarine and waiting for a chance to strike. The American sub guarding our convoy had managed to get into position to sink the U-boat without sinking one of our own vessels just as the U-boat surfaced and fired at us.

The torpedo blew a hole in our side big enough to flood a compartment full of new jeeps and equipment. This slowed us down, so the rest of the convoy had to leave us. We were unprotected without an escort, which made us nervous, but I'm told it wasn't terribly dangerous after we passed the Straits of Gibraltar since the U-boats seldom enter the Mediterranean anymore.

The captain said that if the torpedo had hit us square on, we would have gone straight to visit Davy Jones. He talked about running some of our trucks overboard to lighten the load, if the bulkhead of that compartment should rupture (my precious new ambulance!). Also, the sailors said our ship was built in the same British shipyard as the *Titanic*, and it is of the same design, with compartments sealed off from each other. That didn't comfort us girls at all as the *Titanic* sank anyway!

Our men pulled the German sailor aboard, then they sent him over to our sub (our guardian angel!) for interrogation. I was so thrilled that we escaped with no loss of life, and to see the U-boat sunk, that until that one poor sailor was pulled aboard, the truth didn't really sink in: I had witnessed the drowning of several dozen of the sailor's buddies, entombed in their own *unterseeboot* until Judgment Day. Some of our men were laughing about it, but our cook, who has a son in the Royal Navy, said it always grieves him to see a boat sunk and men killed, no matter whose side they're on.

With Love (and a few tears),

Amy

The ticking of the clock on the parsonage kitchen mantel was the only sound heard as Wes Andrews laid Amy's first letter from overseas on the supper table. Papa, who had read it aloud, now removed his glasses and let the tears flow unashamedly.

"Afraid, Papa—for Amy, I mean?" asked Andy.

"Son..." Wes choked, then he tried again. "Son, every parent who has children in the war has fears."

"Well, I'm glad those ol' Germans drowned." Wessie was never shy in sharing his opinions. "They're the bad guys!"

Mama patted Wessie's arm. Impetuous, brash-spoken like herself and Andy, young Wessie in school packed weekly Victory Boxes for "our boys over there." Often he listened to the excited reports from schoolmates who had fathers, uncles, brothers, or cousins off fighting "slant-eyed Japs" or "Hitler-loving Krauts."

Truly puzzled at Papa's assertions that war is evil, Wessie had more than once drawn from his father a simplified version of the conviction which had caused the Andrews family to leave Pennsylvania. Mama, mindful of her own struggles with Papa's pacifism, now stilled Wessie's patriotism.

"I was in college when a U-boat torpedoed the *Lusitania* in '15," Papa said. "Nearly 1,200 human lives were drowned like a sack full of unwanted kittens in less than twenty minutes."

"That could have been our Amy last week," Mama agreed. Her mother's heart had warmed itself to Papa's philosophy of peace now. That her heart and head did not agree did not matter at the moment.

"This sounds funny, I know, since by all human reasoning Amy's ship *should* have sunk when the torpedo hit it. But it could not merely 'have been.' Nothing 'could have been' but what is, since God is absolutely in control of human affairs." Papa was trying to swing the conversation around to the will of God in the affairs of mankind.

"The *Lusitania* tragedy was bad, but the *Titanic* tragedy was worse," put in Jack, who knew his historical details.

"The *Lusitania* was *far* worse." Papa's indignation had begun to rise.

"Weren't... weren't there more than 1,500 drowned when the *Titanic* struck an iceberg?" Jack disagreed.

"The *Titanic* sank because of carelessness—inexcusable but understandable. The *Lusitania* was sunk by hate and greed, and that's murder." Papa was emphatic.

"Papa, you're beginning to sound like one of those recruiting officers on the radio, urging us to enlist." Andy found his father's reasons for not fighting actually reasons to fight. Don't hate and greed need to be resisted? he wondered.

"Hate, greed, and all other sins will someday be dealt with at God's Judgment Bar, Andy. For now, it's not up to us to take revenge."

"But, 'Whoso...'"

"'Sheddeth man's blood, by man shall his blood be shed,'" Papa finished. Father and son had on prior occasions each used the same Bible verse to prove contrary points. "God's injunction to Noah was a prediction, a prophecy—not a mandate to kill in the time of war," Papa stated. He managed to keep his tones kindly and calm, though he was outnumbered. Mama supported Wes's right to his opinion, though she inwardly disagreed. He knew that all three of his sons would willingly debate him on their juvenile—and sometimes adult—levels. Only Amy, he believed, would attempt to see both sides.

"Papa," Andy finally concluded thoughtfully, "maybe God meant Genesis 9:6 to be *both* a prediction and a mandate."

❦ ❦ ❦

Naples, Italy
November 12, 1943

Dearest Family,

Here we are in Naples, south of Rome, today. It still is a beautiful city, though the Germans burned much of it when they retreated in October. I'm sitting on a marble fountain above the harbor, looking at a bay much larger than Samoset Harbor, and it is filled with freighters and war vessels flying Old Glory and the Union Jack. There are several Italian vessels which the Germans scuttled showing above water at low tide, and what there is left for docking area are the antique stone quays as well as the temporary floating docks put in by the army engineers in recent weeks. The Germans sank so many ships here to plug the harbor that they say it looked like the whole Italian navy was at the bottom of the bay until about three weeks ago.

The streets below me are filled with new tanks, jeeps, and trucks of all description. My ambulance is a brand-new GMC six-wheeler with a steel cab, but the body is covered with canvas. I drove it off the boat myself, and the day after tomorrow we will begin a motor convoy north to carry supplies to the battlefront. After this, part of my trips will be shuttling wounded soldiers from the field hospital to hospital ships in Naples for their return to America. The rest of the time, I shall actually be close to the battlefront, picking up wounded boys to bring into the field hospital for emergency treatment.

The bars and nightclubs of Naples will be filled tonight with American soldiers taking a last fling before they plunge into battle. The girls who came with me on the freighter—Red Cross nurses and WACS—will be with them. I suppose it is their right to do this, but one would think the seriousness of war would make them consider their Maker. The same ladies of the night who entertained Jerry (the Germans) only a few weeks ago are now entertaining GI Joe and Tommy (the British). Some of the girls in my outfit find this very funny, so you see I am learning a new angle on humor.

Just now a group of Tommies went by on drill parade. And—would you believe it?—they were wearing the same ridiculous short pants they wore in North Africa. The fellows all wore berets, and they had a guy playing a bagpipe as a Scottie dog skipped along beside him. He was cute (the bagpiper, not the dog!) but his skirt (kilt?) made him look pretty silly. The Brits really do go to war in style. I've heard the reason they still use those First World War tin-pan helmets is so they can cock them at a jaunty angle.

Everywhere are beggars, though as yet there is no serious starvation. Naples was a free city until the Germans took it in September. They moved on after only a month's occupation when General Mark Clark's American Fifth Army came. The Germans took the food supplies, and they torched whole neighborhoods, so half the city is homeless. The children are particularly pathetic, in their cast-off adult clothing and bare feet. Our GI's do give these kids what they can of their own supplies, though it's hardly a wholesome diet, I'm afraid. Our boys are issued cigarettes, but since many of them don't smoke, they give them to the begging children. I wonder how many Napolitans will in future years trace their tobacco addiction to the American occupation!

Love,

Amy

🐞 🐞 🐞

Somewhere in the Apennine Hills of Italy
November 17, 1943

Dearest Family,

Since our letters are heavily censored, I can't say where I am, except that we have been pushing Jerry north toward Rome. But these mountains are rugged, and reports are that German Field Marshal Kesselring's army has dug in from coast to coast, and we may wait until spring to try to pry them out. So far, my unit is still convoying supplies.

I sleep in my truck at night, and each morning I use my helmet as a basin to heat water for washing and coffee. Once we get to the combat zone, we are under strict orders to sleep *under* our trucks, since the cabs and especially the canvas compartments in back are little protection against shrapnel. Last night I sat up after midnight watching the firestorm in the hills up ahead. I could see the flashes of the artillery fire, though we are still too far off to hear the explosions.

We stopped to refuel by a little country village, and the locals crowded around to greet us. Everywhere they kept shouting, *"Vive gli Americanis!"* They did not beg as did the people in Naples, but they gave *us* food—fruit, vegetables, preserves, homemade cheeses. Our Yanks returned the favor with the only thing they could spare from their packs: cigarettes. Oh, well.

How can I drive this truck, you asked, Mama? I almost couldn't. Papa taught me to drive Mr. Keay's Reo, and when we got to the training school after Fort Dix, we girls who had volunteered as ambulance drivers were told to prove we could drive by wheeling old army trucks around the parking lot. That was it! The rest of our three weeks' school we spent learning how to do splints, tourniquets, and first aid.

One day out of Naples I was sure I couldn't drive another mile. My left knee was so stiff from clutching that I could scarcely walk. I had to pull *up* on the steering wheel just to push *down* on the clutch. But an army mechanic rescued me by adjusting the pedal, so it's softer.

Love, as always,

Amy

❧ ❧ ❧

The Winter Line, Italy
November 19, 1943

Dear Mama, Papa, and Boys,

I have rope burns on both hands, just when my knee is getting better. We set up a seventy-bed field hospital today. I helped pull the tents up. Silly me! The other WACS unpacked utensils and helped the nurses stash medicines and bandages for easy use. Finally, we have a place to call "home"— for a while, at least. Our tents are half a mile from the supply depot, and they have red crosses on the roofs, which is supposed to keep Jerry from shooting us up with his dive bombers. My truck is marked the same way, and we have been assured that the Germans will keep the terms of the Geneva Convention and respect medical facilities.

Love,

Amy

❧ ❧ ❧

The Winter Line, Italy
November 21, 1943

Dear Family,

I took my first load of wounded GI's back to Naples for transfer to the hospital ship today. It was pretty much routine driving, except that it rains most of the time and the roads are a sea of mud. Going into Naples, I made out pretty well, for it was downhill much of the way. But coming back empty (the two nurses' aids who had ridden in back with the boys rode with me in the cab), I had a terrible time getting through the mud. The vacuum wipers on this truck don't work uphill, except when I let up on the gas to shift, which fortunately is pretty often.

So far, our wounded boys must be dragged from the battle lines on their stretchers to the field hospital behind pack mules, since the trails are impassable for motor vehicles. The engineers are putting a road through with bulldozers, though, so I may soon be asked to drive into the firing zone. "Italy is mud, mules, and mountains, and the mountains have Jerries with Mausers," our soldiers say.

Love and Affection,

Amy

❦ ❦ ❦

The Winter Line, Italy
December 5, 1943

Dearest Folks,

Kindness and cruelty are found in odd places in war. There are many stone farmhouses in these hills, and when these houses are behind either line, both the Germans and Americans leave them alone and let the country folk live unbothered. But when a house is suspected of hiding a sniper or a reconnaissance man, either side will shell it without warning the inhabitants to get out.

Sometimes the Italian resistance guerrillas will use these places to hide out when on sabotage forays to blow up German supplies. A little girl was brought into our hospital today with her hand nearly shot off. The Germans had followed two resistance fighters to a farmhouse. Although the men surrendered to protect the farm family who had sheltered them, they killed everyone in retaliation but this child, whom our boys found hiding in a cupboard riddled with machine gun bullets when they went in to drive the Germans out.

Then one of our Mountain Infantry units found an American soldier atop a cliff where he'd been left by the Germans.

The Jerries were so impressed that this GI had the guts to scale the cliff alone, that after they'd shot him in the leg, they patched him up and left him with a blanket and a canteen of water until his buddies could rescue him.

I do get to spend some time in the hospital, helping wherever I can, since the fighting has stalemated and I usually have only one trip a day back to Naples. Yesterday they brought in a German lieutenant and three troopers. The troopers weren't hurt too badly, for they'd surrendered without a fight when caught on a sabotage mission behind our lines. They were laughing and smoking American cigarettes our boys had given them, and you could tell that they were glad the war (for them) is over. A lot of these guys spent the winter of '42 in Russia, and they look on fighting in "sunny Italy" as a sort of picnic. But being captured by Americans is even better, apparently.

Their lieutenant was another story. He was a tall, handsome, arrogant fellow who spoke flawless English. His arm had caught a couple of bullets, and he was bleeding pretty badly. Our surgeon, Dr. Larry Rothberg, is a little guy, and the lieutenant says, "In our army they send runts like you home as unfit for front-line duty."

Doctor Larry, with a straight face, answered, "No kidding? The worst of it is, I'm Jewish. Now do you want me to patch that arm, or would you rather bleed to death?" Well, the German officer required a couple of pints of plasma, and he even had the gall to complain that it might have come from "a nigger or a Jew." Doctor Rothberg says, "It's genuine American blood—we don't use anything else. When we're done with the transfusion, you'll be singing 'Yankee Doodle.'"

Christmas is coming. I shall miss celebrating our Lord's birthday with you all.

Love,

Amy

❦ ❦ ❦

Naples, Italy
December 21, 1943

Dearest Folks,

My hand is shaking so badly as I write this, that I doubt
that the transcribers will be able to figure out enough of it
to type it for you to read. Yesterday we came into Naples in a
convoy of three ambulances loaded with wounded boys to
be transferred to the hospital ship *Newfoundland* for the
trip to the U.S. We had just rounded a bend in the hills above
the city, and we could see the harbor and even make out the
red crosses painted on the sides of the *Newfoundland*.

Just then a roar drowned the sound of our truck motors,
and two American Mustang P-51 fighter planes came out of
the hills and zoomed in so close it looked as though their
propellers would strike the treetops. In a second, we could
see that they were after a German dive bomber—a Junk-
ers-88, I heard later. Of course we stopped. But the JU-88
dropped its bombs on the *Newfoundland* and hit her amid-
ships. She split in half and sank immediately. I didn't think I
could feel good about seeing anyone get killed, but when
the Mustangs caught the dive bomber and blew it out of the
sky without the crew being able to escape, I was at that
moment glad.

We took our GI's to a civilian hospital in Naples, then we
drove to the waterfront to see if we could help. A couple of
motor launches met us, and they had rescued exactly seventeen soldiers and two nurses from over 400 invalid soldiers
and several dozen Red Cross nurses on board the *Newfoundland*.

Last evening, shortly before sunset, I decided to return
alone to the waterfront. I parked the ambulance above the
harbor, for I was sure the MP's wouldn't let me through
without orders, and I walked to a strip of beach between the
docks. The tide had gone out, and I thought I'd look for
anything that might have washed ashore from the wreckage.
I nearly stumbled over a body face down on the sand.

It was a woman. I turned my flashlight on her and I
believe she must have drowned, for she had no visible

injuries. My first thought was to report the location of the body, then go back to the hospital. But I turned her over. It was Maxine Chapman, a Red Cross nurse who had come on *The City of Chicago* with us from Norfolk! Her bunk had been next to mine on the boat. I managed to carry Maxine to the stone steps up from the beach, but I could not get her up on the quay. Two MP's came by just then and solved my problem.

Love and Tears,

Amy

❦ ❦ ❦

The Winter Line, Italy
January 18, 1944

Dear Mama, and Papa, Andy, Jack, and Wessie,

I am kept busy every day now, carrying the wounded from the front lines in my ambulance. The engineers did finally get a motor route back into the hills. Too, with the freezing weather it does not mud up so much, so there is less danger of getting stuck. The battle is heating up with heavy shelling, and we have made some advances on the Germans. Only yesterday I met several of our Yanks marching more than fifty German prisoners out of the hills. The Krauts seemed to be happy enough to march along toward our field hospital, so I guess they are no danger to us.

There is little danger to my ambulance from shelling, but we have been warned to watch out for land mines, which the Germans left aplenty when they retreated. As long as I keep my truck in the wheel tracks I used coming up, I won't hit a mine on the trip back down. The engineers are constantly sweeping for mines with regular mine detectors as well as tanks equipped with huge rollers on front which look like giant noodle cutters. We are under orders to follow the tank tracks for safety.

Amy's letter ended abruptly. With tears in her eyes, Mama read the note from a Red Cross nurse which had been enclosed with Amy's last letter.

Dear Reverend and Mrs. Andrews,

I found this letter among Amy's belongings, which she evidently intended to finish, since it had not been signed. I'm not sure how much will be in the army report to you on Amy's death, but I wanted you to know that I visited the spot where Amy's ambulance ran onto a German land mine. Her truck was upside down in a mountain stream, and because of this several bodies, including Amy's, were never recovered. There was evidence that a unit of Germans might have been in the area just before the explosion, and Amy might have taken this side trip just a little off the path to avoid them. The officers think it's a case of "Missing in Action—Presumed Dead," and I'm afraid I'll have to agree.

Amy was the favorite driver among our nurses. She seems to have made fast friends with several nurses on the boat trip from Norfolk, and those friendships continued until the last. Some of the WACS whom we work with are silly visionaries, but Amy was level-headed and sensible as well as a lot of fun. She cared for the boys she brought in and when necessary gave them medical attention until the doctors and nurses could look after them.

I guess I was not surprised to learn one day that Amy's father had been a chaplain in the last war. From time to time we'd see Amy reading a Bible to soldiers with bandaged eyes or even praying with them. God knows we could use more girls here who know how to pray!

Some day, perhaps when this awful war is over, I can come to Maine and visit you in Portugal.

Yours Affectionately,

Mary Towers, RN

In the weeks following Amy's death, Wes Andrews buried himself in a righteous campaign of his own. He found himself more and more putting the school in charge of his assistant principal, Mrs. Gladys Hussey, the fifth- and sixth-grade teacher, as soon as the music teacher arrived from her high school duties in East Portugal to relieve him from his seventh- and eighth-grade teaching responsibilities for the rest of the day.

Bible in hand, he would slip behind the wheel of the grand old Packard Clipper. The machine's mighty straight-eight would take minister and car, its whitewalled balloon tires and winter Weed snow chains contrasting with the body's slick, ecclesiastical black finish, into the frozen back reaches of the hills above Samoset Valley. Here Pastor Andrews would minister to a winter housebound widow or an elderly farm couple whose only contact with the world were a crank-and-holler phone and a battery-powered Atwater-Kent which drew in the distant voice of Walter Winchell to report on the advances of the Yanks under Eisenhower or MacArthur.

On some of these occasions, Wes would sup with his hill-country parishioners, dining on boiled 'coon, fried potatoes, canned dandelion greens, and blueberry pie. He would then turn toward home, plowing through snow drifting across the open spaces of old pastures to fill the road between the stone walls and rail fences. Cresting a mountain grade, Wes's car would break out of the ever-shifting snow from a recent storm to where stars and winter moon so gloriously lighted the northern evening that he would sometimes cut the Packard's lights and roll homeward by moonlight.

On one such occasion, Wes climbed in second gear to the crest of a north-facing hill. He had spent some moments fighting a half-mile stretch of blowing drifts between open fields, double clutching and shifting, throttling the heavy car in low through the drifts, praying that he might not meet a farmer fool enough to tackle a winter road only a minister-teacher from the lowlands of southern Pennsylvania could be dumb enough to take on, trying in his agitation over his driving difficulties to drown his grief over the loss of his Amy. The drifts ended where the fields ran out into a long stretch of road shaded by bending hemlocks and stately pointed balsam firs, and the one-track lane pitched upward and wound northward for another quarter mile to the top.

The moon had not yet risen on this evening though the stars shone across the cloudless night. Wes stopped at the pinnacle, set the hand brake, and cut the headlights. Below in the valley the road angled to his right, back toward the southeast into Portugal where it joined Route One toward home. He was glad to see that this narrow lane, protected on the windward side by a thicket of cedars, was passable, and he could expect easy travel the last mile to the village.

But directly ahead he faced a mountain, gleaming white in the starlight. It was the long back and shoulder ridge of Hogback, whose rump reared above the sea across the road from the parsonage. Above Hogback Mountain Wes Andrews saw, or thought he saw, the hem of the skirts of God as it trailed across the starlit mountainside. Undulating waves of ethereal pink and lavender swept across the winter night sky; fingers of fire flashed upward from beyond the long hill, reaching nearly the top of the starry canopy above. The sight took Wes's breath away, and for some moments he sat, enraptured in the beauty flashing outside the windshield of the car, forgetting his grief and his labors, forgetting even that he had a family at the parsonage who awaited their father's safe return and his welcome, melancholy voice as he read to them the Scriptures and prayed with them before bedtime.

Aurora Borealis. Wes knew the scientific term for these northern lights, though he had never seen them in his native Lancaster County, far south. Nor in his winter past in Maine had he seen this magnificent electrical show. He had, in fact, dismissed as local boasting tales which Down-Easters told of the glories of clear winter nights in years gone by. The northern lights, Wes had believed, were visible only in Arctic Canada.

But here, as sure as Noah's rainbow following the Flood, God was saying, "I have great blessings for thee yet. Take heart. Trust Me. Be not afraid."

10

The Scandal

"*You're spending a lot of time* at the Trask place these days, Althea," Wes remarked mildly. It was the third February evening in a week that supper for Wes and the boys had been chicken pot pie from the capons Mrs. Andrews had canned in the fall of '43. Though Wes had no complaints about this simple meal, it occurred to him that his wife ordinarily fixed more elaborate repasts for the one daily meal when the family could all be at the same place at the same time.

"I don't know what we can do for Orin," Althea sighed at last. "Since you buried his grandmother right after Christmas, he's been beyond grief. Perhaps I'm helping him more out of my desire to forget my own loss than to help Orin with his," she added softly.

"Have you told him about Amy?"

"Yes." Althea suppressed a sob. "I don't suppose it was right to expect him to share our loss—though I thought he'd want to know. But when I told him the news, he just stared at me as if I'd intentionally done him wrong. And I'm sure I couldn't get three words out of him all afternoon when we were trying to sort through his grandmother's things." She paused for a moment, her eyes staring blankly at the food before her. "I had a really odd thing happen today though," she said at last.

"Oh?" Papa raised his eyebrows.

"I found a stash of letters among some of his grandmother's papers in a kitchen drawer. Thinking the papers might be valuable, I began to separate them into piles. One was written to Cora

117

Trask from Italy—it was from Amy. I wasn't surprised and I was about to ask permission to read it when I found two more with an APO return address. Amy had been writing to Orin!" Mama's eyes brimmed with tears.

"Well!" Papa sighed, unable to put coherent words to his feelings about this revelation.

"Orin saw them, too," Althea continued. "He grabbed them and crammed everything back into the drawer."

"Was he angry?"

"I don't think so. Embarrassed, evidently."

"Perhaps someday he'll share them with us." Feeling emotions rising in him he did not wish to deal with at the moment, Papa quickly changed the subject. "Is he still staying in his cabin on the mountain?"

"No. He gave that up right after the heavy snow came the week they brought us the telegram about Amy. He's camping out in the kitchen."

"The kitchen? He's got...you said fourteen rooms?"

"Except for the one Mrs. Trask used, they're hardly livable," Althea answered quietly. "Plaster's coming down. I expect the roof leaks. But the kitchen's plenty big for a man by himself. He's got his bed in the far end, and he heats with the cookstove."

"I've been meaning to see if he needs any help putting his legal papers in order. That's quite an estate he has there—640 acres, a full square mile, he once told me."

"He seems all set, Wes." Althea admired her husband's well-intentioned concern. "He showed me the deed Mrs. Trask kept folded inside her ledger. His father signed over 635 acres of woods and fields to him before he died, years ago."

"The other five?"

"The other five is the front lot—just the house and barn and gardens. Grandma Trask had a life lease on that. But Orin has a legal, separate deed, quit claim from his grandmother on those buildings and the five acres with no encumbrances, valid on her death. And there don't seem to be any other heirs to step in and stake a claim."

"You know," mused Reverend Andrews, "if we could just get that boy into church, I believe he'd come out of his shell and blossom like a normal human being."

"I know. I'll work on it," said his wife. "But no fancy promises."

❧ ❧ ❧

"If we can't get the sheriff to run 'em off, we should go in there ourselves. I'd fix his ol' tractor so it won't run until spring." Wessie was feeling the indignation that rises in the male psyche at puberty. Mama had come home moments earlier with bad news from Orin Trask that evening.

"I've seen that 'Little King' Thurston playing pool in the barbershop," Jack interrupted. "He's as slippery as a greased pig and twice as dirty. They say around town that Thurston's no fool, though, and anyone who deals with him will get dirty, too."

"Orin needs a lawyer." There was conviction in Althea's voice, a certainty which overcame her own confusion about the whole affair. "He's been swindled, and Thurston and his loggers'll take thousands of dollars worth o' logs off that mountain before anyone can stop them."

"How much property did you say is involved?" Wes asked, trying to focus on the issue.

"All 635 acres—willed Orin in the deed his father made out when Orin was a child. Nearly 600 of it is in old-growth forest, and the rest in fields and pasture. Orin has a clear title to only the five acres which the house and barn are on."

"An entire section, then, isn't it? A square mile all told. Those old land grants were usually for a quarter section, but wealthy men sometimes bought up surrounding acreage—and they say Captain Giles Trask was wealthy," Wes mused.

"It looks as though his grandson and namesake squandered more than just the bank account and boats," Althea remarked tartly.

"I'm not so sure," Wes replied. "Giles Trask III was an alcoholic, alright, and he didn't keep the buildings in repair. But from what Orin has told you, Althea, his father did leave things in good order for Grandmother Trask. And Orin's father passed away nearly ten years ago, so if anyone else had dibs on Hogback Mountain timber, it's not likely they'd wait until Cora Trask died to move on it. Something smells as fishy as Bessey's sardine plant in July." Wes sighed and stood up. He shuffled toward the closet where his overcoat hung. His family waited in silence as he pushed his beaver-fur trooper hat over his ears and pulled on his gloves. "I won't be long. I want to see Orin Trask before he goes to bed." With that, a determined Reverend Andrews strode off into the night.

❧ ❧ ❧

Mrs. Alice Metcalf was the substitute Wes called to teach his junior high classes next morning. "Just keep a lid on things," he told the older woman with a grim chuckle. Then he turned to face the class. Motioning for eighth-grader Junior Higgins to follow him into the hall, he prompted Junior, the class clown, with a private admonition to keep a diary of all goings-on in his absence. "You're ready for some responsibility, I think," Wes told young Higgins. "But keep what you write down private. I'll read it over tomorrow and take whatever action is necessary."

Alice's husband, Willard Metcalf, was Portugal's tax collector and treasurer, and also the senior deacon at Samoset Valley Chapel. Wes found Willard at his desk in the cubbyhole which passed for the town office behind Samoset Harvest Grange No. 19. Besides Metcalf's rolltop desk and swivel chair, this tiny room held a safe, a tiny coal stove, and three kitchen chairs. The town office doubled as the boardroom for Portugal's three selectmen during their twice-monthly meetings. Those were the days before open business sessions had become the law of the land, and like all small-town officials in New England, Portugal's executive body preferred to conduct business in strict secrecy.

At any rate, Portugal's some 300 registered voters got their fill of democracy once each March when they crowded into the grange's main hall for town meeting. "Mistuh moderatuh," one citizen after another was heard to say, "effen the town kin appropriate $300 fer plank an' timbuh t' rebuild the bridge out ouah way, I'll give the ruhd crew enough quarried granite fer new abutments frum the old cellar hole on my place jest faw haulin' it off."

Metcalf stared at a crack in the unpainted plaster behind his desk and seemed to be choosing his words as he attempted to answer his pastor's earnest query about how the "Little King" had come into possession of Orin Trask's forest lands. "I assure you, Reverend," Metcalf stated slowly and emphatically, "Prince Thurston bought that propitty fay-ah an' squay-ah on a tax lien."

"For how much?" Wes pressed.

"For $6,000. 'S a mattuh of record. You kin verify my word at the county register of deeds."

"I'll take your word for it, Willard," Wes answered, mustering his most pleasant manner. But indignation returned to his voice when he added, "But that's not even ten dollars an acre."

"No, it's not." A defensive tone had crept into Metcalf's words. "Land prices have bin bad hereabouts sence the last war. We're too far east for much agriculture—not like y' eastern Pennsylvania dairy lands where the market's on yoah doorstep, practically!"

"But we're talking old-growth forest," Wes insisted. "Orin Trask says the mountain was last cut by his grandfather's sawmill crew in the last century—Cora told him that before she died."

"True. True enough. But that's hawdly the issue. Effen the taxpayers don't think we chawged enough, then it's the taxpayers that should complain, 'n' yoah pasnidge don't pay no taxes!" Metcalf turned in his swivel chair, and for a moment he glared accusingly into his pastor's face.

"When did Giles Trask pass away?" Wes inquired, shifting his approach.

"May 18, 1935. Collapsed in the pool hall behind the bahbuh shawp—cirrhosis of the liver, doctuh sed. An' old Giles II died of a stroke in the wintuh of 1893. I wuz a kid then, helpin' him split up his woodpile the day he kicked the bucket. The Captain, Giles I, died in 1837—I've seen it on his headstone. Which Giles do y' mean?"

"Orin's father—the Giles whose signature appears on the deeds Orin showed me last night. The papers were dated March 4, 1933—the day President Roosevelt was inaugurated." It was the minister's turn to be as specific as an attorney in court, though there was no rancor in his tone. But he decided if his deacon were to engage in a battle of wits, he'd give him a good one. "I'd like to see the annual reports for the Town of Portugal, from 1936 to the present, please," Wes pressed firmly.

"Shoah. They're public records. We keep bound copies, ten yeahs to a volume. But prob'ly you kin find loose ones ovah there to take with you." Metcalf pointed with his pencil to a cardboard box in the corner.

"I'd like to conduct a brief research project right here, if you don't mind."

"Suit y'self, Reverend." Metcalf turned back to his desk and began noisily to punch the keys and yank the lever on a mechanical adding machine, studying his ledger as he worked.

Wes worked down through a pile of stapled booklets bound by rubber bands, each one titled, *Annual Report of the Town of Portugal.* He soon found a copy for each year, backward from 1943 to 1936. Quick perusal of each edition revealed the same notation under "Unpaid Taxes": "Orin Trask, $150, for forest and tillable land at 17 Shore Road." The entry for 1943 was followed by the eight consecutive years beginning in 1936, with taxes listed as unpaid each year. The Andrews' parsonage was at 18 Shore Road, the local designation of U.S. Route One, Wes considered as he examined the reports, though addresses were seldom used for mail delivery purposes since mail carrier Donald "Ducky" Drake knew each householder by name.

"Excuse me?"

"Ya-a-a-a-s?" Metcalf did not look up from his work.

"Has Orin Trask seen these reports?"

"Doubt it. Trask never comes t' town meetin', an' he's nevah registered t' vote," the deacon honestly admitted. "Don't know's he kin read!"

"Doesn't state law require property to be auctioned off for unpaid taxes after three years?" the minister inquired, with no trace of intimidation in his voice.

"Permits it. Don't require it."

"Aren't you derelict in your duty to the other taxpayers by *not* offering tax-liened real estate for sale?"

"Now see here, Mistuh..." Metcalf turned around, but he avoided looking at Wes. "Times has bin hahd since the Crash o' '29. We've got indigent widders in this town ain't paid no taxes sence their husbands died ten, twenty yeahs ago. We gen'ly bay-ah with 'em til they're dead an' buried. Then effen the relatives don't wish to redeem their estates, we sell it. Not only does this keep widders offen the pauper list, it's Christian charity to do so, don't y' think?"

"Cora Trask's taxes have always been paid on time, quite evidently. There's no mention of her house and barn and five acres in the delinquent lists," Wes insisted. "Why *did* you wait until this winter to take action against her grandson? And was Orin ever properly notified? The state attorney told me on the phone this morning that the law requires an annual notice of delinquent taxes—besides a warning by registered mail at least ninety days before the tax auction."

"Mr. Orin Trask wuz duly an' properly notified of enny impending auction on our tax lien!" Mr. Metcalf's voice raised a notch. "You kin tell the state attorney that fer me when you crank up Augusta agin. Tell Governor Sewall, too!"

"Did you send a registered letter, and do you have the receipt?"

Metcalf paused, and Wes felt a thrill of pity pass through his own body as the tax collector visibly trembled. "Certainly," Deacon Metcalf affirmed. "But sech doc-u-mints'r not public record. They can be produced when subpoenaed by a court of law, of course," he added almost inaudibly.

Late that morning, Wes found Portugal's R.F.D. #1 mail carrier, Ducky Drake, unpacking his leather pouch in the post office, his route completed. "Nossuh," Ducky stated, pausing to let a stream of tobacco juice squirt into the brass spittoon at the end of the mail cage, "I have a pritty good mem'ry for sech things. I've been t' the front door o' the Trask mansion jest once in twenty-seven years with a registered lettuh. That was Orin's draft notice in '42. And as you know, he couldn't pass an army physical because of that short leg."

"Could a substitute carrier have delivered the tax auction notice?" Wes asked.

"Last time I hed a sub wuz '35, in Januerry. Broke m' arm crankin' a Ford when the batt'ry wouldn't turn 'er ovah at thirty below."

"Would you testify to that in court if you were put on the witness stand?"

"Now see here, Reverend!" Ducky's tone had grown indignant. "What're you drivin' at?"

"Exactly what I asked," Wes replied calmly. "Someone appears to have been tricked out of some property. It may go to court."

Drake eyed Pastor Andrews warily. "I don't want t' get in the middle o' no lawsuit," he answered at last. "But I guess if I wuz put on the witness stand, I'd state truthfully that young Trask ain't nevah received no registered tax notice frum the town office."

Wes found The Little King taking a nooning with his crew at the end of a forest auto road evidently bulldozed with the blade of the Lombard diesel crawling tractor parked between two huge piles of pine sawlogs. Half a mile of crawling on tire chains had brought Wes to a clearing where eight grizzled men in plaid wool and corduroy hunkered around a bonfire of dead limbs.

Thurston, Wes noted, was impossible to mistake. He was so short that, were it not for his belly which protruded farther only than his gigantic Cuban cigar, it seemed that the tops of his fur-trimmed overshoes reached almost to the wide brim of his greasy, rumpled black homburg. A ridiculous beaver-fur coat hung loosely down his back where it fell nearly to his ankles. The coat was open to reveal that The Little King wore a vested business suit of gray wool sharkskin, a once-white shirt now gray as the suit, and a tie of flowered silk. A week's growth of white whiskers were stained brown from his mouth to his throat, and his gold teeth glinted wickedly between sneering lips.

The man glared at Wes from dark eyes sunken into well-larded cheeks, his eyes seeming even more evil under the shade of his ebony hat brim. But Wes had already walked on coals that day in dealing with Deacon Willard Metcalf. *At least this man makes no dissimulation of leading a godly life*, the minister considered, striding forth to meet Thurston halfway between the Packard and the logger's equally luxurious, though grime-covered, Pierce-Arrow coupe.

"A gentlemen's agreement is all I ask, until the court can determine whether the Town of Portugal had a legal right to sell the Trask property," Wes explained evenly, after he and Thurston had exchanged greetings.

"Well, Je...hosaphat! I'm a businessman, Reverend. I play by the rules of business. You're a preachuh of the gospel, an' if yoah parish ast you t' quit preachin', you'd preach ennyways—right?"

"I spoke with Mr. Metcalf this morning, and he ..."

"Metcalf kin go t' Hades with the rest o' the church-goin' hypocrites!" The Little King huffed. "He likes t' hev his palm greased as well as the rest o' your deacons and the other Elmer Gantrys around town."

In his wrath, Thurston had revealed more about his dealings with Metcalf than he had intended, and Wes quickly followed up on this *faux pas.* "How much did you give him to arrange the deal?" Wes could not believe his own boldness, and his eyes caught the old sinner's catty eyes, who for half a second manifested less duplicity than Samoset Chapel's senior deacon.

"Five Franklins." Thurston paused. "I didn't say that. Effen enny o' you log choppers sez I did, I'll kick your bee-hind clearn ovah to St. Johnsbury, Vermont." Turning back to Wes, he added, "I'll cease an' desist when I get papers from the court. Meantime, you tell Mr. Metcalf for me where to go, an' it ain't purgatory!"

"Thanks." Without another word, Wes Andrews strode for the Packard.

❦ ❦ ❦

"Don't you feel you're taking a chance—hiring The Little King and his crew to cut your logs after he tried to rob you?" Jack Andrews had befriended Orin Trask during the trial, and they sat together in Orin's snug mountainside log cabin as they spoke.

"I had to ask myself, 'What would Jesus do?'" Orin straightened from feeding a dry limb left by Thurston's loggers into his cast-iron Clarion parlor stove as he spoke. He tossed his tousled, red curls away from his face and grinned in boyish innocence.

How could anyone think this guy feebleminded or foolish? Jack thought as the slanting February sun through the frosted cabin window illuminated the countenance of Captain Giles' great-grandson. Aloud he said, "I guess you're giving eight men work and making a profit, so long as they don't cheat you."

"They won't. At any rate, I'm over to their yarding place several nights a week to count logs. Bessey's sawmill gives me a count as they are delivered, and so far it's always agreed with mine. The mill pays me by the thousand board feet, and I keep good records." He pointed to a new ledger on the cabin's single table by a kerosene lamp. "Tell me, what's happened to Willard Metcalf? I'm glad he got off with a suspended sentence."

"Well, he's walking now. He had to sell his car to repay the nine years' taxes he cheated the town out of to gain possession of your mountain. And he's out of a job with the Town of Portugal.

"The Little King told me that Mr. Metcalf even gave back the bribe Thurston paid to fix the bids. Can you believe that a man of his position in the community and the church would risk his career and reputation for a measly $500?"

"That's not all that's hard to believe," Jack added. "Mr. Metcalf resigned as deacon at once, and he made a full confession before the congregation along with the restitution. On Papa's recommendation the church has hired him to audit its books this year, as in the past. And with so many folks around the county having to file Federal Victory Tax papers, Willard has taken out an ad in the *Samoset Valley Gazette* offering to do tax forms. Mrs. Metcalf tells Mama he's got a good number of paying customers already."

A thoughtful Jack Andrews tramped on snowshoes down the mountain and across the road to the parsonage that Saturday afternoon. The events of the past two months had shaken his ideas of Christianity to its roots. He had watched Willard Metcalf's repentance and confession with skepticism, and at seventeen, Jack considered skepticism to be wisdom. Would it be just a matter of months before the now-humbled Mr. Metcalf became his old conniving self, trying to manipulate and bully Papa as he fed the flock of God in this small country church?

Then there was Orin Trask. Jack had known Orin to be good ever since the Andrews had come to Portugal in the summer of '42. Jack could accept that Orin might have a moral goodness born of affection for his grandmother and revulsion for his father's profligate living. And Jack had not failed to notice that Amy had been awed with the man's goodness and kindness, which had been missed by most of their neighbors.

But Orin's allusion to Sheldon's *In His Steps*, his evident glad willingness to share the love of Christ with the filthy, pompous, evil Prince Thurston—this startled Jack. Orin's grandmother had been a member of the Federated Church, which had years ago been Congregational—but the guy doesn't even go to church! Jack mused as he made his way home in the chill winter air.

11

Over There

"*I know, Mama!*" Andy Andrews lay his head on his arms as Althea ran her gnarled fingers through his locks, dark and tousled like her own auburn waves. It was a blustery February evening in 1944, and the old clock ticked quietly on the mantel behind the kitchen's cast-iron range as mother and son tried to read each other's thoughts in the sputtering glow of the kerosene wick. Wes Andrews had gone into the hills for an evening pastoral call, and Jack and Wessie played dominoes by the sitting room's heating stove beyond the archway.

"When this war's over, Central Maine Power can take better care of its lines," Andy changed the subject. " 'S the third time in a month that the juice's been off all evening. If we cooked on an electric range, like in Pennsylvania, we'd 'a' had a cold suppah."

"You're beginning to sound like a real Down-Easter—or is it Down-Eastuh?" Mama chuckled.

"We shouldn't have t' draw the shades, either," Andy added indignantly, ignoring his mother's attempt at being lighthearted. "Papa says the whole air raid blackout thing is silly. The *Luftwaffe* hasn't any zeppelins left, and Germany's long-range bombers can't reach North America. Why doesn't President Roosevelt try appealing to the real concerns of patriotic Americans?"

"How long has it been since that U-boat was spotted in Fundy, just off Nova Scotia, opposite here?" Mama's tone had turned from teasing to pleading once again. "And there's that U-boat that tried to sink Amy's ship!"

"Mama, you've been listening to the news, same's the rest of us," Andy sighed. "You know that the Germans haven't had a submarine west of Iceland since last fall—any battleship, for that matter. After the *Bismarck* went down, our Navy mopped up the Atlantic. The United States has ruled the seas since the fall of '43!"

"And you wish to help America . . . rule Europe."

"That's one way to put it," Andy agreed. *That's not fair*, was what he restrained himself from saying. "What will I tell my children if I don't . . . don't take Amy's place?" he pleaded. "I'm eighteen next week. I've *got* to enlist!"

"Your graduation . . . couldn't you wait until June?"

"Mama, I *know* how you feel. No . . ." Andy paused. "No, I probably don't. Losin' a big sis isn't quite like losin' an only daughter, is it?"

Both were crying now, and Mama hugged Andy tightly. The warmth of the matronly arm that had cradled the child to her breast years earlier now circled the broad, muscled shoulders of the young man.

"Did . . . did Papa enlist in '17, or was he drafted?" Andy asked.

"Papa enlisted, and with his seminary schooling they made him a chaplain," Mama admitted. "He was a conscientious objector, but if he'd held out for official conscientious objector status, he might have been sent to a munitions plant to build guns, which in his eyes was the same as shooting them." Fiercely, Mama added, "If I were a man, I'd volunteer. I'd be a bombardier in a Liberator B-24, and we'd dump the whole load on Hitler's head!"

"Then . . . then you won't protest if I did enlist?"

"My heart will protest, Andy. I'm still your mother. My heart aches for Amy every day. But . . ."

"But?"

"My will says, 'Go, with my blessing!'"

❧ ❧ ❧

England's weather in April 1944 is *rimy*, Andy thought, recalling Dickens's terminology. In fact, the phrase "April showers" must have been coined in England as well, he considered, hugging his khaki oilskin raincoat under his chin and settling his helmet deeper onto his head. The helmet had recently been issued for use in the invasion of Europe rumored to be planned for sometime in the spring. Already Andy had learned that a military helmet, besides offering protection from shrapnel, served other purposes: It was a pot to boil water on the battle-field, where safe drinking water was not to be found, the army instructor at Fort Dix had explained. And it was useful, too, for shedding the "blasted Henglish drizzle" described by another British writer, Kipling.

Wethersfield, England, is a dreary little village, Andy thought as he trudged from the boardwalk, which led out to Camp Pershing, onto the paving stones of the ancient sidewalk. Not like Maine, he considered, recalling the elm-shaded village streets of Portugal. Only here and there did a naked oak fling its rain-driven arms wildly skyward along this narrow lane of shops and taverns. *Coal*. Andy sniffed the air, catching a whiff of the ever-present odor of English towns in winter. To tell the truth, Andy had become fond of the aroma of wood smoke which permeated the atmosphere about Portugal, though he had lived there only two years. Though England seemed to have plenty of farmland, he had not seen a forested area since he arrived.

Andy trudged a few paces further, then he looked up. A sooty sign above a door portrayed a caricatured rooster and fox in animated conversation. Chaucer's Chauntecleer and Russel—everything in this town reminds me of English Lit class at the academy, Andy chuckled to himself. He pushed open the door of *Ye Cock & Fox* and hurried inside.

From somewhere behind the bar, "Over There," a First World War tune, was coming in on a radio fuzzy with static. Andy smiled grimly. "Over there," he knew, referred to France. He had come in winter across the stormy North Atlantic only to be stuck, waiting for weeks in wet England until Eisenhower's high command should order them into Europe.

"Wot'll it be, Yank?" A ruddy-faced waitress had hurried up as Andy joined two other GI's at a table near where several soldiers were tossing darts. "A mug o' stout?"

"No ale, thanks," Andy answered pleasantly. "Hot chocolate on a rainy day such as this. Fish and...uh...chips." Andy dared not refer to English fried potatoes by their American name, "French fries." They were "chips," though certainly not what passed for chips in the U.S.A.

"British booze too strong for your stomach?" chuckled Mickey Shozenski, a soldier from Andy's barracks.

"Naw. Andrews is a teetotaler," cracked Hal Harrelson, who bunked next to Andy in the steel Quonset hut which was their home at Camp Pershing.

"T. Total abstinence, or totally tea," Shozenski chortled. "Hey, missy, our friend here wants tea!"

"Comin' up!"

Andy was served tea instead of hot chocolate with his fish and chips that April evening at *Ye Cock & Fox*. He paid for the unordered beverage good-naturedly and showed no offense at the joke at his expense.

"Missed you at drill this morning," Harrelson observed after Andy had been served.

"Had to work." Now it was Andy's turn to tease.

"'Work' as in w-o-r-k?" inquired Shozenski. "If you're cuttin' drills, the sarge'll have you on KP from now until the Fourth of July!"

"Been building bridges," Andy chuckled. "Major Hall has taken me off drill practice." Andy spread out his hands in triumph. Several tiny wood splinters, along with callouses, proved his point.

"What for?" Shozenski was incredulous.

"'There are twenty miles of rolling sea,'" Andy quoted gleefully. English literature was in his system, and it just seemed to pop out today.

"Cut it out! We ain't goin' t' cross no channel on wooden bridges—not built by no farm boy from Maine," protested Shozenski.

"You'd have us use the Brooklyn Bridge, maybe? I hear every time a Maine farm boy goes to New York, you guys try to sell it to him," Andy laughed.

"A point well made," observed Harrelson. "But why *are* you building bridges? It must be important for you to be yanked out of drill practice."

"Actually, the army had nothing so ambitious in mind as invading Europe by bridge. We expect the Germans to dynamite every bridge in France as they retreat, so we're constructing portable bridges here in England out of Canadian pine timber. They'll be parachuted onto the riverbanks across Europe where the Allies need to cross. I'm on a special deployment crew to build them here, then assemble them in France and Belgium."

"Lucky stiff! No foxholes."

"Use your head, Shozenski!" Harrelson interjected. "What d' you think the Krauts are going to be doing while Andy's unit is bolting their bridges together? Handing them the wrenches?"

Paris, France
August 26, 1944

Dear Mama and Papa, Jack and Wessie,

This city is filled with rejoicing today as General Charles de Gaulle parades with his troops through the city. It has been just a week since we put the Jerries on the run and made Europe's queen city once again free. I'm afraid some of the spirit "Libertie!" manifest in the streets came from Paris's wine cellars rather than the people's hearts. And many of our soldiers are as guilty of this as the locals.

I'm seated on a park bench near the Arch of Triumph, and it is marvelous to see that this beautiful city, which the Arch symbolizes, has been untouched by war. After seeing town after town in ruins in our more than two months of pushing the Germans across France, it's swell to find a place that hasn't been bombed and vandalized. I've heard that Hitler was an artist before he got into politics. I find it incredible that God put into the heart of a man as evil and ambitious as *der Führer* such a love for beauty and art that he ordered Paris spared.

I've purposely not told you about the exploits of my unit in June and July in my previous letters because I didn't want to worry you. But that is all past, and it looks like clear sailing to Berlin. Oh, there'll be a bit of shooting, but we'll be firing at Jerry's heels. General Clark is keeping one

German army busy in the Alps, and Ivan (the Russians) is keeping Jerry busy in the east. So our generals, Eisenhower, Bradley, and Patton, aren't meeting all that much resistance.

My unit splashed ashore at Omaha Beach in Normandy on June 9, three days after D-Day. Since the Germans had been pushed away from the coast by then, not a shot was fired in our direction. We kept our trucks moving just behind the front lines, and after a week's travel, we set up our portable sawmill and workshop and began to build more bridge sections.

We were asked to bridge a couple of rivers which, fortunately, were past the spring flood stage and well toward their summer low. We had got our pontoon sections about two-thirds of the way across the stream when the Jerries opened up with a machine gun hidden under some willows on the opposite bank. We were standing chest-deep in water, and the only place we could go for protection was to dive beneath our bridge—which was open toward the side where the Germans were waiting for us. Fortunately, the Krauts were too high up to shoot directly into our prison, and our boys were doing a pretty good job of holding them off by artillery fire from the bank on our side. After about ten minutes, a couple of guys used grenade launchers to blow the machine gunners out of their nest.

I was wounded in that episode, but I am fine now. I picked up some pretty good splinters in my left shoulder when a couple of machine-gun bullets tore through the planks. I was still ambulatory and no bones were broken, but my left arm was in a sling for a week, and it was another week before I could rejoin my unit to build and assemble bridges. I haven't had any bad scares since then because our artillery men have been able to cover us whenever we've gone in to put a bridge in place. I am thankful for the Lord's protection, and I know each day that I am here in France because that's where He wants me.

I came here to fight, though, and I do find it frustrating that I'm doing noncombative work while the war rages around me. I guess there's something in me that says, "They got my sister; I want to get 'em back." Perhaps the Lord is trying to deal with this, and He's letting me see fighting and killing for what it is without actually being involved. I do carry my government-issue M-1 rifle, though when we're working up to our armpits in water, it's necessary to leave our firearms on high ground to keep them dry.

I go from here to Belgium. By fall we expect to be in the Ardennes of eastern Belgium, mountains which they say are much like the Alleghenies of western Pennsylvania. Since we'll be spanning mountain rivers and gorges, we're already working with pre-fab truss construction for practice. The floating pontoon bridges we have used in France just won't work in the hills.

Already the boys in my unit are talking about being home for Christmas. They figure to chase Jerry across the Rhine and into Germany by then, and once in Germany, Hitler will probably sue for peace. Between our bombers and those of the British we have pounded many of Germany's larger cities to rubble without an Allied foot ever being set in that land. And since the Russians recaptured Stalingrad, they have been steadily pushing the Germans westward. It looks as though the Third Reich's great empire should be squeezed entirely back within the borders of Germany by Christmas, at any rate.

Wessie will be old enough to get a hunting license this year, won't he? He can use my shotgun in partridge season, so long as Papa or Jack go with him.

Love,

Andy

12

A Healing of Wounds

Jack Andrews held his breath as the stooped old man pushed open the heavy rolling door in the ell connecting the Trask Mansion to its barn. The man slipped inside, and Jack waited until the white-haired fellow in the green-billed cap shuffled past the window before following.

Except for Orin's pickup truck, there was no auto in the Trask drive, so Jack had been startled to spot the intruder when he rounded the corner of the verandah. The fellow was dressed neatly enough, so he was hardly a hobo. An old, but well-oiled pair of heavy work shoes adorned his feet. The man's denim overalls, though faded from several washings, were neither frayed nor patched. Curiously, the legs appeared to have been creased like dress trousers. His chambray shirt, likewise, was pressed and starched as stiffly as a banker's.

Did he have malicious intent? Jack was aware that many folks about Portugal, though they had never had a hostile encounter with Orin, feared this recluse. Fear, Jack had learned, is a powerful motivator and may even lead to bizarre behavior.

Orin's newfound wealth from the sale of his logs had brought out the worst in several local scalawags. Orin, who never had driven an auto in his more than thirty years, had become the owner of a dilapidated Model T Ford pickup in a fifty-dollar deal with an elderly farmer whose failing eyesight would no longer permit him to drive. Papa had aptly described Orin's flivver as a "death trap"—two-wheel brakes, carbide headlamps, canvas top, a mule kick which would break an arm if the operator forgot to retard the spark before hand-cranking the motor. "Its only redeeming value," Papa remarked ruefully, "is its road speed—fifteen miles per hour, flat out. At that speed, he probably won't kill himself while he's learning to drive."

Only last week Jack had had to rescue Orin from the menace of Moose MacFarland and Jupe Jenison. Moose, driving his father's '33 Victoria V8, had overtaken Orin as he chugged toward home along Route One, and Moose decided to entertain himself at Orin's expense. Jack, in the big Packard and himself newly licensed to drive, was rumbling along in the dust cloud a respectful distance behind the Victoria.

Moose and Jupe went sailing past Orin's plodding Model T, then without warning, MacFarland cut the ancient pickup off, sluing to a stop in a shower of gravel. Orin's frantic "Onka! Onka! Onka!" on his rubber-bulb-and-brass horn failed to clear the road, and the flivver's two-wheel binders couldn't stop the pickup in time to avoid a collision, breaking a taillight on the Victoria and a headlamp on Orin's Model T.

Two can play that game, Jack told himself. He parked the Packard behind the two cars and slid from beneath the wheel. Moose, spouting profanity and hinting at lawsuits and prosecution, likewise hopped out of his vehicle. "Yeah," echoed Jupe. "Dutch Boy an' Retard here'll both go t' jail!"

"It'll be *your* license for reckless driving and assault with a motor vehicle! As you can see, we've got witnesses." The soft-and-precisely-spoken defender of Orin's rights was Cinnamon Gurney, petite, sloe-eyed, fifteen-year-old daughter of Harvey Gurney, chief deputy sheriff of Samoset County. Cinnamon was Jack's passenger that July afternoon, planning to join Jack exploring Sabbathday Brook by the same route Amy had followed a year earlier. "My daddy knows the district court judge pehh-son'ly," she cooed. "Iffen you want t' make somethin' of it, I'll jest use the pasnidge phone t' call the station right naow!"

Jack stood speechless as Moose and Jupe dived into the old Victoria. "I hope they get home in one piece," Jack muttered, as

Moose, his throttle foot all but in the V8's carburetor, disappeared around Hogback Mountain at the head of a column of road dust.

Jack had taken it unto himself to check up on Orin's comings and goings on a regular basis after that episode. He feared for his friend's safety, though Papa once remarked that his concern was "four-fifths teenage paranoia." This afternoon he had decided to visit Orin just at five o'clock, when he knew he could find him seated on his three-legged stool, head down against the belly of old Molly as rivulets of cream-rich Jersey milk flowed into a stainless steel pail between his knees.

So, with apprehension, Jack slipped through the shed door. The interloper scurried ahead of him toward the barn, evidently unaware that he was being followed, and Jack hurried behind. The tie-up now held Orin's Red Durham oxen, a heifer, a steer destined to become steaks, and cats without number. The old man moseyed past all of these. He stopped, hunched over, hands in his deep pockets, behind the milker on his stool. "Mr. Trask," the man at last uttered, his voice barely audible.

Orin, startled, must have pinched a teat, for Molly stepped aside so suddenly that he nearly tumbled into the gutter.

Jack recognized the voice at once. But he was used to seeing the man in a wool business suit, shiny at the elbows, topped with a neat though worn gray felt homburg.

"Yes?" Orin regained his perch and faced his visitor.

"I've come...I've come to..." The voice trailed off.

If anything, Willard Metcalf is meeker than on the evening he confessed his crimes before the congregation of Samoset Valley Chapel, Jack thought in amazement as he hung in the shadows.

"Good to see you, Mr. Metcalf!" Orin's remark was intended to fill the awkward pause, and it was spoken in tones as rich and warm as the milk in his bucket. For never having had opportunity to develop social graces, it seemed to Jack, Orin was somehow marvelously charming as he put the broken old man at ease.

"I..." Metcalf began again, "I've come to apologize an' t' beg your forgiveness."

"Friend," Orin responded, rising and setting his pail on a shelf by the window, "brother, you owe me no apology. You've unlocked my grandfather's treasury of timber so that for the first time in my life I have cash enough for my needs—and more." Then, sheepish at having spoken so freely of his newfound earthly wealth, he continued, "We who know the Lord are all rich in Christ Jesus." Jack gaped in amazement as Orin's long arms clasped the little old man in a bear hug and squeezed him so that Jack expected to hear ribs popping.

"I'm so sorry," Mr. Metcalf stammered on. "I tried to cheat you out of what was rightfully yours."

"Hey, don't worry about it," Orin countered. "It all belongs to our Father." At this point he spied Jack and smiled in his direction.

"Can...can I take the milk into the house for you?" Jack suddenly felt a need to make himself scarce.

"Sure!" Orin replied good-naturedly. "Cream settlin' can's in the bottom of the fridge. An' tell your ma that ennytime she wants t' come over, I've got at least a gallon o' cream that's startin' t' turn. She kin put Wessie onto the churn's crank handle, an' we both kin have buttah!"

Orin's spirits have sure perked up since last winter, Jack told himself as he ambled back through the long ell toward the kitchen. I guess maybe getting into the village with his truck to meet folks has helped, now that he doesn't need to keep his grandmother company. Any fellow needs friends.

When Jack returned to the barn, he found that Orin had already turned his cattle into the pasture for their nighttime forage on grass. He now busily plied his manure shovel in the gutter, pitching the cow droppings into a wheelbarrow to push outside. Willard Metcalf, ignoring Orin's protests, scraped the stalls with a large hoe. Jack quietly watched the men work for a moment, then slipped out and went home.

❧ ❧ ❧

"You don't say!" Papa snapped the Atwater-Kent off and sat up in his maple-arm easy chair where he had been listening to Mutual Radio's announcer report how the Allies were steadily

chasing Hitler's *Wehrmacht* across France. Thumbtacks in a map
of Europe behind the radio showed the progress of the armies of
American General Ike and British Field Marshal Monty. "Here,"
Wes Andrews had only yesterday remarked, pointing at Andy's
position on the map, "lies a large chunk of my heart." Further
down the map, a tiny cross in central Italy south of Rome bore the
India-inked notation: "Amy—with Jesus."

"You don't say," Wes repeated. "Willard Metcalf helped Orin
clean out his cow stalls—and he apologized?"

"He's already made a full confession before the church, Wesley,"
Mama, who had heard Jack's report, reminded her husband.

"I've been bothered by that," Wes admitted. "Willard sinned
against the church, to be sure. But his offense was *primarily*
against Orin Trask. Is there any real repentance until the person
primarily offended has been reckoned with?"

"Churches across America would be much stronger if that
principle were carried out, I'm sure," Mama agreed.

"And our nation as well," Papa added. "We're at war, and war is
a result of sin, no matter how shiny a coat of patriotic varnish we
may choose to give it. Men like M.R. De Haan and Charles E. Fuller
are calling for repentance," Wes concluded. "Would that other
Christians get the message as thoroughly as Willard has!"

"Did you know Amy had been writing Orin?" Jack quietly asked
as his eyes drifted to his sister's cross on Papa's map. "There are
several letters from her in a holder on top of his refrigerator."

"You didn't touch them, I hope." Mama paused, and Jack could
see that she was crying. "Yes. I've seen those letters," she said at
last. "Orin kept them hidden for months, but I think he now
leaves them out after rereading them to remind himself that God
was good enough to let him know her. Amy had dates with Eddie
Bessey, but I think she may have realized a kinship with Orin she
herself didn't understand. That man has a heart of solid gold. If
only he'd get involved in church—and the community."

"After what I saw this afternoon, his responding so kindly to
Mr. Metcalf, I think we may see that yet," Jack remarked. He rose
and held Mama close. Mother and son wept together.

Papa was silent.

❦ ❦ ❦

Dear Son in France,

Wes Andrews, man of letters that he was, ordinarily added a few lines to Mama's letters to Andy rather than write his own. Tonight, though, he was moved to pen an epistle to Andy unburdening his heart from a load he'd carried for some months.

> I've been wanting to write to you for some time now, Andy. And something happened today which reminded me to do so.
> We learned after Amy died

Here Wes's fountain pen blotted the page as he stopped for some seconds.

> that she had been writing Orin Trask. Jack was visiting Orin today, and he spied the letters and asked us about them. Thinking of Amy and her letters prompted me to sit down and share with you what's on my heart.
> I've wanted to tell you that I'm proud to have a son in the U.S. Army. I pray every day that you'll never have to take a human life. And I pray harder (God knows my heart!) that your life will be spared through the war. I'm sorry that we didn't discuss these matters face-to-face before you left.
> I have come to believe participation in war to be a personal choice. In God's unfathomable wisdom, I find it possible for two Christians to take opposite positions on some issues while still maintaining their Christianity. Moral issues are another matter, of course. Stealing, lying, and adultery are wrong. Those who practice such things without repentance will never inherit the kingdom of God.
> The same holds true for murder. For me to kill, even in war, would be—was—murder. But God has forgiven me. I suppose I shall wrestle to my grave with why God permitted me to choose between killing and seeing a buddy killed that October day in 1917. Was his life more precious in God's eyes than the life of the young man I killed? I learned from the fellow's ID card that he was a Lutheran—a Christian. Since no German chaplain was present, I conducted

his funeral from a German Bible and prayer book, using the German my mother had taught me as a child. I suppose he and I may have a good laugh in heaven over the Baptist-cum-Mennonite chaplain who shot the Lutheran!

So as Saul went forth to slay the Amalekites, and David the Philistines, if it becomes your lot to kill German soldiers, do so to the glory of God! I shall pray that you do not have to, of course. Meanwhile, God bless the bridge-building business. I'm doing my best to build a few bridges here on the home front.

Love,

Papa

13

The Captain's Heritage

"*We kin sell all the white spruce* your crew cuts offen that mountain, Mistuh Trask." Parker Hamlin, Lloyd Bessey's sawmill foreman, was obviously delighted at the most recent load of logs Orin Trask's hired truck had hauled over to the mill. "Mountain grown, an' the wood is tough, not soft or rotten hearted, like some trees grown on wet ground."

Orin's logs, in fact, had earned Bessey's Lumber & Building Supplies a government contract to furnish framing timber for GI housing at a rapidly expanding air base in Aroostook County. Mr. Bessey and foreman Hamlin had days earlier traipsed with Orin and The Little King over Orin's forested acres. Up and down the mountainside the men had gone, on foot, on The King's old Lombard log hauler, or on a pung pulled by one pair of The King's three teams of Clydesdale draft horses. This day, Orin had hitched a ride to the sawmill with the trucker hauling his logs, hoping to elicit a report from Hamlin on whether he could expect continued sales of his timber.

"Best logs I've seen in thuhtty ye-ahs. He-ahs yoah check, an' it's got a bonus for extry-fine timbuh," Hamlin exulted.

"Now I can give Bessey some business," chuckled Orin, glancing at the sum on the bank draft. "I've hired Charlie Fuller and his boy to put a new roof on my place and give it a couple o' coats of paint. On Will Metcalf's advice, I'm acting as my own contractor, so I'll need to order my supplies directly from the mill. Soon's Charlie gets the measuring done an' gives me the particulars, you can expect me back with an order!"

As the weeks passed, sheet after sheet of gleaming new copper capped the roof of the Trask place. First the house with its porches, next the long ell, then the grand barn with its cupola shone with new metal roofing so that lobster fishermen, who had for years depended on the lighthouse on the breakwater to guide them into Portugal Harbor, now began to set their bearings by the copper-crested buildings ablaze at sunrise above the low sea-fog as the early rays of Old Sol set the roofs agleam.

The barn, clapboarded like the house and ell on the side facing the sea, was, in the fashion of rural New England, shingled in unpainted cedar on its other three sides. These weathered and curled shingles were removed and replaced by new ones from Bessey's mill by Fuller & Son, and at Orin's invitation, Wessie Andrews pushed endless wheelbarrow loads of old, dry shingles into the parsonage woodshed for Mama to build biscuit fires on cool summer mornings.

🐚 🐚 🐚

"Your crew is really making that house look spiffy—white paint, green shutters, and such," remarked Wes Andrews. He turned from his shaving mirror beside the kitchen window to strop his razor on the strap hung on its brass hook against the wainscoting before he attacked the lathered bristles on the other side of his face.

"Charlie Fuller is as good at painting as he is at roofing," chuckled Orin. He stretched and yawned in the parsonage's kitchen rocker as the mantel clock struck half after five. "If I had known how good Althea's biscuits are," he teased, "I'd have given you folks a shed full of old shingles years ago—even if it'd 'a' meant leavin' my barn exposed to the weather."

With a squeak of cast-iron hinges, Althea opened her oven door and removed a baking sheet laden with baking-powder biscuits. "Butter from your Molly moo cow and strawberry jam from our garden coming up!" Mama sang out. "Breakfast is ready."

"Sure nice of you folks to ask me over f' breakfast," Orin remarked almost apologetically, after swallowing the last of his fifth hot biscuit. "By the way, in the process of cutting sawlogs, The Little King has had to take out a good number of hardwood trees suitable for firewood here 'n' theyah. Theyah's enough piled along The King's yardin' roads t' heat both our houses f' several wintuhs. If I kin borrow some young muscle, I'll hitch up ol' Red an' Ron, and we'll get that firewood out."

Wessie flexed his muscles to show off his developing biceps.

"Red and Ron?" Mama quizzed.

"Orin's oxen," Wessie explained importantly.

"How about it, Wessie?" Papa asked. "Can you give a few hours a day till school starts to the cause of heating our house? I'll pitch in fifty cents a day."

"Hrumph!" Orin cleared his throat in embarrassment. "I'd intended to pay him a dollar a day. So he gets a dollar and a half?"

"Why not?" agreed Papa.

"And I've got Grandfather Trask's old buzz saw in the ell," Orin continued. "My Model T has a power takeoff on the drive shaft. Ed Norton down at the Flying A has told me he can fit it with a belt pulley, so we've got power to drive our saw. We'll have a bee some Saturday this fall and cut up our firewood."

"Chug, chug, chug," mimicked Wessie, remembering the many times he'd heard the Model T pickup labor up the steep Trask driveway.

Papa shot Wessie a stern glance. Orin only laughed.

❦ ❦ ❦

Portugal Federated Church was a conglomerate of half a dozen denominations, which, as Down East religious life waned in the years between the Civil War and World War I, had merged, torn down, or sold its old buildings, and finally maintained only one, a fine example of New England Congregational church architecture, for the few faithful who remained. The Trasks had been faithful Congregationalists, so long as the local church remained faithful to its evangelical Puritan heritage. But when the sturdy doctrines which had given pulpit fire to Cotton Mather and Jonathan Edwards were replaced by the wisdom of Freud and

Niebuhr, Grandmother Trask simply chose to maintain her simple altar at home.

Under the care of Grandmother Trask, the good seed of the Word took root, grew, and flourished in the heart of young Orin like the pure white hepaticas, which bloom under the melting snows of March, blossoming long weeks before the rival, more gaudy violets awaken from their winter sleep. The hepatica, or white liverwort, is a hardy, solitary flower, needing only the slightest thawing of snow, only the merest rays of sunlight, to blossom in the silent forest, smiled upon only by the face of God.

Thus with Orin Trask. Ignored by the garden variety of Christian, who requires much weeding and the hot rays of June to bloom, abused by the ungodly, who sprang like tares in his way whenever he should venture into the village, Orin nonetheless developed an inner beauty of the type discovered beneath the feet of the solitary woodland wanderer in the season when the thawing days and freezing nights of early spring command the sweet sap of forest sugar maples to yield their nectar.

And so it began to occur to Orin that his newfound wealth, owed as it was to God who giveth every good and perfect gift, ought to be used, in part, to build God's earthly kingdom. Orin was returning from Bessey's mill one afternoon with his groaning pickup laden to capacity with split cedar shingles, a keg of nails, and a five-gallon pail of paint crowding the cab floor space of his Ford Model T. He turned past the village green, then he drew up before the ancient edifice where as a child too young to recall he'd been sprinkled "In the name of the Father, the Son, and the Holy Ghost." He cut the spark on the magneto, and the engine gasped, coughed, then died.

Orin surveyed the old building and its glass-faced sign which advertised: "Federated Church—Services Twice Monthly Under the Ministry of Northern Theological Seminary Students—Miss Gertrude Saltonstall, Clerk." The granite steps leading to the double doors were lichen-crusted with only a narrow path down the middle kept smooth by the slippers of a few aged ladies, its sole parishioners. Orin's eyes followed line upon line of peeling paint up the steeple. A hideous gray stain from the open belfry showed that assorted gulls, pigeons, bats, and swallows made their roost there, their daubing unchecked by any wire netting until the steeple had become totally disfigured.

The wooden sign was held in place by large screws, and it hung at a slight angle, the weight of its boxed glass front having wrested the screws part of the way out of their anchors. Here was one feature of the church he could repair easily enough, Orin decided. Unfolding the screwdriver blade of his scout knife, he hoisted the sign into place with his shoulder and set to work. The first screw, rusty as it was, turned grudgingly in its anchor, and after some wrenching which nearly broke his blade, Orin succeeded in resetting the screw. The second, however, moved a quarter turn, then snapped in two. At this point, Orin realized he would need a stepladder to tighten the ones higher up. He let go of the sign, expecting it to rest peacefully on the remaining screws. But, loosened from their lead moorings by his lift, the screws let go, and the sign somersaulted over his shoulder, landing with a shattering of glass and rotten wood.

As Orin surveyed the mess on the granite at his feet, he noticed out of the corner of his eye a rust-encrusted iron plaque set into the wall; for half a century it had been hidden by the wooden sign. Cleaning the corrosion to make this sign readable, however, would need to wait.

Orin took the bits and pieces of glass and wood into the foyer where he got his first look at the interior of a church building since infancy. What he saw distressed him, but it did not surprise him. The plaster was gone from much of the ceiling, uncovering great stretches of naked, hand-split lathing of the same vintage as the bare laths in his home's upstairs bedrooms, and exposed for the same reason: a leaking roof had loosened the plaster.

All but the two front pews, padded with velvet cushions and sawn from sturdy oak, were covered with old bed sheets. The church had no piano, but a high pump organ stood at one end of the platform. Most distressing, however, was the church's "Record of Attendance & Offering," posted in a wooden sign on the front wall: 6 present; offering, $1.29.

Whatever thought processes moved Orin's mind, emerging as it had begun to do from three decades of near-somnolence under the shadow of Hogback Mountain, to visit the elderly Miss Gertrude Saltonstall and propose that his roofing and painting crew top Portugal's oldest sanctuary of worship with a new copper roof, paint the building, and repair the shutters and plaster, remains a mystery. In later years, Orin himself could never quite figure out why, when a sixty-member evangelical church just down the street struggled to pay its pastor and maintain its building, he had chosen instead to bankroll a landmark—spiritually dead, nearly ruined, and sparsely and seldom attended.

Perhaps it was the iron plaque. Orin had scraped the flaking rust away with his knife and found that it proclaimed, "First Congregational Church. Erected 1809, a Gift From Capt. Giles Trask to the Town He Loved & Founded." Perhaps, after counting the pews and determining that some 300 worshipers could comfortably sing the Lord's praises here, Orin had been moved by the possibilities of restoring the building's spiritual heart even as his hired crew was restoring its body of wood, stone, and metal.

Then Orin made a remarkable discovery. Following the advice of Willard Metcalf, one of the few citizens of sleepy Portugal shrewd enough not to share the popular fiction that church edifices, along with the heady salt air from the Bay of Fundy, belong to the people, Orin learned from Miss Saltonstall that the Federated Church belonged to no denomination, that—though several ladies attended the twice-monthly lectures on moral philosophy—it had no official membership roll. Orin was determined to discover to whom his gift of roofing, painting, and interior decorating of the grand old Puritan meetinghouse had been given. To God, certainly. But who owned the building? Who was the rightful earthly steward of this heaven-spired edifice?

A trip to Samoset County's Register of Deeds uncovered an interesting entry dated "Oct. 18th, in ye yeare of Oure Lord Eighteen Hundred and Nine." It stated that the church building had been built by Giles Trask on land registered in his name. A "Perpetual Lease" left it "In truft to ye Congregation of ye Firft Congregational Church, to hold in Perpetuity untill ye holie services shall ceafe for ye space of one yeare." At which time the property was to "Revert with its Buildynges and alle Appurtences to ye faid Giles Trafk, or to his heirs."

14

The King Is Dead

"*Kin I hev yoah p'mission* t' swamp a ruhd through the gap on the Hogback?" The Little King, Jack thought, could be decent and polite enough when he tried. Were it not for his habitual pomposity, he could even be easy to like. This evening Jack was observing with keen interest Orin's dealings with the man who'd once stolen his woodlot, then had relinquished it under legal duress.

"Certainly—if it's something you need to do." Orin was kind, perhaps a little gullible. But Jack figured it was better to err on the side of gullibility than to play the hard-nosed, perhaps offensive, businessman.

"That fellow needs the Lord," Orin had told Jack only days earlier. "One of these days, I'm going to catch him relaxed long enough to chat, then we're goin' t' have a talk on eternal matters." Now, apparently, was not the time. Orin merely let The Little King explain that he'd bought cutting rights from Wilfred Wellington to 40 acres of pine on the back side of the mountain. The old private drive up from Hardscrabble Road, near the Wellingtons' abandoned tumbledown house, was drifted in because of early snows, the King explained. But since he already had roads up Orin's side of the mountain, it would be just a matter of cutting through a couple of hundred yards of cedar thicket—more timber for Orin to sell—to get at Wellington's pine.

Bill Wellington's fortunes had changed for the better in the months since his young daughter Fannie's death. Reverend Andrews, knowing that Portugal already had the Wellington brood on their pauper list, appealed to the selectmen to let the family live in a spacious, though run-down, abandoned farmhouse that the town had taken on a tax lien.

Bill's training as a railway engineer and experience as a fireman, it had occurred to Wes, ought to suit him for operating a stationary boiler, if the work was not too demanding for a man with a bad back. As things turned out, Lloyd Bessey needed a night-shift man to sleep in his Down East Cannery's furnace room and toss in a shovel of coal now and then to maintain steam pressure in the warehouse. This arrangement suited Bill well, for he was not only able to escape the continual carping of Ruth, but he could contribute to his family's welfare and maintain dignity before his neighbors as well. And since, in Ruth's words, Bill had "got religion" at the Samoset Valley Chapel, where he was now a faithful, baptized member, she was filled with loathing for this new Bill, who had exchanged his pipe for spearmint and his profanity for "Praise the Lord!"

Fannie's death had cut Bill Wellington to the quick. Only weeks after Fannie's funeral Wes Andrews had the privilege to share with Bill the words of the apostle Paul who wrote, "If thou shalt confess with thy mouth Jesus as Lord, and shalt believe in thy heart that God hath raised him from the dead, thou shalt be saved." Bill believed. He confessed his sin and repented. Christ became his Lord, and from that moment on, Christ would rule his life. Once a coward, unwilling to seek medical help for his dying daughter, Wilfred Wellington was now washed, sanctified, and justified in the name of the Lord Jesus, by the power of the Holy Spirit of God.

It was now the week before Christmas, and Jack had crossed the road that afternoon to bend his ears to Orin's shortwave radio set which brought in the British Broadcasting Company's twenty-four-hour coverage of the war's progress. Frightening new developments in the snowbound Ardenne Mountains of Belgium had begun days earlier, as the Germans, firing with artillery and slipping through the forest under camouflage, pushed the Yanks back dozens of miles in just days. Thousands of Americans had been killed and wounded. Andy, the family knew, was in the thick of things in Belgium, but Papa's Atwater-Kent would pick up only the Bangor AM station, WABI, with its five-minute, top-of-the-hour newscasts. Orin Trask, however, had a new shortwave radio, purchased mail order from Montgomery Ward with funds from the sale of his timber.

So as Prince Thurston lingered in the Trask kitchen, Jack bent again to the squawks and squeals of the radio as Orin adjusted the dial, trying to better bring in the distant, British-accented voice of the BBC's announcer. The newscaster made mention of "craters" left in the terrain by artillery fire, and this remark stirred Orin's memory. He turned again to Thurston. "You're aware there's an old cellar hole and a well in those pines," he said. "I've been through there on foot many times. I'll go with you and show you where it is, if you'd like. It could swaller y' log hauler right out o' sight, if a man gets careless."

"Found it awreddy," The King growled, going from polite to surly. Plainly, he did not care to be warned of dangers. He was a man who could take care of himself.

❧ ❧ ❧

Bill Wellington went home to his wife and children on Christmas Eve. Though his meager paychecks had left him nothing to play Santa Claus with, Bill was clever with wood-carving tools, and he made good use of the long hours when his duties at Bessey's cannery consisted primarily of watching pressure gauges and opening or closing steam valves. Blocks of red cedar from Prince Thurston's logging operations became a fire engine, a truck—with wheels that really turned—and dolls with joints which bent in all the proper places. Bill carved a section of cedar tree trunk with a couple of limbs left on into a good-sized cross. This he decorated with a relief of a young girl in slumber, hair spilling across her shoulders as she slept. "Frances Ann Wellington, 1932-1943, Our Darling With Jesus," he added underneath the child.

A pensive Bill Wellington carried the cross, a piece of iron pipe, baling wire, and borrowed tools out to an unmarked grave in Maple Grove Cemetery the day before Christmas. With an old axe, he drove the pipe several feet into the grave's soil which fortunately was loosely frozen gravel. The cross he then wired to this upright metal post. "That'll last a few years, until Ruth an' I kin git a proper headstone made o' marble," Bill muttered, surveying his work. Few stone carvers, though, could have rendered their artistry as lifelike as Bill's labor of love.

Tears were frozen on Wilfred's scarf and the cuff of his mackinaw as he trudged for home. These were tears of sorrow, yet strangely, tears of joy. Besides Jesus, who had died for Wilfred's sins and then ascended to the right hand of the Father, Bill now had another light in a heavenly window calling, gently calling, sweetly calling him to come.

Bill managed to maintain a modicum of civility while among his loving children and perpetually angry wife that Christmas Day. How his heart ached to have Ruth forgive him for ever letting Fannie be hurt! He supposed, though, that Ruth's implacable meanness was in part an attempt to bury her own guilt in also refusing to send the desperately ill child to the hospital in Bangor for a lifesaving shot of penicillin.

Bill returned home from the cannery each morning from Christmas Day to New Year's. The weather had turned milder, and he spent several hours each day repairing the powerful but badly worn motor of his '28 DeSoto. He could walk to work. Ruth and the kids, however, needed transportation to trade in the village, to visit with Ruth's mother, or just to get away from the stifling confinement of a farmhouse full of kids in winter.

New rings, rod bearings, valves ground, and a new battery—hard to come by in the war years—went into the old car. Ruth soon had her wheels, albeit a ragtop which let the breezes through the side curtains as she motored along.

On New Year's Eve, Ruth let Bill out at the cannery for his all-night shift, then she drove to her mother's place with the children. Bill's conversion had taken away his appetite for "ringing in the New" in the tradition of Portugal's rabble crowd. Ruth would have to celebrate by herself this year; and he knew that she would find men capable of swinging her around the spangled hardwood at the Bear Trap Pavilion as Big Al's Dance Band tooted out the strains of "Auld Lang Syne."

"When you hit a patch of ice at eighty, something's got to give," Sergeant Stanley Corson, Maine State Police, commented later that evening. He lounged against the leather saddle of his big Indian motorcycle and lit a cigarette. Corson had written out his report, and he was anxious to be on his way—just as soon as the coroner got the body into the hearse and Norton's Flying A wrecker got the auto on the hook.

"Phew!" Sheriff Harvey Gurney rammed his three-cell flashlight into his coat pocket. "Stewed to the gills! Iffen I hadn't been occupied with a fight at the dance, I had planned to take her to jail. I had no idear she come in her own cah, er I'd 'a' snapped the cuffs on her an' chained her to a post 'til I was reddy t' go."

"Looks o' that ol' tourin' cah, ain't nobody goin' t' drive it home t'night. That's one Ed Norton ain't goin' t' put back on the ruhd, even with a war on," Sergeant Corson observed. The DeSoto lay on its side, bent nearly double against a gigantic elm tree at the bottom of the hill below the Bear Trap Pavilion. "Mebbe even have t' cut the tree down t' git the old crate loose, way the frame's twisted."

"Have t' use his torch, ennyways." Gurney flipped his light on and studied his wristwatch for a moment. " 'S quarter t' twelve. I'll go over t' the cannery to tell Bill the news, then I've got t' git back to the Bear Trap. Hog rassle'll be cuttin' the mustard till the proprietor cuts the lights at two."

"I'll be along soon's I kin." Corson took a long drag on his cigarette. "If this pile o' junk is screwed onto the tree as bad's it looks, I'll tell Ed t' fergit it til daylight. We can't have anymore drunks skiddin' around in the middle of the night."

🕊 🕊 🕊

The day of Ruth Wellington's funeral, her mother, though ailing, took the children home and made it plain that her "high-an'-mighty religious" son-in-law was not welcome past her threshold. What few possessions Wilfred had, he stored in his shack on Hardscrabble Road. After his twelve-hour night shift, Bill could often be found chatting in the plant's employee lunchroom or sitting in a corner reading a Gideon Bible.

From time to time, Bill would hike out to the Andrews' parsonage. After a pleasant, but melancholy, visit with whomever he happened to find at home, he would sometimes climb aboard Prince Thurston's log hauler and ride with him back to the Wellington pine woodlot to check on The King's progress at cutting lumber. If he could realize enough profit to pay his taxes, pay the undertaker, and put headstones on the two graves now on the Wellington cemetery lot, this broken man told Wes Andrews, he'd be more than satisfied.

"Be back by 5:30, Bill. Althea doesn't like to wait supper and we can't be late for prayer meeting," Wes Andrews told Wilfred a February afternoon in '45. Wes was in high spirits today. He had just received a good letter from Andy, telling of his exploits at building bridges. The *Bangor Daily News* had earlier reported that the German Bulge had broken right after Christmas. Now, more than a month later, the radio reported daily that the Allies had the Jerries on the run, and in several places the Americans had advanced across the borders of Germany.

"Sure thing, Reverend Andrews. You want me to invite Orin Trask f' suppah, too?"

"Bring him along. With both of us working on him, maybe we can even get him into church," Wes chuckled.

Bill hiked up the hill across the road where he found Orin repairing horse stalls in his barn. Prince Thurston had kept his six horses in the Trask barn since he had begun cutting logs under arrangement with Orin. Now that his crew had moved across the mountain to the Wellington lot, he continued to use the Trask barn for a paddock at a dollar a week per horse.

"Seen the King?" Bill inquired.

"'S been a couple of hours. He should be back anytime now with a luhd of your logs. Goin' back with him?"

"Yeah. Not that I don't trust him. But work inspected is better done than work expected, if y' know what I mean," Bill smiled.

"You're right," agreed Orin. "Here. Can you hold this board while I drive a nail?"

Just at dusk, The King's Pierce-Arrow pulled up beside Orin's barn. Ruby Thurston, The King's wife, was behind the wheel, and she parked next to a beat-up Hudson pickup belonging to one of her husband's employees. Like Bill Wellington, she was waiting for The Little King to come out of the woods, so she made no move to leave her auto.

Moments later, two pair of Belgians driven by two French-Canadien loggers standing on pungs behind the horses trotted out of the woods. Orin rolled the barn door open to let men and beasts inside, and Ruby followed behind. "Where's y' boss?" Bill asked the men. "I've been waitin' for a ride back to the woodlot."

"Ze Little King—*le roi*—he has not been out?" The logger was startled. "King, he say he go for another sleigh o' lumbair, two, mebbe three hour ago!"

"It's not like my Prince to be late for his supper," observed Mrs. Thurston mildly. Her voice had a worried pitch which made Orin and Bill uneasy.

"Jacques Violette, he back there with the othair hosses. He'll look aftair The King," the logger remarked. The men tossed their tools into a corner and turned to leave. "You an' *le roi*, you'll bring Jacques home, *non?*" inquired the loquacious French logger.

"*Oui*," Ruby answered crisply. "Tell Jacques's wife he may be late, *s'il vous plaît.*"

Ruby Thurston was a compact, well-kept woman of about forty. She wore a Harris Tweed coat with a mink-dyed rabbit collar, calfskin gloves, and lined leather boots. Not ostentatious like her husband, she nevertheless dressed in keeping with Prince's earnings, well above the standard of Samoset Valley. Her hair, like that of the village wives, had been professionally set, and it had been tinted so that the gray streaking the honey blonde had vanished, giving her an appearance of youth complementing her beauty of figure.

Orin fished his silver-case Waltham, once his grandfather's timepiece, from his watch pocket. "A quarter to six," he remarked.

"Hey, Althea Andrews was expecting me at 5:30 for suppah—you, too!" Bill exclaimed.

"Well, we can't just leave Mrs. Thurston here alone."

Orin's boyish sincerity in his concern for her brought a smile from Ruby's ruby lips, which Wilfred did not fail to notice. Conscience smitten at once for admiring the beauty in the face of another man's wife, Bill built on Orin's concern. "C'mon, Mrs. Thurston," he suggested. His recent trauma and the Lord's strength had buoyed him to heights of new confidence. "The

Andrews have a big table. If Prince an' Jacques get back right away, they kin jine us."

"Well, the Lombard *does* have headlights," she sighed. "I guess he'll be able to see his car across the road. Climb in, boys!" She flashed them both her sweet smile once again.

It was a quarter to seven, and Althea Andrews was just serving seconds of chiffon cake garnished with canned strawberries from the parsonage garden when there came a pounding at the kitchen door. "It's horses!" cried Wessie, who had tipped his chair over in his haste to beat the adults to the door.

"Le roi est mort!" screamed an excited, nearly incoherent Jacques Violette. *"Le roi est mort!"* The King's body lay lifeless on the pung behind Jacques's horses.

As the excited Jacques gained his composure, he explained that his employer had got the log hauler mired in a hillside drift on the overgrown farm where they were logging. Jacques and Prince had shoveled snow for more than an hour, then, with the help of Jacques's horses, they had worked the heavy tractor free, but by then it was dark. The Lombard had headlights so The King went on ahead. Jacques followed with the horses.

The Little King, angry at having to leave his last load of logs in the forest, took a shortcut across an open space overgrown with a tangle of raspberry bushes. The collapsed walls of a farmhouse buried in drifting snow appeared as another hummock among many on the night hillside. Though Thurston had seen the ruined farmstead from its uphill side, he had lost his bearings. Onto this pile of rubble he drove, Jacques and the horses following a short ways behind. The rotten boards and timbers gave way, and man and machine pitched into an abyss cut into the bedrock of the hillside, once a farmhouse cellar.

A scream above the clatter of the machine, then silence as the tractor turned over, killing the motor and crushing the life out of The Little King—that was all. Had Jacques not had the flashlight from the tractor's toolbox in his pocket he would have had to leave Prince's body until daylight. In fact, without the flashlight, he said, he might not have been able to find his way out of the forest with the horses that moonless evening.

"The King is dead" soon went out across the telephone wires of Portugal as members of the Samoset Valley Chapel phoned one another to report that there would be no prayer meeting. Doctor Abbott examined Prince Thurston's body on the parsonage sitting room couch where Orin and Jacques had carried it; then it was taken away by hearse to await Mrs. Thurston's decision in the morning.

Next morning at eight, Reverend and Mrs. Andrews drove out to the Thurston residence, a seaside home with several rental guest cottages on a peninsula below Portugal. They were surprised to find no car in the drive. But since they had promised to accompany Ruby to the funeral parlor, Althea rang the bell.

"Oh, the car—I told Wilfred to take it over to the cannery, since you were coming for me anyway," Ruby explained quite matter-of-factly.

Wes knew that folks can get overly generous in times of grief, but he said only, "Bill will take good care of it."

At this, Ruby smiled and remarked, "Bill is a very kind man."

Wes later learned from Bill that he had asked only to ride with Ruby to the village, expecting to walk out to the cannery for the night shift. But Ruby insisted that Bill drive, and that he take her home. "I can't bring myself to go into that empty house unless someone goes ahead of me and turns the lights on," Ruth had said sadly. Bill not only turned the lights on, but he built fires in both her stoves and filled her wood boxes before he left.

Wilfred Wellington and Prince Thurston had been mere business acquaintances until Prince's death. Bill now, however, felt an unexplainable urge to attend The King's funeral. "I don't own a suit, though," Bill had confided to Wes. "And the undertaker has attached my lumber checks until my wife's funeral is paid for, so I can't buy one."

Wes understood. "I've got an extra black suit you can have," he said simply. He eyed the diminutive man, eight inches shorter and fifty pounds lighter than he. "Althea's going to have some fun cutting my old suit down to fit you," he chuckled.

It was Bill Wellington who sat with Ruby Thurston at Prince's funeral. It was he whose elbow she clasped at the graveside that raw day in February. And in the weeks to follow, the Pierce-Arrow was parked overnight at the cannery as often as it was kept at Ruby's home.

Bill retained The King's logging crew to cut his pine the rest of the winter. By the end of March, Bill not only had paid off the undertaker, but he had gotten respectable gravestones for his family lot as well. And even with buying shoes and groceries for his children and mother-in-law, he was able to open a modest account at Samoset Trust Company.

The Pierce-Arrow was parked in the lot next to Samoset Valley Chapel each Sunday morning after Prince Thurston's funeral. Ruby saw to it that Bill, in Wes's old suit, was parked next to her in a front pew each morning worship service and usually for evening services as well. Her second Sunday in church, Ruby, who had been a fifteen-year-old perfect-attendance Sunday school girl until running away from home to escape an abusive father and becoming the child bride of The Little King, knelt at the altar and reconfirmed a commitment to follow Christ made many years earlier.

February melded into March, and reports from Andy in Germany were good news in every letter. His unit moved eastward day after day as the Allies steadily pushed the German armies toward Berlin. And in Samoset Valley, Maine, the arrival of spring brought thawing days and freezing nights along the Atlantic coast. The sap was rising in the maples in an old grove behind the Trask mansion. Orin honored a custom begun by Grandmother Trask in the last century, and he tapped two dozen of these trees, boiling the sap into syrup on the kitchen range.

Rising, too, was a strange romance, which had set the tongues of local gossips awag. The lovely, well-to-do widow of a recently deceased successful entrepreneur, a fat, rambunctious, and filthy fellow missed by few, was being courted by a twice-married and twice widowed widower a dozen years older than she, a man brought to poverty through no fault of his own. "At least he's clean," commented a doughty housewife one day, shopping at Farrington's Grocery.

"Clean, mebbe, but poor as Job's turkey. Hardly equal to her," said another.

Wilfred Wellington was, in fact, clean. Since the day he had taken the job as engineer of the cannery's boilers, he had rigged a shower above a drain in the furnace room, and hot showers, a luxury not available for most of his fifty-three years, had become a nightly ritual after the other workers left.

April arrived, and with it the robins. Mourning doves, a love-bird not found in Maine's frigid interior beyond Hogback and the other coastal hills, cooed from the telephone lines around Portugal Village. Tulips and daffodils pushed up to bloom in the sunny corners of white-picketed yards. And Bill Wellington, though like the daffodils his romantic feelings had lain frozen for a long season, bloomed in Ruby's presence until one day she suggested that his accommodation at the cannery, a cot behind the boiler, was too drab and narrow.

"Move into your spare bedroom—it wouldn't be right," he protested.

"Actually, I had something better in mind," she cooed. Ruby perceived Bill as a man who, though not actually hesitant about matrimony, might be bashful about putting his desires into words.

Ruby had considered her motives carefully before this April morning when she and Bill met for breakfast at Whitcombs Cafe. She was *not* offering him her guest room. That had been Prince's since, dirty and drunk each evening, this was the only way they could live under one roof. To make it sound like she was offering for Bill to share her bed without holy vows before their church and guests from the community was unthinkable.

Ruby now patted the blushing Bill's left hand with her own left hand, without her wedding band and diamond for the first time since her husband's funeral. Bill still wore his wedding ring, as he deemed this proper for a man responsible to feed his six children. She touched his ring. "Is it engraved inside?"

"Why...yes."

"Do you mind if I see?"

"G-go ahead." He moved to remove it, but Ruby beat him to the draw.

Holding it up to the sunlight she read, "'Size nine.' I'll have to remember that."

"Wha-what *are* you getting at?" Bill stammered.

Ruby smiled, and when she did so, she touched her lip with her left hand.

Bill saw, finally, that her pretty, perfectly tapered fingers were bereft of jewelry. His jaw dropped, then snapped shut. "Yer rings! I mean, would—would you wear *my* ring?"

"Is that a proposal?"

"I—I love you. Will you marry me?" he whispered.

"You *know* I will; and I love you, too." Both Bill and Ruby laughed with delight as they basked in the warmth of their declared love for each other. "Pomerleau's Jewelry is having a spring sale on sets of rings," Ruby continued. "And I don't see any reason why I should have to wait to wear both rings—if Pastor Andrews has a date open in the next week or so."

The last Saturday in April the sun rose bright over Samoset Harbor. The bells at the chapel rang at ten o'clock, as the strains of *Lohengrin* pealed from the pump organ. The bride, beautiful in a powder-blue suit which matched her eyes, walked the aisle on the arm of her brother. Pastor Andrews waited at the altar. As matron of honor, Althea stood beside him in a pink suit which matched the bride's.

Orin Trask could no longer be bashful about entering a house of worship. Stiff and awkward in new shoes, black trousers, and rented white dinner jacket, Orin stood beside Wilfred Wellington in identical dress outfit. Identical, that is, except that the best man had opted to leave off his black bow tie. "What's the point of putting it on?" he had asked Bill, as they dressed together at the Trask mansion. Bill agreed when Orin demonstrated that his red beard covered not only the tie, but most of the front of his ruffled shirt.

After the wedding, after the bride had been kissed and an interminable line of guests had shaken hands and offered congratulations, after the groom had the first piece of wedding cake mashed into his face, after the luncheon at noon, at which Bill's mother-in-law grudgingly conceded to permit his two oldest girls to wait on tables to honor their new stepmother, after the Pierce-Arrow purred off down Route One with tomato cans bouncing behind on baling wire, the Andrews family, exhilarated in their shared happiness, piled into the Packard and motored toward the parsonage.

The family approached the Andrews' residence to see a new, drab-khaki Chevrolet sedan pull into their drive from the other direction. The auto had a white star painted on its driver's side door. A man in khaki uniform climbed from under the wheel, an expression of infinite sadness on his face.

Wes and Althea had been met by a messenger like that once before—just over a month before Andy had enlisted in the United States Army in March 1944.

15

"Quiet on the Western Front"

"*And who might these be,* Corporal?" Lieutenant Engle affected the voice of an aged maiden aunt, then he spat a string of oaths around his Cuban cigar.

"My prisoners, sir!"

"I said, 'Take no more prisoners,' Andrews. You were under orders!"

The chill Andy felt as he held his carbine on the backs of the three ragged *Wehrmacht Panzer* corpsmen was not from the cold of late December 1944 in the Ardennes of eastern Belgium. It was the frigidness of the fear of facing the wrath of a superior officer rumored to be capable of the oldest dirty trick in military history: sending a soldier who crossed him to the most vulnerable frontline spot under enemy fire.

Too, the knots in Andy's stomach were in part a reaction to an episode of three days earlier which had caused Lieutenant Engle to issue his rash order. Engle's unit had come upon more than fifty American soldiers facedown in the snow. They had been disarmed, then shot one by one in the back of the head. Andy had helped tag and photograph the bodies for retribution by a military tribunal after the war.

"That's what happens when German soldiers have been on the Russian Front," Engle had snarled. "Well, if they wish to behave like barbarians, we'll give 'em a taste of their own medicine!"

Andy had prayed then that he might be spared having to make a decision about obeying Lieutenant Engle's order.

"Line 'em up!"

"Yes, sir! *Achtung!*" Andy snapped at the tall blond one whom he had learned was named Hans. They were ragged, desperate men, these German warriors. By their tough demeanor, Andy guessed they were among those elite forces transferred on Hitler's orders from the Russian Front to the Western Front to create this bulge in the Allied lines. Battle-weary, these near-crazed German divisions sought to push the Americans back to the Belgian seaport of Antwerp and cut off Allied supplies vital to the rush to cross the Rhine. They had forced General George Patton and General Omar Bradley to withdraw their armies some sixty miles, just when the Yanks thought the war was about over.

A few hours earlier, Andy had rushed to aid a buddy fighting the three Germans who had miraculously escaped from a *Panzer* tank stopped by a bazooka. But Andy arrived too late. Hans had shot the American who had destroyed his tiger on caterpillar tracks, then out of ammunition, he had surrendered himself and the other two to Andy.

"*Ja?*" the blond eyed Andy evenly.

"Over there." Andy gestured with his gun muzzle toward a wrecked American tank. Fear filled the *Panzer* leader's eyes, but he obeyed and the others followed.

"Now shoot them," Engle ordered.

"Sir," Andy protested. "That star," he pointed to a white star on the gun turret of the ruined tank, "that star represents my country. We signed the Geneva Accord, which supersedes your orders."

"Can't do it? I've seen scared little boys before."

"Before God, I won't." Andy's fear was about gone, and he now felt the calm assurance of being right.

"Then I'll shoot the Huns myself." Lieutenant Engle carried a German nine-millimeter Luger pistol which he liked to boast he had taken off the body of a Kraut he'd finished with a bayonet. He now unbuckled the holster and began to draw the weapon.

"Engle!" Never before had Andy impolitely addressed an officer without using his title.

Two mechanics repairing a jeep nearby wiped the grease from their fingers and lounged against its fenders as they lighted cigarettes and watched in cautious interest.

The lieutenant's eyes narrowed as he stared at Andy.

"If you murder these prisoners, sir—in cold blood—and I live through this war, there's going to be a court-martial. These men are under my protection." Andy kept his composure and he spoke calmly, though he again felt cold fear working up a fever in the pit of his stomach.

"You're threatening me, soldier!"

"No, sir! That's not a threat! That's a promise, and I intend to keep it." Andy nodded toward the two mechanics who watched the exchange in slack-jawed amazement. "Spearrin and Hayward, there, they'll be subpoenaed as witnesses at your trial."

Engle bit his cigar in two, then he uttered a vile string of oaths. But he froze in his tracks and dropped his pistol back into its sheath. "Andrews, you've got guts," he growled at last. "Put these Heinies on the next truck to Antwerp."

Trois Ponts, Belgium
January 16, 1945

Dear Mama and Papa, Jack and Wessie,

Things started moving so fast right after Christmas that I haven't had a chance to write. Anyway, there's been no mail out of here until recently. I'm sitting in a charming little inn near the juncture of three mountain streams in the forest of Belgium. It is a beautiful, snow-blanketed place, much like Hogback Mountain and the hills around Samoset Valley in winter. The forest is hardwoods, bare of leaves, with clumps of pines and firs green against the white hillside. Were it not for what man has done to this mountain hamlet, I believe Trois Ponts would be next door to heaven!

American tanks—*our* tanks!—are rumbling across a new bridge my crew finished just this morning after working two days around the clock. You will be fortunate to get my letter if I can stay awake long enough to write it. The front of this inn was torn off by artillery fire, so I have a ringside seat on our procession of tanks, trucks, and jeeps.

My outfit got to Trois Ponts the day after New Year's. Though the village was occupied by the Germans (most of the residents had fled), it hadn't yet been touched by fighting. The Germans had decorated the place for Christmas with fir boughs cut from the snow-covered hillsides around. Every sign, every lamppost, every chimney was decorated with evergreen garlands. They had even swaddled several of their tanks with greenery. I really felt bad at having been sent in to spoil their fun!

The situation was this: The *Wehrmacht* had advanced to Trois Ponts, then it stopped. This area provides good forest cover to hide in, and they didn't wish to expose themselves to our artillery by moving farther down the mountain. Most of the heavy fighting was south of here, and neither side felt the roundabout forest road through here was worth committing a lot of men and equipment to control. So the Germans stopped in this village, wired the bridge with explosives, and dug in. If we had put our tanks on the road up the mountain, they knew they could blow us apart, and so did we. If we outnumbered them, they could always destroy the bridge and retreat, blasting away at our artillery from the mountaintop, and we would have to bridge this river under fire.

But the German "Bulge" toward Brussels and Antwerp began to fall apart the day after Christmas, after ten days of heavy fighting. General Bradley gave orders to push into Germany and cross the Rhine while we had them on the run, and we were to attack on all fronts, including Trois Ponts. My unit was sent on foot over an old mountain trail into Trois Ponts at night to soften up the resistance as best we could. We didn't plan to blow the old stone bridge, only to knock out a couple of their tanks with bazookas, then we'd take cover while the Allied artillery opened up on the Krauts.

As things turned out, we discovered that the Germans had planted explosives under the bridge before we got there. We figured *we* should decide if and when the bridge would blow. So we found and cut the wires to their detonator, then we wired their explosives up to *our* detonator, using about a quarter of a mile of wire so we wouldn't get hurt when the bridge blew—but I'm getting ahead of myself.

Three of us were under the bridge making the connections at about two in the morning, when we heard motors starting. Their tanks! If they crossed the bridge, they'd mess up a pretty lot of our artillery before our boys down the mountain could get into position to fire. It would take at least fifteen minutes to string our wire and get out of there. So I volunteered to go above and blast their lead tank with a bazooka. This would plug the road for maybe fifteen to thirty minutes until they could winch the damaged tank out of the way with a cable.

You can imagine me waiting behind a tree next to the bridge. The Germans seemed to be taking their time— hatches slamming, wishing each other good luck, revving engines to warm them up, no hurry to move—and no point in my blasting away until my target was plugging this old one-lane bridge. I checked my watch (it has a luminous dial). I'd been there fifteen minutes. My guys would set the charge off any minute now, and they had no way of knowing where I was. I would blow up with the bridge! I looked around, but there was no place to take cover. The tanks had finally begun to move, and if I left my post before I used my bazooka or the guys blew the bridge, our mission would be wasted, and American boys down the mountain would be killed. I had a job to do. I had to stay at my post.

Things happened so fast, I'm not sure what followed. As near's I can remember, I fired at the lead tank with my bazooka just as it started onto the bridge. One track (caterpillar type) tore off, but the tank itself did not explode. The hatch popped open, and the crew piled out. I guess they figured we had them surrounded, and they expected to be blown up inside. The bridge should have blown by now, but the Germans didn't know that. They were sweating for nothing, but I had reason to sweat!

The moon was still behind the hills, so it was very dark. I stepped in among the *Panzer* tank crew and said something in German I'd picked up from prisoners about "Those dirty Yanks." (I hope it wasn't profane!) Then I scrambled into that tank and slammed the hatch like I owned the thing! The bridge blew at the exact moment I jumped into the German tank, and being on top of the explosion, what I heard was a rumble and a roar. The tank plunged into the river with me inside. When it quit tumbling around, you can bet I got out of there and hightailed it for the American lines!

I guess the Krauts must have decided they were sitting ducks because they turned and went back east over the mountain above Trois Ponts. Next day the trucks arrived with the portable bridge. My crew and I set it up over the next two days. The good people of Trois Ponts now have a two-lane American bridge to replace their old stone one, which almost certainly would have fallen apart in a few days under the weight of military traffic.

Love,

Andy

"It all sounds so businesslike—not like war at all." Jack was thoughtful as Mama put the letter down.

"How can you say that, when Andy came so near to being killed?" Mama missed Jack's point in her motherly concern over Andy's narrow escape.

"Jack is right, of course." Papa launched into a tack on the topic different from either Jack or Althea. "Bridges blown by remote control; steel tanks against steel tanks. In some battles, there's not a human being in sight. That's the really sinister aspect of sin. It can be made to look so glorious that the sinner forgets he's dealing with death."

"Weren't you in Belgium for a while, Papa?" Wessie wanted to know.

"Not that part of Belgium. We were in the lowlands around

Brussels, further west. The countryside was much like our old home in Lancaster County."

"Such beauty," Mama recalled. "And Andy is right. God creates. Man destroys."

❦ ❦ ❦

Somewhere in Germany
February 24, 1945

Dear Folks,

We are taking increasing numbers of prisoners as we push eastward into Germany. A lot of these are soldiers that realize they have lost the war and are just tired of fighting. While Hitler's orders to the *Wehrmacht* are well known—fight to the last man—some German officers are surrendering whole units, not only the wounded and ill but healthy soldiers as well. We put them on trains back to Antwerp where our supply ships take them to England or America. I picked up a story a while back that several thousand of these guys are being kept in lumber camps in northern and eastern Maine where they are put to work cutting wood for the pulp and paper mills. Have you seen any German POW's around Portugal?

Our intelligence is interrogating a female POW who claims to be a displaced American named Amy Andrews, of all things! I've seen her, and she's certainly not our Amy. It's the opinion of our people that she's probably not even an American, but a German who somehow got hold of dog tags belonging to an Amy Andrews, hoping to use them as a free ticket to the U.S. Maybe there's more than one Amy Andrews in the WACS. This woman has been taken behind our lines, so I don't guess I'll ever find out if the serial number on those tags belonged to my sister. But then, do you suppose? It couldn't be!

Until I See You All Again,

Andy

"You're not being rational, Althea." Wes was angry at Mama's insistence that he contact the War Department about the prisoner Andy had written about. "Do you know how many thousands of people there are in the country with the Andrews' family name? And how many Amys there could be?"

"But Wes, we've got to know!"

"Requests like that may take two years or longer, even in peacetime," Papa huffed. "And then we'd have to see a Congressman to get action. You've forgotten how long it took just to check on the status of a parishioner in Pennsylvania who'd lost his discharge papers and needed treatment at a VA hospital!"

To tell the truth, though, Papa feared learning for certain what he already believed true—that the dog tags had been pulled off Amy's lifeless body by a Nazi soldier who passed them on to a girlfriend. He feared the truth more than he dreaded the inquiry process, and from time to time it wore on him, and he tore angrily at those God had given him to love. Wes had tried to drown his grief in church work. Why dredge it up for examination?

🐾 🐾 🐾

Elbe River Front, Germany
April 19, 1945

Hello Folks,

It is Patriot's Day in Maine! How I wish I were home! I suppose there'll be a parade of old soldiers in Portugal, even if it rains.

You should be able to find the Elbe River on any good map of Germany. I can write this since it is no longer a classified secret that the Allies are holding their Western Front here. The Russians under Field Marshal Zhukov have advanced to the Oder River in the east, and on Monday, April 16, they opened up with artillery fire to soften Berlin up for their invasion with troops. So we have Berlin in a pincers between us and the Red Army.

There is some shelling back and forth across the river, but for the most part it's pretty quiet around here. We must now deal with hordes of refugees, civilians who fear the Russian advance on Germany's capital city, as well as soldiers by the thousands still surrendering.

Will we invade Berlin? That's the question everyone is asking. I sure hope not. It is expected the battle will be bloodier than last winter's Battle of the Bulge in the Ardennes. I see too much of death every day to wish to inflict more suffering on those who took Amy from us.

The refugees are particularly pitiful. Most of them are afoot. Some have horses, oxen, here and there an old auto or truck. Many have bicycles or pull carts loaded with all the possessions they could drag. Occasionally there is a motorcycle. Mostly these refugees hate Americans for bombing their cities. But they come to us because they have heard that the Russians will rape them like the Red Army is said to have raped the women in Poland, and eighty percent of these people are women. The rest are children and old men. I can understand why they fear, because the Germans destroyed so much of Russia. They now expect the Russians want revenge.

Hate and fear—what an awful way to live. I've heard it said that fear of death is mankind's most powerful motive. I joined the army as much out of hate for those who killed Amy as out of love for my country, I'm afraid. It's times like these that make one examine his own heart. The fear I see every day in the faces of these refugees has changed my attitude. I'd like nothing better than to return here after the war and help rebuild this beautiful, bombed-out land—after a few months of R & R in dear old Samoset Valley!

Is it wrong to get sentimental over a drinking song? One of the guys has a 78-RPM record of Rudy Vallee singing "The Stein Song," and when Vallee sings the line, "We'll drink a toast to dear old Maine," I sometimes shed a few tears. I know it means the university not the state, but it takes me right back to Portugal—to home!

Eisenhower has told our troops that Berlin is the supreme prize we've been fighting for, but I believe Ike is wrong. For me and a lot of others, the supreme prize is peace.

Dear Reverend and Mrs. Andrews,

By now you will have received a telegram informing you of the death of my dear friend, Corporal Andrew Andrews. Later there will be several medals of honor from the War Department, I am sure.

I found this unfinished letter among your son's things, so I am adding my own thoughts, as I think he'd want. Andy was known as "Preacher" to some of the guys, though the fellows who called him that didn't mean it as a put-down. To me, he was just plain Andy, and I share his faith in Jesus Christ. It's funny, but I never knew Andy to preach. He did live a consistent Christian life, and he stood up for what he believed in. Andy has told me that you, Reverend Andrews, were once a chaplain, so I guess you know what I mean.

Andy died a hero, just before the war is expected to end. We hadn't seen much fighting for quite a while. In fact, we've been making the Russians unhappy by shipping all German soldiers who surrendered to us safely west of the Rhine rather than let the Soviets send them to one of Stalin's slave-labor camps in Siberia.

One morning out of the river fog Andy's unit was temporarily overrun by several dozen Germans who had managed to sneak across the river on inner-tube rafts. They lobbed a hand grenade across a sandbag barricade manned by Andy and two other guys. Andy saved those two men by using his body and a sandbag as a shield.

Andy lived for three days in the field hospital after this. The doctors refused to ship him back to Antwerp for treatment because he had internal injuries which would have hastened death if they had tried to move him. At least he got to die here among his buddies.

One of the guys whom Andy saved came up to me later, and he was pretty shook up. "Sarge," he says, "you're a Christian like Andy. I want to become one, too." Isn't that swell?!

We had some excitement in camp the day Andy passed away, which I thought might lift your hearts. The boys heard bagpipes playing. Sure enough—in marched nearly 3,000 Allied POW's the Germans had been holding, some of them since '42. Most of these were British aviators from a prison camp called Stalag III. Several hundred were Americans, and there were even about thirty women in the group, mostly U.S. WACS. It seems their German guards got tired of trying to evade the advancing Russians, and an English officer (actually he was a Scotsman, a Lieutenant McBrierty) talked them into marching west and surrendering their prisoners (and themselves) to us.

One of the WACS from this group of liberated prisoners had evidently met Andy earlier in the war. She spotted him when she went into the medical tent for a checkup. There was hugging and kissing that reminded me of Evangeline finding Gabriel on his deathbed. How fortunate I'd be to have a beautiful woman like her to love me like that when I'm dying! I didn't get her name, because she got on a truck for Antwerp next day with the other liberated Americans, but I expect you'll be getting a letter from her.

I'll be praying for you and your family. Andy will be greatly missed.

Yours, Respectfully in Jesus' Name,

Sergeant Kenneth Prescott, U.S. Army

16

Reverend Andrews Meets Himself

When Wes Andrews heard of Andy's death, his very soul seemed to die. As with Amy, there would be no funeral. Andy's body would be buried in Europe. Wes hoped it would be in Flanders Fields, in Belgium. He had been there; he could visualize the white crosses, row on row, and he had buddies from the First World War who awaited the resurrection there.

Wes told himself that he was now the father of two: Jack and Wessie. Serious, academic Jack, the joy of his parents, would be the pastor of a large congregation or perhaps a college professor teaching seminary-level Greek and Hebrew, Wes liked to think. And Wesley, Jr.—Wessie—born after an extended hiatus in Althea's childbearing which had been interrupted by a miscarriage, was his mother's image. Like her, he was short, dark, and even as a preteen beginning to show muscles. Wessie, the independent, the imp, the undisciplined daredevil, the spoiled-rotten brat. He'd make a business leader, or perhaps an FBI agent, or even a rodeo cowboy. If it required derring-do, Wessie had it.

This was Wes's little family—two children, no more. Never any more. He would live on through them. Amy and Andy? They had never been; they were mere phantoms.

It had not been his privilege to bring his grief to the graveside, to weep as the caskets were lowered, to hold Althea and to be held by her as together they mourned. So, instead of burying his children, Wes determined he would bury his grief.

There were closets Wes refused to open because a skirt, a pair of skates, an old football were there to open closets in his memory. There were shelves he avoided glancing at, photo albums he refused to pick up. Somehow it would not be right to suggest to Althea that she ought to remove old photos from their frames and put them away. But Wes, by habit, glanced downward more often than upward, downward at his books and sermon notes, downward at his research and correspondence. He found navigation through the sitting room manageable, though he always hurried through and avoided sitting there. He preferred studying in the rocker by the kitchen's south window.

May was a hard month from the beginning. Amy had been born in May. He forgot her birthday. Althea did not. The morning of May 10, 1945, Wes awoke at dawn to find Althea sitting on the edge of their bed, weeping. "What's the matter?" he asked gently.

Althea rubbed her stomach and groaned in agony. Her only answer was a long moan.

"Why are you crying?"

More moans and sobs.

"Are you in pain—cramps?"

"Oh-h-h-h-h-h-h-h-h-h-h-h-h!" In reply, Althea only shook her head. Twenty minutes of hugging and prying finally brought Althea to verbalize, in part, the cause of her distress. "Do you remember where we were twenty-one years ago this morning?" she wailed.

Wes *did* remember and his blood ran cold. They were in the Elizabeth Swartz Maternity Home in rural Lancaster County, Pennsylvania. There had been hours of labor pains and groanings not unlike these he now heard from his wife of twenty-two years. But that morning had been a time of joy and not of grief, when the midwife, beaming, had told Wes, "You've got a beautiful little girl!"

May was Wes and Althea's wedding anniversary month as well. And May meant Memorial Day. While the world of nature sprang with a riot of spring life, dying old soldiers would tramp Portugal's five blocks of downtown under battle flags to remember the boys who followed Pershing at Ypres, or Eisenhower at Normandy, or long ago rode with Teddy Roosevelt at San Juan Hill. Portugal's last leaf from the Civil War, Gus Wiggin, hale, lean, and snow-bearded at 104, who could still wear the trousers he marched in in 1863, would sit bolt upright in his moth-eaten Union Army blues in the open backseat of Eddie Bessey's convertible, remembering companions who died at Bull Run or Gettysburg.

The parade would pause in front of a monument and a Civil War cannon on the town common. "Salute the dead," an American Legion commander would bark. The voice of death would roar from a dozen .30-'06 Springfields, and the mournful music of death would waft out of a trumpet from the steps of the Federated Church.

Memorial Day was also the day folks in Samoset Valley planted their gardens. Wes had a large garden planned, so he would skip this year's parade. Gardens deal with life.

May brought constant news reports of the war in Europe, reports which Wes could not ignore, reports which reminded him that he had a real stake in the killings over there. May began with a report of the death of Hitler on April 30, that *Führer* whose hate had unleashed misery upon so many millions. On May 2, Berlin surrendered to the Red Army, that city of which Andy had written. On May 5 came the announcement that hostilities had ceased in Italy—too late for Amy. V-E Day was May 8, with the signing of the surrender papers. Johnny would soon come marching home again. But not Amy and Andy.

On the Friday following Amy's birthday, Wes and Althea decided to drive to Calais to watch Jack's baseball team play their arch rival. The family was not disappointed. Jack hit a double in the top of the ninth, giving the man on third a chance to cross home plate, breaking a tie with a lead of 8–9. In the bottom of the ninth, Jack struck out Calais' best hitter, the first man up. After this, it was two more strikeouts, which assured that SVCI would face Calais again in the tournament.

"Let's take the coastal route home," Althea remarked. Papa agreed. Route One meandered sixty miles from Calais to Portugal, but the road had been kept graded and it was paved through the villages. The inland trip, thirty-five miles through the woods across potholes and ruts, had taken them nearly two hours, and it had caused them to miss Jack's first pitch.

With Jack and Wessie holding down the rear seat, Wes held the Packard at a steady forty-five where conditions permitted. The family enjoyed the ride; Althea, in fact, remarked how blessed it seemed on such a marvelous spring afternoon to ride in a fine, trouble-free auto.

"Let's make Hitler/And Hirohito/Wish that they/Were like Benito/He needed/*Burma Shave,*" Wessie sang in glee as the little family neared East Portugal. America's best-known shaving cream manufacturer had recently discovered a stretch of highway not adorned with one of their famous slogans, and they had chosen to combine clever advertising with patriotism.

Jack found Wessie's glee amusing, and he laughed. Mama, only irritated, was silent. Wesley, Sr. was shocked. "What Benito Mussolini needed was Christ and His love, not execution," Papa intoned firmly.

Wessie was quiet for a moment. "Papa," he inquired at last, "then why did Amy and Andy have to die?"

There were no more words that day between Wesley Andrews and his namesake. Wessie's question was one he could not answer. Amy had died, he believed, helping save others' lives, even as some twenty-five years earlier he had himself gone to Europe to save souls. Andy had died in saving his buddies from the senseless act of a German soldier, who, though the war was lost, determined to take one more life before he should be killed or captured. Yet Andy had thrown himself on the grenade, protected only by a single sandbag. Might such a death be considered suicide? Wes suffered great agony of soul whenever it came to mind.

On Monday, Wes excused himself right after breakfast. He strolled to the back porch and looked out to sea. Beyond the harbor breakwater, where Sabbathday Brook's estuary entered the Bay of Fundy, a rocky peninsula reached eastward toward

Canada. Farther out was an island rife with ancient, pointed firs. Ragged Island, it was called. It would be filled from June to Labor Day with "summer people," as the locals called them—professionals, artsy types from New York or Connecticut who owned cottages and evidently had nothing better to do all summer than swim, stroll on the sand, or paint pictures of gulls and terns. It was desolate now. Here, Wes decided, he could wrestle with God alone.

"Something's troubling you, Wes." Althea put her arms about his waist. She dare not say "Amy" or "Andy," for that would only bring on one of her husband's philosophical tirades, leaving him angry, her crying, their problem unresolved.

"Yes," he admitted.

"Do you want to be alone?"

Wes pointed to Ragged Island in the distance. "There's nobody out there this time of year. I can rent a rowboat at the wharf behind Whitcombs Cafe. I'll be back before dark."

Althea wept silently as she watched Wes leave, his Bible, a blanket, a Thermos of coffee, and a paper sack of oatmeal-raisin cookies in the basket of Wessie's bike.

An hour and a half of steady pulling on the oars on a choppy ocean brought Wes to the island. In half an hour more he reached the seaward side where he found a south-facing cove with a beach sandier than any mainland shore near Portugal. He pulled his boat up to the high-tide line, spread his blanket in the sun, and fell fast asleep.

Wes's nap by the sea brought on unfathomable rest and infinite calm. It had been ten-thirty in the morning when he lay down, perhaps a hundred yards from the tossing sea. He awoke with wet feet, fully refreshed, at two o'clock in the afternoon. Wes was caused to think on the experience of the Old Testament prophet who, huddled in a booth beneath a gourd vine, waited in anger for the Lord to destroy the wicked city he had just railed against. But the city, filled with the prophet's enemies, repented. To demonstrate His right to destroy or create life, the Lord directed a worm to kill the gourd vine, Wes remembered, dragging his blanket, Bible, and lunch above a line of dried seaweed along the beach.

"Doest thou well to be angry for the gourd?" the Lord had asked the prophet, who had resisted learning a spiritual lesson even after three days in a whale's belly.

"I do well to be angry, even unto death," Jonah had raged in God's face. Wes had lost more than Jonah's gourd vine, he realized, looking up from his Bible. His eyes searched the heavens above him, considering God's tender care for him in his time of loss and distress.

"The Lord gave, and the Lord hath taken away; blessed be the name of the Lord." Wes had often intoned the words of Job at a gravesite, where family members mourned the loss of spouse, parent, or child. Now the Lord was asking him, Reverend Wesley Andrews, who had often comforted others, to wrap himself in the Lord's consolation. The Lord who "comforteth us in all our tribulation" was here, even now. Yet the ache, the hurt, the agony of having his dearest possessions ripped from his heart in so short a space was nevertheless real also.

Then it dawned on Wes: Amy and Andy were not his and Althea's to own. They were God's to lend and to take, as the one to whom they are lent has need of them or in God's wisdom no longer has need of them.

Wes thought on Jack. Like himself, Jack was an academic super-achiever, a true scholar. But Wes was an introvert, and despite his proficiency in Greek and Hebrew and his vast knowledge of Scripture, Reverend Andrews felt condemned to small parishes in out-of-the-way places. But Jack had his father's brains *and* he could charm crowds. In Jack, Wes could envision all that he himself had wanted to be. Wes pastored in tiny Portugal. Jack could, in maturity, lead the largest congregations in Pittsburgh or Philadelphia, Wes considered.

Yet Wes had to confess that in his heart Jack had become a surrogate for Amy and Andy. To love Jack for Jack's sake—though he did love Jack—had not entirely been the case. He loved Jack a little for his own sake. But Wes loved him a lot more as the replacement for his two eldest, and for what he hoped Jack would become.

Had Wes ever truly loved Amy and Andy? It pained him to consider such a question. And what if the Lord should choose to take Jack?

Amy was his only daughter, and he loved her for that. She was the eldest, and Wes was partial to his firstborn. And Amy's delicate yet hearty femininity gave Wes a contrasting perspective on the aggressive personality of Althea. He couldn't quite put his finger on it, but he loved Amy for that as well.

And Wes loved Amy for Amy's sake. But he had to admit that his loss was largely in that he now found himself stripped of all the qualities he had admired in Amy rather than being bereft of his loving Amy herself.

Then there was Andy, the second-born. Andy was smart, but he had always refused to settle down. Andy had a head for science and higher math, but he lacked the patience to teach others. Andy, like his mother and Wessie, was a practical one. If it worked, it was good. But whatever did not work on the first try, Andy cast aside as so much excess baggage.

Wes knew that it was the Althea in Andy that he had loved— that brusque, sensible nature that said, "Let's get things done!"

Wessie, Wes knew, was cut from the same bolt of cloth as Andy. But further down the roll, the Lord seemed to have snipped Wessie from the tightly wound inner piece. Everything Andy was, Wessie was to excess. Youngest children, especially the tagalong born after the next oldest has reached middle childhood, can be hard to raise. Let run like an untamed vine, they can crash colossally. But directed and nurtured by parents who have not learned to take their own advancing years too seriously, youngest children can be the most effective leaders in God's economy.

John and Charles Wesley, whose name Wes and Wessie shared, were fifteenth and sixteenth in their family, Wes mused. Benjamin Franklin, perhaps the most accomplished American of the eighteenth century, was the fifteenth of seventeen children and, like the Wesleys, born after both his parents had reached middle age. Joseph the patriarch, who grew up the youngest of eleven sons—Benjamin yet to be born—became the prime minister of Egypt and his family's savior. Wes smiled when he thought on these things. His own Wessie, he realized, was missing out on the love of a father too busy in the ministry, too enraptured in his idolatry of Jack.

"My thoughts are not your thoughts," Jehovah had admonished Isaiah. *Could it be*, mused Wes, *that I have been listening to myself, not heeding the still, small voice of the Lord?* God's admonition to Isaiah was followed by a promise of blessing, that the Word of God in Isaiah's—Wes Andrews'—life in time would "accomplish" and "prosper" His perfect will. And "joy," "singing," and a fruitful ministry were promised as a result.

🐚 🐚 🐚

"I met myself, and I didn't like what I saw," Wes told Althea that evening. "But then, meditating on God's Word, I met the Lord afresh. My heart may still ache, but from this time forward, it'll neither be angry nor bitter."

The sun had set behind Hogback Mountain as they stood that evening on the porch. Wes took up the old blanket he had tossed on the porch glider when he had returned. He wrapped it across his wife's shoulders, then drew it around himself. Cheek to cheek, locked in an embrace, the couple stood until the last rays of the sun of springtime were gone and the night chill dampened the wool about their shoulders.

Wes took one last look at the sea in the starlight before he followed Althea into the kitchen. The angry whitecaps which he had fought with his oars that morning were gone, and the salt surface spread smooth as glass to the horizon.

17

The Girl at the Phone Booth

"*Parker's comin' in t' Bang-gaw* station tomorrow 'bout noon." It thrilled Althea Andrews to hear this report from the widowed Bernice Copeland at the ladies' prayer group Wednesday evening. Like Althea's husband, Harry Copeland had fought in the First World War. He had left his pregnant bride, Bernice, to enter this "War to End All Wars." Harry, however, was killed in action while driving the Kaiser's army out of France. Parker Copeland had been born May 17, 1918, and Thursday, May 17, 1945, was his twenty-seventh birthday, Mrs. Copeland related to Althea.

"But I guess that'll have to wait till Friday," Parker's mother concluded. "The Down East Railroad train into Portugal is only twice a week, you know."

Althea did know, of course. She also knew there was no bus service from Bangor. She often found it odd and amusing to hear old-timers speak of the stagecoach runs from Bangor's railway terminal in the days before the narrow-gauge train's twice-weekly freight and passenger runs had made Portugal a viable community. "When I wuz a boy," Willard Metcalf would often fondly intone, "the coaches ran frum Bang-gaw mornin' an' afternoon. Fo-ah hosses—put on six in bad weathuh! But all that ended when they laid the rails in '99."

"I'll see if Wes knows of anybody driving to Bangor tomorrow," Althea comforted Mrs. Copeland. Parker, she knew, had joined the army with Andy in March 1944. *What's one more day, after more than a year?* her reason argued. Yet her heart quickly rebuked, *I'd want to be there to meet the train, if it were Andy coming home.*

Wessie and Jack's school bus had just rumbled off when Althea and Wes climbed into the Packard Thursday morning. "You called Mrs. Copeland?" Wes inquired.

"Yes. I told her to skip breakfast since we'd be stopping at a restaurant in Ellsworth. We'll be there way ahead of the train, if we *don't* stop. At least one person will lose their mind if we have a long wait at the depot."

"More'n one," Wes agreed.

As things turned out, Mrs. Copeland came prepared with a basket of egg-salad sandwiches and a chocolate layer cake. "Plenty f' everybuddy," she exulted. And she also had eaten an early breakfast. "I can never eat mid-morning," she apologized, but she did order blueberry pancakes at the Ellsworth Inn. "How did they manage to make 'em without gettin' the batter blue?" Bernice asked in genuine surprise.

"Restaurants use frozen berries, I'm sure," Althea answered pleasantly.

"In many stores in the populated areas they offer frozen fruits and vegetables as well as ice cream," Wes explained.

"Well, what will they think of next!"

Wes knew that Bessey's cannery had only last year added a frozen food locker to its operation, so he only chuckled at Mrs. Copeland's amazement at modern technology.

The Maine Central Railroad's *Flying Yankee* diesel locomotive had been chartered by the U.S. Armed Services to bring a long passenger train of discharged Maine servicemen north from Boston, Wes, Althea, and Mrs. Copeland learned from a gentleman at the depot. Since Bangor was the special train's last stop, there would be plenty of empty seats going south to Boston, he had chuckled.

Moments before train time, eight large buses, all painted military khaki—even the side windows had been painted—

pulled into the depot. Two MP's stepped out of each, their semi-automatic M-1 rifles with long clips of ammunition at the ready.

"I don't like this," Wes told Althea.

"Them fellas don't look's though they could be fooled with," remarked the gentleman who had told Wes about the chartered train. "I wonder what's up." The MP's were standing with bayonets fixed, so Wes decided he'd keep his distance and just watch.

Parker Copeland was one of the first off the train. He carried a duffel bag of clothing and another of bulky items as he sprang down the steps, dropped his bags (Wes noticed uncomfortably that one landed with a clatter), and seized his mother. He swung her in his arms and kissed her. The noisy bag was filled with captured German Mausers, Lugers, and other small arms, it became evident, as Wes hoisted it into the Packard's trunk.

The U.S. servicemen were all off the train, Wes noticed, as he unlocked his auto. The MP's now opened the buses. Marching single file, a line of young men in gray uniforms, military duffel bags over their shoulders, walked toward the train. Many of these men had sandy hair, Wes saw, unusual in Maine with its predominance of people of English or French ancestry. Then he realized that several of them wore jackets of the *Wehrmacht*. "German soldiers—POW's!" he exclaimed. "Andy heard in Europe that we were holding prisoners of war in Maine woods' lumber camps, but I never really believed it."

"They're Krauts, all right," Parker agreed, looking up from his mother's attention. "And what *they've* got to go home to!" He shook his head sadly.

Then Wes spotted a couple of POW's who had broken from the line. They were standing by themselves beside the train, engaged in conversation with a young lady in a khaki WAC sergeant's uniform, who was resting one hand on her upended duffel bag. Wes caught a distinct German phrase from the girl's lips as she shouldered her bag and struggled toward the depot. The two POW's quickly ducked onto the train to avoid being hassled by an MP striding in their direction.

Wes watched the girl for a moment. She was lithe and pretty, with a bun of ash-blonde hair beneath her cap which was fastened at a jaunty angle with bobby pins. She's somebody's daughter. Why isn't anybody waiting for her? he mused.

Turning to Althea, who by now was seated in the Packard, he said simply, "There's a lady that just went inside. I'm going to see if she needs help."

Althea pleaded with her eyes for a moment for Wes to hurry. "Don't be long," she remarked with a sigh.

Wes spotted the girl in a phone booth as soon as he stepped inside. She seemed to be fishing in her purse for change, and she evidently could not find the correct coin—a nickel. The girl bit her lower lip in animated frustration. Wes had seen that facial expression before.

"Sergeant, may I help?" he offered crisply.

She turned to face him.

Wes felt his knees turn to jelly, and he grabbed a marble column holding up the depot's vaulted ceiling for support.

"Daddy!"

Wes's jaw worked open and shut. His mouth formed "Amy," but no sound came out.

❦ ❦ ❦

"Why didn't you write? Other parents whose children were prisoners got letters exchanged through the Red Cross," Mama asked later that evening. Wes, for his part, felt he had been given so much back from the war in the goodness of the Lord that he could only sit and listen.

"I was a prisoner at Stalag III, near Berlin, for less than a month before the armistice," Amy explained. "Typically, it takes six months for a POW's letter to work through channels. And I was so afraid—after being thought dead all this time—to even phone you from New York. I was about to hire a taxi to drive me to Portugal when Papa found me at the phone booth."

"But where were you, Sis? What were you doing?" It was Jack's turn to inquire.

"Working as a practical nurse in a hospital in Munich," Amy replied. "And they allowed us no contact with the outside world. The Germans held badly wounded aviators there—their own *Luftwaffe,* RAF, even a few Americans. I hated the *Luftwaffe* pilots at first, after what they did to our boys and the nurses on the *Newfoundland.* Then I decided if that was the Lord's will for me, I could save lives, no matter which side they were on."

"Like Edith Cavell?" Wessie had recently read in school the story of the Red Cross nurse who was executed for helping British aviators escape from a hospital in occupied Brussels during the First World War.

"Wessie, it's a *long* story." Amy paused, a faraway look in her eyes. "They did stand me before a firing squad for execution in a convent courtyard in Bavaria, but God intervened. I was sent to prison camp, instead, the first week of April."

"Let's let Amy rest," Papa interrupted. "She's had a long day, I'm sure."

"Papa?" Amy slid to the floor and eased over to his reclining Morris chair. She placed her head on his lap and began to sob. At last she raised her head. "Andy . . . Andy died in my arms. I found him in a field hospital on the Western Front, just before the armistice."

"Andy's sergeant wrote that he had seen Andy with a girl—a former POW," Papa's voice choked with emotion. "But we didn't dare believe it could have been you."

"It . . . it was, Papa."

Mama now knelt with Amy and embraced her. "Did he know you?"

"Yes, Mama. He called my name."

For some moments, only the ticking of the mantel clock through the kitchen archway was heard in the sitting room.

"Andy . . . Andy joined the army to rescue me," Amy said at last. "But he said he could no longer hate the Germans for what they've done, after all he'd seen. He said we should love them, as Christ loved us . . ." Amy's voice trailed off into weeping.

Finally she added, "He said to say good-bye to Mama and Papa and Jack and Wessie." She paused to look at each member of the family. "He was so brave," she whispered.

18

The Recluse of Hogback Mountain

"'*Dead' WAC Reunited with Portugal Family*," screamed the *Bangor Daily News* headline. *Missing 1¹/₂ years,* the subheading continued. "Local Minister's Daughter Was Forced to Nurse *Luftwaffe* Pilots," announced the banner in Portugal's weekly *Samoset Valley Gazette*.

School bus driver Judson Harding had seen Amy emerge from Papa's Packard on Friday when he had let Jack and Wessie out at the parsonage. Not to be upstaged in carrying the news about town, Harding had gone straight to the *Gazette* office as soon as his bus run was over. Editor Russ Cookson was also a local news stringer for the Bangor newspaper, an arrangement he maintained only by publishing his own weekly's story—usually in considerable more detail—days after the daily ran its article.

Cookson had come unannounced to the Andrews' home on Friday afternoon just in time to snap several press photos of Amy and her family on the parsonage steps. Though he had barged rudely into the tearful homecoming, he was "blessedly brief," as Mama put it later. Five or six sentences of basic information, and Cookson went on his way.

Russ Cookson spied the *Bangor Daily News'* delivery truck

when it rolled into town Saturday with the weekend edition, just after noon. He found the driver munching on a hot dog on a stool at Whitcombs, and he shoved a large manila envelope labeled, "Photos—Do Not Bend," under his nose. "This one's front-page material," Russ emphasized. With his index finger he tapped the two-dollar bill clipped to the envelope. "On Ye Ed's desk tonight—*please!* He wants it for Monday's paper." Russ grinned magnanimously at the truck driver. "Piece o' pie with that dog, on me?"

Russ did not tell the *News'* delivery driver that the editor—who had already gone home for the day by the time Russ had interviewed the Andrews—was not actually expecting the glossy black-and-white photos he had developed Friday evening. But Russ knew news when he saw it.

Sunday afternoon Amy got a long-distance phone call from the *Bangor Daily News'* news editor, who remarked mildly that he "needed to write a blurb to go with your photo." But his startled, "Repeat that please" and "Were you forced to work, against the rules of the Geneva Convention?" soon gave Amy an inkling that the editor might use more than a caption with her picture. To her surprise, she was the main feature on page one in Monday afternoon's *Bangor Daily News.*

Cookson waited until Tuesday to interview Amy for his story, since the *Gazette* published on Thursday. Not to be outdone by the daily's page-one story, Cookson gave Amy the entire page and two columns continued inside.

"I'm going for a walk, Mama," Amy remarked tiredly after glancing briefly at the *Gazette* Jack had purchased in the village on Thursday. "At least in Munich I could have some privacy."

Amy crossed the road to the Trask place, intending to follow one of the logging roads cut along the side of Hogback Mountain by The Little King and his crew. Far, far up the face of the mountain she had often noticed a rocky bluff which stood out from the pines, spruce, and hemlocks, and from which she believed she might get a grand ocean view. Never had Amy attempted to hike that far, even when rabbit hunting with Jack, since the dense forest had seemed forbidding. But Jack had told her of the new network of horse-and-sled skid roads, and she felt certain she could get quite near the bluff itself before having to plunge into the underbrush. "You *can't* get lost, Sis," he emphasized. "Just keep the mountain at your back and walk downhill. You'll always find the highway. I've done it many times."

The climb was steep, and though the woods were cool on a May afternoon, the exercise soon caused Amy to perspire so she peeled off her sweater. Midges and mosquitoes, the menaces of the Maine woods in May, soon found her sweating cheeks and neck. She wrapped her face in her kerchief to protect herself. Amy had forgotten this feature of northern New England woodland hiking. But no matter. If she could find a sunny clearing where the loggers had opened up the mountainside, the vicious pests would leave her alone, and she could rest for a few minutes on a stump.

She passed a bend and came out at a wye in the road. A newer but more deeply rutted branch went to the right, across the face of the mountain. The left branch, which seemed to be several years old, angled uphill and back behind the Trask Mansion. Shallow wheel ruts, which showed narrow tire tracks, fresh today, followed the older forest road.

Glancing up the road less traveled by, Amy thought she discerned sunlight—perhaps a good-sized clearing—uphill a ways. The other road went on and on in an uninviting tangle of brush. She chose the steeper but pleasanter path.

Presently, Amy found herself at a set of cedar bars set into a rail and rock fence. Here, a mountain meadow of perhaps three or four acres was lush with spring grass and dandelions. The wheel tracks crossed the field, and on the far side a handsome cabin of peeled and varnished logs, its stone fireplace giving forth a curl of blue smoke, faced the sea. In front of the cabin, to her surprise, an ancient Model T pickup, its top folded down, was parked in the sun.

Amy sat for a moment on the bars eyeing the cattle grazing on the green. The Jersey cow and her calf would offer no challenge, so long as she did not get between mother and child, Amy knew.

But what were these? Huge red brutes with broad, brass-tipped horns grazed directly between her and the cabin. Then Amy remembered—Orin Trask owned a pair of Durham oxen.

They were gentle, harmless as kittens, she had been told. Amy had braved machine-gun fire, land mines, and aerial strafing to save lives in Italy. She had returned a braver and wiser woman, but she was still possessed of common sense. With the pocket-knife she had borrowed from Wessie, Amy whittled herself a stout cudgel from a green alder before she ventured into the pasture.

Amy had not taken a dozen steps when a man emerged from under the Model T. He seemed to stand only with some difficulty. Fetching a walking stick from the Model T's truck body, he hunched over it and limped lamely and painfully into the cabin.

Who was this? She knew that Orin walked with a limp. But Orin's step, though uneven, was quick, firm, and youthful.

And the auto? Jack and Mama had told her about Orin's change in fortunes, and Mama had even mentioned that Orin had a pickup truck. But this was not a truck a young man would buy in 1945, was it? The vehicle beside the cabin was of First World War vintage, the type of antique only a few elderly folks still chugged around in. Orin, she concluded, must have rented his cabin to an old man while he himself lived comfortably in the renovated mansion.

So who was this old fellow who crawled under Model T's and walked with a rheumatic limp? Did he have a wife? Amy envisioned being greeted at the door of the mountain cabin by a diminutive, stooping granny in full apron, cackling, "Come in, my dear. We don't get many callers in these parts." Amy pushed up the mountain meadow in anticipation.

Suddenly she stopped. Four large brown eyes framed by four huge horns were staring at her. Three tons of beef and bone on eight agile, steel-shod hooves opposed her. Would these monsters charge? She readied her club. The ninety pounds of woman that had once held off a drunken Nazi SS officer was about to do battle, if need be, with these terrors of the grassland.

The animals took their time, ambling on ponderous hooves, lowing like milch cows at milking time as they came. Amy stood her ground.

The beasts drew close. Amy raised her stick to strike. Then she thought better of it. War breeds war—how well she knew! "So-o-o-o-o-o, bossy! Easy bossy!" Amy called calmly. "Good boys!"

One red snout sniffed her face, its grassy breath rich with bovine digestive juices. A tongue, great, gray-and-pink, sloshed its saliva across her eyes. "Help!" Amy managed one word before freezing in her tracks.

She looked up to see that the man had emerged from the cabin. He had evidently seen her plight because he bent at the Ford's crank, gave it a tug, then limped into the backfiring vehicle, taking far too long to suit Amy. As the Model T chugged across the field, Amy was horrified to see that the man was masked. A red bandanna covered most of his face!

Whatever the fellow was up to, he had rescue in mind for Amy. He stopped behind the oxen and pounded furiously on the rubber horn bulb: "Onk-a! Onk-a! Onk-a!" Amy laughed as the oxen, either one of which could easily upset the Ford alone, ran like frightened kittens for the far side of the pasture.

The mysterious meadow motorist now swung his truck in front of her, and he popped the passenger door open. "Hop in!" he invited in muffled tones.

Amy pointed her club at his face. "Remove the mask first, mister!"

"Not until you take yours off!"

Amy blushed with embarrassment at the thought of how she must look with her face swaddled in her kerchief to protect against the biting midges.

"Together?" he suggested, with a laugh. He hooked a finger inside his bandanna.

Amy undid her kerchief, then she took a close look at her rescuer.

"What moves a pretty maiden to brave the flies of May and visit the recluse of Hogback Mountain?" he chuckled. Then he stopped, as astonished as if he had seen a ghost. "Amy?" he sputtered.

"And you *are* Orin!" Her mind was envisioning a rheumatic, gray-bearded octogenarian behind the bandanna. Had she been gone for fifty years—stepped through a time warp, perhaps? Amy pulled a wisp of her own hair before her eyes for a look. *Still blonde—no sign of gray.* Then her eyes saw. Orin was still red-bearded, youthful, virile. Tall and lean, he towered above the Model T's steering wheel.

"Yes," he admitted at last. "I am who I've been all along. But is it really you?"

"Oh yes. I am Amy Andrews—still Amy, forever Amy." A moment of silence hung between them. "Why were you masked?" she asked at last.

"I was about to crawl back under to tighten the brakes on this contraption a bit more," Orin explained, obviously relieved to be talking about more everyday subjects. "And I don't care to have a face full of rust, grease, and road dirt." He held up a wrench. "The only way these two-wheel brakes will hold on this mountain is if they're *tight*," he emphasized. "And since you're obviously not the Big, Bad Wolf disguised as Little Red Riding Hood's grandmother, I assume that *your* mask is to fend off the biting no-see-ums."

"You got it," Amy nodded, climbing into the Model T.

"Now, Miss Ghost from the War, will you let me fix you a cup of tea?" Orin mashed the high-low pedal to the floorboard, and they lurched toward his cabin.

Moments later, as Orin swung his legs out and grasped his cane, Amy discovered that he had bandaged his knee with strips torn from an old sheet. "What *ever* did you do to your knee?" she asked

"Hurt it loggin', last week. If it hadn't been for my oxen, I'd 'a' still been lyin' in the woods. They dragged me out on the pung."

"Logging? But I thought..."

"Well, The Little King got the sawlogs, but his crew left perhaps a hundred cords of pulpwood in pine and spruce tops all over the place. I can trim it up with an axe, haul it down to the roadside with the oxen, then take it on my truck over to the railroad siding to ship to the paper mill. 'Waste not, want not,'" he chuckled.

"The wisdom of Franklin," she agreed. "You should realize a few hundred dollars, then."

"Oh, of course." He paused. "I'd invite you in, but..."

"But a gentleman never takes a lady into his lair without a chaperone—or aren't you the world's tidiest housekeeper?" she teased.

"No, actually I keep a very neat house."

Amy thought Orin sounded a bit defensive. Then she remembered, and it was her turn to be embarrassed. The sole companion for this lonely man had been his grandmother for most of his life. Orin was uncomfortable when the companionship of a female passed from the intellectual to the social level.

"Wait here," Orin remarked, pointing with his cane to a split-log bench in front of the cabin. "I'll get you a cup o' pennyroyal tea."

Amy was tired from her hike, and she saw by her watch that it was after six. The climb to the exposed bluff could wait another day. As she drank her tea with Orin, she briefly told him about her disappearance and return.

"And you, how are you keeping yourself?" she asked, turning the conversation away from what she found tiring to talk about.

"God is good to me," Orin replied. "Better than I deserve. I've gone from being hated for being poor and so crazy I belong in a mental institution to being well-to-do and hated for my wealth."

"You're evidently not given to conspicuous consumption." Amy motioned toward the Model T.

"Best I could do, with the war on," he laughed. "Oh, they say there's late-model cars at the dealers in Bang-gaw. But they're bringing twice what they cost brand-new. You see, the Lord knew exactly what I needed. With this hurt knee, I have no way to climb up to my cabin where I can be alone, without this old crate."

Alone? Amy puzzled. How alone could one possibly wish to be? The mansion was empty now, except when Orin chose to spend a day or a night there. Orin was not merely "alone" in his cabin— he was virtually a hermit, the only sign of other human life being the distant boats on the sea. The only sound he could hear being the lowing of his cattle, the rush of Sabbathday Brook tumbling down its waterfalls to form a pool, then to gurgle across the meadow, then plunge in a series of rapids until it splashed past the mansion toward the bay.

"I couldn't drive up here with a streamlined model," Orin continued. "Which reminds me..." He slid off the bench and beneath his truck on the seat of his pants and began to tighten the brake bands. "There!" he declared at last. "Now I kin take you home in style!"

❧ ❧ ❧

"Orin Trask has hurt his knee," Amy told Mama that evening.

"I know. He was suffering so badly last Sunday that he missed church. First time he's missed since he was best man at Bill Wellington's wedding."

"Wilfred Wellington?" But that was a story Amy could catch up on later.

"Orin has spent some months supervising the renovation of his mansion, then directing the redecorating of the Federated Church," Mama told her. "And the Federated people ceased entirely to hold services right after Orin put a new roof on the building last year. According to the old records, his great-grandfather built it, and it reverts back to the Trask heirs, aka Orin, in just a few weeks."

"But you said Orin's been attending Papa's chapel?"

"Every service! He's among the candidates for immersion next month. We're using the millpond."

"But what does he intend to do with the Federated building?" Amy wanted to know.

"The community has taken it over—most folks think it belongs to the town of Portugal. They've used it for art fairs and plays. There's even been talk of tearing out the pews and holding dances." Amy could hear a tinge of disgust in Mama's voice. "But by Labor Day, it will be a year since church services have been held there—and the register of deeds says it's his. He intends to have a judge render an opinion, though."

Amy caught her breath. "That is such a fine building. Before I went to Italy, our chapel badly needed a new foundation. Does it still?"

"Papa says it's in such bad shape that the cheapest thing to do is to tear it down and build a new building," Mama sighed.

"What if Orin gives the Federated building to *his* church?" The possibilities awed Amy.

"We're hoping and praying, but the decision must be from his heart, in the Lord's will. Papa steadfastly refuses to approach him about it." Amy couldn't tell if Mama necessarily agreed with Papa's decision.

"I learned some marvelous things about God's dealings during my months as a nurse in the hospital in Munich," Amy consoled.

"But what will Orin do now that he's sold his timber? That money won't last forever."

"No-o-o-o," Mama said slowly. "And his life as a recluse is standing in the way of his adjustment to public worship. The Bible says that it's not good for man to be alone. We're trying to help him solve that need by getting him involved. He's very outspoken in Sunday school."

"Does he ask . . . intellectual questions?"

"He's worse'n Papa," Mama chuckled. "He knows his Bible— and he's read St. Augustine, Spurgeon, and about every Bible commentator between. He even invites Papa to come over and help him dust off some of the books in the library that belonged to Grandmother Trask's father, Professor Chamberlain—intellectually dust 'em, that is!"

"Maybe he should try college. It appears to be in his blood," Amy mused.

"Maybe he should *teach* college," Mama added wisely.

Orin Trask was a wild chestnut burr beginning to open, Amy decided. She would not be forward about helping where she was not wanted. But if God opened the door, she'd step through and help her reclusive neighbor emerge into the light of day.

19

Memorial Day

Amy awoke at six on the Saturday before Memorial Day to the "putt-putt-putt-putt-putt" of a two-cylinder John Deere tractor in the parsonage backyard. She stumbled sleepily to the window to see elderly Allen Keay, one of Papa's church members, bouncing along on the high seat of the old green machine, black furrows of garden soil turning up behind his double-bottom plow.

Only the evening before, Papa had squeezed Amy fondly, kissed both her cheeks, and teased, "Now that we've got another mouth to feed, we're planting a really *big* garden this year. And since you're not Popeye," he said tickling Amy's too-obvious ribs, "we're planting more than spinach! I've got a peck of o' Pontiac red potatoes for seed. They'll put some meat on your bones if you eat 'em with Orin Trask's Jersey butter!"

"You're right, Papa," Amy gladly agreed. Already she had gained back five of the pounds she had lost on the near-starvation diet of wartime Germany. Two pounds a week, Amy figured, would exchange skinny for svelte in four or five months.

It was no use to try to sleep with Keay's tractor clattering and coughing beneath her window, so Amy slipped on her dungarees—taking a tuck in the waist with a safety pin—grabbed a blouse, and headed for the kitchen. Papa was there already, sorting through garden seeds left over from last year. He had spread the stuff on the kitchen table, and he was busily collating it with the new packets of seeds which had just arrived from

W. Atlee Burpee Seed Co. "Papa, I thought you were waiting until Memorial Day to plant—that's the thirtieth, next Wednesday."

"Exactly so," Papa agreed. "But there's no rule that says I can't get *ready* today. There's tools to repair, rocks to pick in the garden, raking, and staking. Mama's coming to fix breakfast right away, and with Jack and Wessie's help, I want to tackle that garden as soon as Allen is done plowing and harrowing!"

This was not the Papa Amy had remembered from before the war. Mama was a doer. Papa was a thinker, given to long contemplations before action. Once in a while, the time for action had passed before Papa was finished with his planning and contemplating.

"What's happened to Papa?" He and the boys were busy with a wheelbarrow, removing stones from the freshly plowed garden plot as Amy helped Mama with the dishes.

"Papa . . . Papa spent a day alone with God just before you came home. He's been a kinder, nicer man ever since," Mama affirmed.

"But the energy?" Amy was perturbed. Papa's burst of physical vigor seemed to go beyond reason. "At nights he's *so* tired and gray."

"I know, Amy." There was worry in Mama's voice. "I . . . I think he's so happy to have you home that he can't contain his joy."

Memorial Day arrived, and Wes Andrews determined to take his family to the patriotic parade after all. "It's my war, too," Papa explained. "The Lord has given us our Amy again, and He let Andy die gloriously saving lives, rather than taking them."

❦ ❦ ❦

The flag went by, followed by a line of young men from all over Eastern Maine in World War II uniforms. Homburgs, fedoras, Panamas, straw boaters, and billed caps along both sides of the street were held over hearts as men who had been in the service and men who had not remembered their comrades who had given their lives for their country and the cause of freedom. Men—dozens of men—wept freely as they stood at attention, thinking, perhaps, that on Okinawa and in the Philippines where General MacArthur had returned as he said, the battle still raged and young men still died for the grand old flag of forty-eight stars and thirteen stripes.

A second flag went by, and this time the men who marched behind it were of Papa's generation: They wore puttees and breeches, American Expeditionary Force campaign hats, and natty, collarless jackets—those old soldiers who could still button them up! Springfield bolt actions with bayonets, instead of M-1 semiautomatics, were borne proudly on leather straps across their shoulders. It was too much. Papa found himself weeping uncontrollably as his mind reeled back a quarter of a century to the trenches of France. Had he dabbed his tears moments sooner, Papa would have seen that most of the other men of his generation were weeping as well.

A third flag came by, this one carried by a calvaryman with gray temples beneath the rumpled, high-crowned hat that had shielded his head from the Cuban sun of '98. Two others rode with him; their marching days were done, but they still sat tall in the saddle as they recalled chasing the Spanish tyrant from the Caribbean.

A fourth flag was waved bravely by a granddaughter of the Grand Army of the Republic from the front of Eddie Bessey's red convertible. As Eddie later told Amy, she "should have had the honor," but Amy was presumed dead at the time he asked the girl to ride with him. Gus Wiggin, bolt upright on the backseat, once again wore his blue flannel Civil War Union uniform which was faded and moth-eaten beneath his flowing full beard. He had laid down his sword and musket for pitchfork, axe, and scythe eighty years earlier. But as he had told editor Russ Cookson on his last birthday, "Pushing 105 is battle enough for any man."

❦ ❦ ❦

"One of these days, Lord willing," Papa remarked, "we're getting a garden tractor." He straightened up from digging the trench into which Amy was dropping seed potatoes, mopping his face with a handkerchief.

"That's what kids are for," Amy laughed. "And once we've moved on, you and Mama won't need such a large garden."

This was the third year Wes Andrews had planted a garden since coming to Portugal, and it was pretty much his only physical recreation. "What you need is a year-round activity," Doctor

Abbott had once warned him. "Take long walks. Or take up fishing. It's not much exercise unless your fishing hole is a mile back in the woods, but it gives a man a chance to relax from the pressures of dealing with people."

While Wes neither smoked nor drank, and his 180 pounds were well-distributed over a lean, six-foot-two frame, a bout of rheumatic fever as a teen had taken its toll on his heart. Though his only illnesses over the years had been the usual—the flu, colds, occasional bronchitis—times of heavy stress and lack of sleep would bring on what Mama termed "The grays." Papa had had the grays during the summer of '42, when he was trying to put back together the shattered crockery of his ministry in Lancaster County, Pennsylvania.

Irregular heartbeat and shortness of breath sometimes accompanied a pallid complexion at these times. Althea, remembering that her own father's death was preceded by long stretches of gray complexion, was concerned. "I feel fine. I'm just a bit tired," Papa argued. "Hard work never hurt any man."

The garden planting went well that Memorial Day, 1945— early and late potatoes, early, late, and mid-season sweet corn, Progress Number Nine peas, Burpee's Big Boy tomatoes (started indoors in March), Straight Eight cucumbers, squash (five varieties), cabbage, cauliflower, and Swiss chard. Then the beans: Tendergreen string, Kentucky Wonder pole, and Lowe's Champions for shelled beans. In all, half an acre stretching from the back porch steps to the outhouse comprised a garden plot which had tripled in size in three summers.

"Stuff grows so much faster in Maine than in Pennsylvania," Mama had noticed.

"A shorter growing season here is balanced off by longer hours of daylight," Papa explained. "If you plant a garden north of the Arctic Circle, you can plant at lunch, then harvest it in the afternoon for supper," he chuckled.

"We seem to have almost as many frost-free days here in Maine as further south," Mama mused.

"Actually," Papa said, "the Samoset Valley, and other Maine coastal regions protected by the hills, have a full month more frost-free nights than inland. We had tomatoes last year almost until October—remember? Folks over on Hardscrabble Road, back of the mountain, lost their tomatoes on the twenty-third of August." He rested, leaning on his hoe. "I'm having trouble breathing today. I think it's the damp ocean air."

But "trouble breathing" soon progressed to mild chest pains and shooting pains in Wes's shoulders and arms. Althea phoned Doctor Abbott, who agreed to come at once.

"Reverend Andrews," Doctor Abbott gravely intoned, folding his stethoscope, "you're having a heart attack. In my judgment it's not major, but it *could* become life-threatening if you don't get a few days' rest. Don't even *think* of preaching a sermon this Sunday. Thirty minutes' mild exercise twice a day, naps—half an hour to an hour without interruption—both morning and afternoon, and eight or nine hours in bed each night."

"What...what can you do for him, Doctor?" Mama asked.

"In such cases, it's what he can do for himself," the doctor replied. "Essentially, slow down. Your husband is not suffering from dietary abuse like most of my heart patients. But his childhood illness took an awful toll on his heart. And he must not get his blood pressure elevated, ever."

"I'll see you tomorrow, Reverend," Doctor Abbott turned to Wes. "If your heartbeat isn't regular within twenty-four hours, I'm putting you in Eastern Maine General Hospital in Bangor."

"*We'll* take care of Sunday services, Papa." Amy ran her fingers through her father's hair as he lay on the couch.

"It's too late to find a replacement." Papa was not grumbling, just being realistic. Until February, Reverend Heikes, a widower in his eighties who had pastored the chapel thirty years earlier, had been Papa's pinch hitter in last-minute emergencies. But Mr. Heikes had had a stroke, and though he lingered on, coherent, in a wheelchair, he would never preach the Word again.

❦ ❦ ❦

"How did it go?" Papa had been reading his Bible in the kitchen rocker when Amy, Jack, and Wessie arrived home from Sunday services on the third of June. Mama had gone only to Sunday school since she had a girls' class to teach, then Jack had brought her home because she felt a need to be with Papa. Mama was adding vegetables to a corned beef brisket boiling on the stove when the children returned.

"Great, Papa! I made pacifists of most of the congregation with my report of nursing for the Germans in Munich," Amy teased. "Actually, it was a testimony, sort of, of how the Lord took care of me and permitted me to serve Him, even as a prisoner. Jack's knees were knocking a little," she laughed, "but he got through his sermon—all ten minutes of it. He even got a couple of amens!"

"What did you tell them about me? You didn't make it sound too bad, I hope," Papa's forehead wrinkled with concern.

"We told them that you needed rest, prayer—and no phone calls for a week." Amy gently touched him on the arm. "Papa, tell me about Bill and Ruby Wellington."

"What's to tell? You already know about their wedding."

"The children," Amy continued. "Ruby has none, apparently."

"No. None at all. Wilfred has six."

"Mr. Wellington stopped me after church." Amy paused, then sighed. "He wants me to help him get his children back. Their grandmother has them, is that right?"

"Mrs. Bouchard is very protective of her grandchildren, and it's a very complex situation," Papa admitted. "I've suggested to Bill that he not sue. Though he could probably get the judge to give him custody, the lawsuit could open wounds which might never heal. His son, Donald, came back from the army, though he's not living with his father anymore."

"Should... should I get involved?" It was Amy's turn to grow concerned.

"Well, it's certainly not a case of meddling, since you've been asked. What does Bill propose?"

"That I go to see Mrs. Bouchard on his behalf. He thinks maybe I can sweet-talk some sense into her. He tells me she gets defensive around men."

"It's worth a try, Amy," Papa patted her hand. "Remember to be kind."

❧ ❧ ❧

"I'll bet you could use a baby-sitter once in a while," Amy found Janelle Bouchard smoking on her porch as the Wellington children played in a yard littered with dog bones, old tires, dented pots and pans, and broken toys.

"Would if I could afford it," Mrs. Bouchard squinted at Amy and blew her smoke into the air. "Help don't come cheap," she rasped. "Who the heck are you?"

"It's Miss Andrews, Gramma! She used t' teach in our school." The three oldest children screamed this out in unison while they hugged Amy for all they were worth.

"Well, if it ain't the devil in disguise!" Mrs. Bouchard hooted. "They sed you wuz dead, kilt in I-ta-ley. Sence we lost our Fannie, I bin wishin' I could meet y'."

"We . . . we tried to save her." The memory of Fannie still touched a place deep within Amy's heart.

"I knowed you did." Mrs. Bouchard sounded almost kind. "If it hadn't been f' that bullheaded daughter o' mine, we'd still have that precious child with us—Ruth too, prob'ly."

"Oh?" Amy was cautiously inquisitive. Was the old lady really placing the blame on Ruth, or did she wish to draw out Amy's opinion?

"You don't need t' be so close-mouthed about it, honey. I know Wilfred's got religion and joined y' ol' man's church. Seems to have done him some good, too." Grandma Bouchard took another drag on her cigarette before flipping it over the rail.

Amy mounted the final step to the porch and sat on the rail facing Wilfred's former mother-in-law, the grandmother of his children. She waited for Mrs. Bouchard to continue.

"The night Ruth got drunk and racked up that car that Wilfred 'd just fixed f' her, she come in here with the kids. 'I'm goin' out an' find me a man t' shack up with, Ma,' she sez, 'one with some hair on his chest.'" Mrs. Bouchard's voice grew tired as she recalled the final conversation between mother and daughter. "An' I sed, 'Ruthie, it's time you quit knockin' the husbin' God gave you around an' let him come home t' bed. You know well's I do he'd 'a' let that ministuh's dottah take Fannie to the hospital, ef you'd 'a' let him.'"

"Mrs. Bouchard," Amy quietly put in, "I remember the afternoon Mama and I met Doctor Abbott at the Wellington place. It's true, as you say, that Ruth resisted taking Fannie to the hospital. I distinctly felt at the time that Ruth wasn't emotionally capable of making such a decision. I'm sure hindsight is sharper than foresight, but it may be that Ruth's heart had been broken so many times and in so many different directions that she was actually in terror of having Fannie away overnight."

"Her ol' man died in the hospital—never bin sick a day in his life, before that." Mrs. Bouchard sighed. "Ruthie nevah got over it!"

"You've got a chance to set *some* of that right now, Grandma Bouchard," Amy softly pointed out.

"Ruthie's gone. No bringin' her back."

"Your grandchildren have a father. He loves them. And they love him, I'm sure."

"I dunno..." Mrs. Bouchard hesitated.

Amy silently asked the Lord for help, then she made a rash proposal. "Tomorrow morning at Whitcombs we'll have breakfast, just the four of us—you, me, Wilfred, and Ruby. I'm paying, and Mama will stay with the kids." Amy paused, trying to gauge Mrs. Bouchard's reaction. "This'll be a friendly visit. You won't have to discuss the children, unless you're ready to. You certainly can, if you wish, of course."

"I...I dunno." Janelle Bouchard was caught by surprise, but she was not without suggestion in regard to the children. "Per'aps Ruby could have the kids *most* of the time, if I could be sure they'd want t' visit their ol' grandma even one or two days a week."

The light of heaven lit Amy's eyes as she smiled at Grandma Bouchard. "The Lord, *He* knows what will make *all* of you happiest. Can I pick you up at eight?"

20

The Class Reunion

Will I ever call this place home? Amy folded one leg under herself as she sat that sunny June morning sipping a Coke in a wire-frame chair in the far corner of Whitcombs Cafe. She smiled with pleasure as she watched a group of teens tumble in, using both the IN and OUT doors at once, not intentionally rude, but in their youthful gregariousness not wishing separation from friends even for the split second it took to enter. Two of the boys wore identical seaweed-green school jackets with white sleeves. The white, intertwined letters SV boldly proclaimed that the young men were varsity players at Samoset Valley Classical Institute.

Amy ducked her head, dabbing at her tears. Only yesterday she had shoved an identical jacket to the back of Jack and Wessie's closet while helping Wessie move his clothing to make room for her stuff in the parsonage's upper room with the sea-facing dormer. "Andy" was emblazoned on that coat in white script, just above his varsity letter. Jack had declined to wear the garment, but Wessie, of a militant spirit like Andy, had claimed it, and he had been promised it by Mama as soon as he grew into it.

Amy smiled and nearly laughed now through her tears as she watched the group of five teens—two guys and three girls. These were clean-cut youth. Village kids, she thought, noticing the saddle shoes on the girls and the well-shined penny loafers on the boys. Though school was out for the summer, and dungarees had replaced creased trousers and pleated jumpers, village youth seemed determined to keep up an appearance. Farm teens wore sneakers.

Appearance, Amy thought. She had come home from Europe after watching men in khaki and men in green play games with Mausers and M-1s far more serious in consequence than baseball or basketball. Yet in these war games most of the players entered the fray with little more thought to their purpose than the sense of loyalty, pride, and camaraderie which motivated the bobby sox Sues and Wildroot Creme Oil Charlies who now sipped their sodas on the stools at the front of Whitcombs. But this is Portugal, Maine, and these kids are home, Amy mused. They belong here. In their hearts they can say, "This is my own, my native land," this little corner of America that most of them have never left for longer than a weekend.

Home! Where is *my* home? came painfully, almost audibly to her mind. While still a teen, she had been torn from her childhood home, the First Baptist manse in Comfort, Pennsylvania, by the unpleasant circumstances of Papa's employment. She had managed to hang onto some of the straws of what she often remembered as *home* by exchanging letters with school friends Hilda Neuenschwander and Karen Schultz, though gradually these letters came further apart and finally they ceased altogether. Grandpa and Grandma Andrews had, of course, continued faithful in their letter writing. She had even managed to visit them while on an R & R from Fort Dix, New Jersey, by catching a train to Lancaster for a weekend at what once had been Grandpa's dairy farm outside the city.

Can I ever really be home again? Amy cried within herself. She turned her attention now to the familiar seascape through Whitcombs' bay window. There were lobster boats bobbing at anchor in the harbor beyond the patio. An antique schooner left over from the last century, once a work horse of the seaports from Portugal to Boston, was moored to its own floating dock. It had retired, and now, glittering with brass and spar varnish, it was a rich man's plaything.

Farther down the harbor, at the water's edge, stood the ramshackle complex of Down East Canning Co.'s sardine dock, from where fish, once sorted, were shuttled by truck to the cannery on the millpond above the village for processing. A truck had just been loaded at the platform, and the driver, who from the distance appeared to be a tall, pipe-smoking fellow in billed cap and blue bib overalls, slammed shut its double back doors, clambered down the steps of the platform, and climbed into the cab.

Though the truck had a van body rather than a stake bed, its high snub nose, green paint, and gold lettering gave it the appearance of the Mack in which she and the rest of the crew had ridden daily to the blueberry barrens on Hogback Mountain in late summer, '42. Could it be? No. The cannery owned several similar vehicles. Just one of their fleet.

A puff of blue smoke from the stack behind the cab indicated that the driver had fired up the engine. Tiny in the distance, the truck with its load of fish began its ascent from the sea, climbing the grade like the trucks in the army convoy Amy had helped clutch and shift across the Apennines in Italy. Like me, Amy thought, those poor fish have been torn from their home while too young to resist, hardly to remember. Then she laughed silently at her own ridiculous comparison. The fish would soon be entombed in tin cans. But she was free to enjoy life, to follow her Lord.

Amy slurped the last liquid in her glass, the melted, Coke-flavored ice. How fine to enjoy the silliness of slurping ice on a hot day, Amy couldn't help but think. This is America; in Europe there are millions who have not so much ice as to keep their meager food supply from spoiling.

The low squeak of heavy brakes at the curb outside now caught Amy's attention. The lean, pipe-smoking truck driver swung from the cab, the extra-long, green transparent plastic visor of his cap shading his rugged features. He wore a sweat-stained tee shirt, and his rippling muscles caught her attention. Don't stare, Amy chided herself. She shifted her glance.

"Gimmie a brown cow in a paper cup, t' go," sang out the young trucker. "An' add a scoop o' ice. I want it t' last till I get this load o' sardines up t' the cannery."

"Gotcha," chirped the soda jerk, a young girl in a frilly red-checked dress and apron. Buried deep in Amy's subconscious was a memory which created jealousy at the girl's familiarity with the trucker. "Bet you'll be glad when y' ol' man kin hire a few GI's so's you kin sit with y' feet up an' enjoy the fan!" Memories from before the war began to shape in Amy's mind as she listened.

"Can't run a cannery with m' feet on the desk," the pipe smoker joked. The merry rumble of his voice gave her goose bumps.

The truck driver took his ice cream soda, but rather than hurry out the door, his deliberate footsteps moved closer to Amy's table. "Amy, is that you?"

Amy looked up at the young man, pipe in one hand, paper cup in the other. He stood grinning at her, his cap now pushed to the back of his head so that the visor pointed at the ceiling—and the cleft chin was pointed at her!

"Yes, it's me," she said through her smile. Amy rose and extended her hand. "I guess I can't ask a busy man to sit down— Mr. Bessey!"

"Eddie, if you please!"

"The Eddie I remember didn't smoke a pipe."

"Ayuh, there are worse vices—like runnin' over land mines." Eddie did not chuckle at his own wry humor, and Amy was unsure if he was teasing or dead serious. "Say, I've got a load of fresh fish that our line of packers is soon goin' t' need. But I'd like to talk with you. Kin I phone you this evening?"

"Sure. I'll be waiting."

❦ ❦ ❦

"We're all going to the academy alumni banquet Friday night," Mama informed Amy when she returned from her Wednesday morning trip to Whitcombs. Mama was still Mama. Two years in Europe had changed the daughter, but Mama had taken up right where she had left off. Amy was still her little girl.

"We?" Amy was still panting from pedaling Wessie's bike up the long grade from the village, and she could gasp out no more.

"Of course. All of us. Papa's heart seems back to normal, so he is bringing the address—if Doctor Abbott gives his okay this afternoon. He's been the academy chaplain since he gave up the principal's job, you know. Jack will be there as a newly graduated senior."

"Wessie?"

"Wessie's staying home," Mama reluctantly admitted. "I suppose he'll have 'Amos 'n' Andy,' and 'The Lone Ranger' on all evening. I guess if he listens to the 'Old Fashioned Revival Hour' with us, those radio operas don't hurt."

"I'm sure I would have welcomed even 'Inner Sanctum' as a replacement for Wagner's operas on the loudspeaker at the hospital in Munich," Amy responded. "Maybe I should keep Wessie company. After all, I'd be a stranger at the banquet."

"Oh, Amy. You missed Jack's graduation," Mama responded with a hurt tone. "I know it wasn't your fault," she quickly added.

Amy had seldom known Mama to cry, so the tremor in Mama's voice caught her by surprise. She hugged Mama, and they both were silent for several moments. Memories came with a rush. Though not having graduated, Andy would be remembered by Samoset Valley Classical Institute's alumni association as an honor alumnus, and Amy's absence from Jack's graduation had been overwhelmingly felt by every Andrews family member. "I . . . I'll be there. Should I wear my uniform?"

"There'll be a lot of young *men* in uniform. You certainly won't look out of place." Mama paused. "But you do what's best for you."

Did Mama mean about attending or about what to wear? Amy decided not to inquire at this point.

The phone rang at supper time, just as Papa had finished asking the blessing, thanking the Lord also for a clean bill of health from the doctor. Amy ran to the living room to answer it. "I'd be delighted, Eddie," Amy's parents heard her say. "The same red convertible? I'll be ready by five-thirty."

"Well, I guess with two invitations to the banquet, I can't refuse!" Amy chuckled, returning to the table. "But I'll be sitting with the class of '41—Eddie Bessey's class."

"We *could* make room for him at the head table, most likely," Mama worried.

Papa came to the rescue. "Seating Eddie with us at the head table could give a message to a lot of people which Amy's not ready to deliver."

"Thanks, Papa." Amy kissed Papa's cheek. "We'll congratulate Jack, and even slip over to sit with you folks during the awards ceremony. That's a promise."

❧ ❧ ❧

Papa chose Galatians 2:20, "I am crucified with Christ," as his text for the evening. Amy had not before heard Papa preach other than in church, and she sat nervously with Eddie Bessey wondering what her minister father would say. She was pleased that Papa had been appointed chaplain to this quasi-public high school, and she assumed that, as in the military, he functioned as an individual counselor or perhaps with a Bible club rather than as a minister to the whole school. The academy's directors had, in fact, made Wes Andrews chaplain over the objections of several strongly humanistic faculty members.

And how will Eddie receive Papa's sermon? Amy pondered.

Papa plainly pointed out that many folks lift this first clause of Galatians 2:20 out of context and try to support a sort of self-crucifixion as a means to earn their own salvation. "As an educator and a student of literature," Papa's voice was clear and strong, "I learned long ago the folly of evaluating an author's opinion on the basis of a single line of poetry or a single sentence from an essay. Longfellow's reference to 'footprints in the sands of time,' for instance, can be taken to mean that he believes that even the influence of 'great men' dies with them, since each changing tide erases all footprints; Longfellow, reared on the Maine coast, knew this well. Rather, he envisioned footprints of a more enduring nature, left far up the beach above the high-water line.

"And so it was with the words of Paul the apostle to these Gauls transplanted to Asia Minor," Reverend Andrews continued. "They were familiar with the Druidic religions of northern Europe, and with the pantheon of gods worshiped by the Romans and the Greeks. But God's high-water line is Christ crucified. Christ, who died, died unto sin once. By crucifixion with Christ is here meant an acceptance of His death, His blood, as our atonement, not in the re-crucifixion of our physical bodies by self-effort, but by recognizing ourselves as having died when He died, a death that becomes ours once and for all by faith, just as if we had been nailed to that cross. 'Having begun in the Spirit' of God—'born again,' as Jesus put it—you are 'foolish,' Paul writes, to attempt to improve on your already-paid-for salvation by your own fleshly efforts."

"This'll be the first time I ever danced with a sergeant," Eddie chuckled later that evening. Amy had decided to wear her uniform. It was part of her—at least for the present.

The speeches and the sermon were over, the awards had been given, and the boys of the junior class, with their fathers, were carrying the banquet tables off the basketball floor. "I came close once before, though." Eddie's eyes danced with amusement.

"When was that, Eddie?" Amy enjoyed their lighthearted bantor.

"When they took me to the Bangor armory for my physical. Doc said I had flat feet and couldn't march, so I didn't get drafted."

"You don't dance in boot camp—you drill," Amy chuckled.

"I expected as much," he agreed.

"But you won't need good feet once you take over the cannery. You can keep them on your desk," she teased.

"You've bin lis'nin' t' that girl in Whitcombs."

Amy laughed and did not answer.

"Don't sit under the apple tree with anyone else but me," the band now played merrily as several couples swung around the floor.

"C'mon. The music is hot and the night is young!" Eddie rose and held out his hands.

"I . . . I guess I'd rather sit. And I know where there's an old sweet apple tree to sit under—if it's still there."

"At Whitcombs—the one on the patio, beside the harbor?" Eddie questioned. "Say, that's where we wound up the last time I took you dancin'. I haven't sat there with a girl since!"

"Can we go?"

"You really don't want to dance?"

"No." Amy refrained from adding, "I'm sorry," for she felt no apology was needed.

"I've grown up some since we were here last, Eddie," Amy remarked when they had been served coffee and doughnuts on the patio by the sea.

"Actually you haven't—you've lost weight," he teased.

"You noticed. On boiled potatoes and an occasional Red Cross box, none of us got very fat at Stalag Prison Camp."

"Not like a concentration camp, I hope."

"Nothing like that. For the most part, the Germans kept the rules of the Geneva Convention on POW treatment. And with International Red Cross inspectors coming through regularly, they had little choice. Things were better at the *Luftwaffe* hospital in Munich, though, but by Geneva rules I wasn't even supposed to be there. But that's a *long* story," Amy sighed.

"Amy, why did you insist we come here? Not to continue your father's religious speech, I hope." There was no anger in Eddie's tone, but his point was plain. Papa's sermon, just as Amy suspected, had been seen as merely a "religious speech" to Eddie Bessey. The truth of the gospel had slid off him like salt spray off a lobsterman's oilskins.

"I need to talk." Amy did not say "we." She did not presume to know his needs. "I watched a lot of men die in Europe, and I became impressed that life is either meaningless, or that God is trying to tell me something about His purpose for my life."

"Marry, raise kids, give them a good chance in the world—then we grow old and die." Eddie was serious. "What more is there?"

"Some men die like in the movies. They go limp, their eyes dilate, they stop breathing."

"Pretty desperate, huh." Eddie was visibly shocked at Amy's description. He had met soldiers who had refused to tell him what the war had been like. Here was a WAC who was telling him more than he wished to hear.

"Others . . . others die in fear," Amy continued. "They feel pains beyond the physical world."

Eddie was silent.

"Then there are some, in pain or not in pain, who in trusting Jesus see beyond the grave. Though for years they have clung to earth, they gladly welcome death as merely a passage into a new life. 'Tell my mother I'll be there to meet her when it's her time'— I've written this for dying soldiers the same age as you and I. And I was glad to be privileged to write letters to these mothers and fathers, whether German or Allied." Amy spoke the last phrase in hushed tones, for she still found herself awestricken when she considered that spiritual conditions crossed boundaries of nationality so freely.

"I guess...I guess since you folks lost Andy it's hard to focus on things of this life." Eddie seemed to be trying to focus on Amy's theme.

"Life isn't fun and games, Eddie, though I do believe in having fun. No more Corn Borers' Balls, though."

"That one was a bummah," Eddie admitted.

Search me, O God, and know my heart today; Try me, O Saviour, know my thoughts, I pray: See if there be some wicked way in me: Cleanse me from ev'ry sin, and set me free. Why are these words running through my head? Amy wondered.

"Like that tune?" Eddie brought Amy back to the present.

"I...I wasn't listening," she answered, vaguely aware of the tinny loudspeaker in the branches of the apple tree above them.

"Play it again, Sam," chuckled Eddie, jingling a couple of nickels together in his hand. "I'll be right back." He hurried inside the restaurant.

Amy now heard the popping and snapping of records changing in the old jukebox. "Maori Melody," the tune of "Cleanse Me," came over the loudspeaker.

Eddie, smiling in the dim light of the Japanese lanterns hung about the patio, now stood beside their table.

"C'mon. One last dance. I want to remember this night always." He offered his hand.

Between the night of the Corn Borers' Ball and the night of the alumni banquet, Amy had graduated from making moral choices "because Mama and Papa say so" to standards that were personal, a part of her being.

"Thanks, Eddie. But no thanks." Amy answered frankly and decisively. "I can never let a man hold me like that again until I am married to him, 'until death do us part.'"

Eddie seated himself again at their table without further comment, but under his breath Amy discerned that he was singing the secular waltz version of the words which accompanied this tune: "Now is the hour that we must say good-bye." Her heart agreed.

Long after Eddie Bessey took her home, the "Maori Melody's" other refrain continued to haunt Amy: "Lord, take my life, and make it wholly Thine: Fill my poor heart with Thy great love divine; Take all my will, my passion, self, and pride; I now surrender: Lord, in me abide."

That evening, Amy sealed her decision to follow the Lord. From a bureau drawer where she had dumped a pile of old papers before leaving for boot camp, she pulled out a catalog and placed it with her Bible on the nightstand for perusal next morning. "Pilgrim Christian College, Lancaster, Pennsylvania," the catalog was titled.

21

The Beachcomber

Amy wrapped herself in the old-country heirloom patchwork quilt that Papa's German mother had given her parents long ago in Pennsylvania. She sat up, finding the braided rug beside her bed with her bare feet. At a quarter to five that morning late in August 1945, the sun's first rays had broken her fitful sleep. Like a soldier, she had slept in her underwear, and now she groped for her denim dungarees she had after midnight flung across the Saratoga steamer trunk she'd been packing beside her bed.

This room, with its seaward view, had been Amy's alone only for the three months since she had returned. The same day in May 1945 that Amy had stepped back into their lives, Wessie had moved into the bunk in Jack's room left vacant by Andy's death.

And Amy, after more than a year in Munich sleeping rolled in a threadbare blanket with patched sheets on a straw pallet, had used part of her military severance pay to purchase a Beautyrest mattress and box spring from the finest furniture store in Bangor. This was her only luxury; her only luxury, unless one considers that on days Papa spent holed up in his study with his books, Amy had almost a free rein with the posh, eight-year-old Packard sedan given the Andrews family their first winter in Portugal. She had taken on half a dozen pupils to tutor during their summer vacation, and between calls in their homes it was her joy to listen to the throb of the car's mighty straight-eight engine as it flattened the hills in the gravel roads around Samoset County.

Amy could not sleep this cool morning two days before leaving for Pilgrim Christian College, her parents' alma mater in Lancaster County, Pennsylvania. She and Papa had chatted late by a low fire in the kitchen stove about things long past in their lives before coming to Maine, about their common experiences in two world wars, about Papa's dreams for Samoset Chapel in its new home, the renovated, grand old Federated Church building, and about Amy's dreams for her future. "I really *have* no plans beyond college, Papa," Amy had insisted. "I'm taking a heavy Bible and social work concentration. I'm moving ahead only as the Lord leads."

"Mama thinks you should try nursing. You've had a year's practical experience at it in the army—even though you were a prisoner. There's room at Eastern General in Bangor, I've been told. The GI Bill would pay your tuition."

"Practical Mama!" laughed Amy. "But I certainly learned a couple of things about nursing in that German hospital in Munich. For one, I wouldn't want it as a career. Then, too, people have needs more real than merely physical, heart needs which medicine can't touch and won't cure." After a pause, she added, "What do *you* think, Papa?"

"I think you must follow your gleam, the gleam which God gives from His Word and the circumstances He sets you in. Not I, nor Mama, must take that from you. God has enabled me to light His lamp in this dark valley because I did exactly that." Papa rose from his chair at the table and extended a hand to Amy in the rocker by the stove. "Morning gilds the skies early Down East. After three years, I'm still not used to it, and the doctor says I've got to get to bed early if I'm going to rise early! I've got a busy day tomorrow."

Amy let Papa pull her to her feet, then she kissed the rough stubble on his cheek. "G'night, Papa."

As she pulled on her jeans and sweatshirt, Amy considered Wessie's record player on the dresser. A single-disk, 78-RPM recording of "Sentimental Journey" was cut back-to-back with "Throw Momma from the Train a Kiss." Even the musical mispronounciation of that Pennsylvania *Deutsch* phrase had not irked Amy as she played and replayed one side of the record then the

other until she had finally fallen asleep. In only two days, Amy
realized, she would begin her own sentimental journey, throwing her own kisses from the train in Bangor, not to *leave* "Pennsylvania Dutch" country, as the song stated, but to steam *toward*
it. Amy had awakened an hour earlier at a quarter to four to the
"pop...pop...pop" of the phonograph needle at the record's
end, and she had been unable to go back to sleep.

Amy now found her way to the ladder Wessie had nailed
in place from the back porch roof to the ground to provide himself a private entrance. But she did not descend at once, for this
was a Maine morning to savor. It had been a fogless and frostless
night, and with the tide at its ebb, Portugal Harbor, beyond the
point which sheltered Sabbathday Cove behind the parsonage,
stretched in a sheet of pure gold toward the breakwater, beyond
which the Bay of Fundy and the open ocean gleamed in glossy,
glassy splendor. Amy took all this in, then she sat on the roof's
edge, one foot on the ladder, studying the empty cove with its
beached boats.

Something about Sabbathday Cove at low tide had the power to
draw out Amy's very soul. Perhaps it had been fixed in her
memory as her first real experience with the sea that first August
morning in Maine three years earlier. Maybe it had been her
embarrassment at her brief, sudden encounter with the mysterious Orin Trask. Perhaps it was that Saturday in May, when angry at
Mama for criticizing Amy's decision to enlist, she had at low tide
found her way up Sabbathday Brook to the high stairs which
emerged onto the Trask patio where aged Mrs. Trask was tending
her peonies. Here, too, the dame of the old mansion had soothed
Amy's wounded spirits with food and pleasant chatter, painted
her wounded legs with iodine, then sent her home to the parsonage with a tale of the old lady's own war experiences, a story
of death and horror too sacred and hauntingly strange to repeat
until Amy understood it fully.

"Now I understand," Amy told herself, descending the ladder
and recalling the incident. "Now I understand," she said again,
half-aloud as she wound along the path toward the sea.

Amy paused at the grand, old wind-blasted hemlock with its
climbing rope by the cliff's edge. "The cove looks so...so naked

without its water," Amy decided at last, talking as much to God as to herself. She scanned the mucky flats but no clam diggers were out. Here a rusted bicycle frame encrusted with barnacles showed its ugliness; there, half an auto tire, no doubt once a bumper on the gunwale of a lobster boat, lay among the shells and stones, a disgusting reminder of the human tendency to create what humans cannot easily destroy.

But it was the utter nakedness of the seascape that riveted Amy's attention. In Italy during the war it had been her task to carry the bodies of the barely living off battlefields stained with human blood. Naked soldiers she had glimpsed on numerous occasions; not naked bodies, actually, for these were draped in khaki, but naked souls. These were the souls of dying young men like those Mrs. Trask and Papa had told her about from their experiences in the First World War.

"Naked came I out of my mother's womb, and naked shall I return thither," were Job's words when bereft of belongings and family. Amy had once childishly believed that this simply meant that you were born with nothing on, and "You can't take it with you" when you die. But the utter vulnerability of these dying soldiers, the barrenness of soul of which physical nudity is but a reflection, was what had impressed Amy in the war. Other medical people might go about tending bodies. But as death forced the dying to focus their thoughts on the few things in life which truly matter, as American soldiers and German aviators spoke their last words to *her,* as they shared with her alone their final thoughts, as she heard the cries of men breathing their last, their heads cradled on her knees, Amy had peered into the nakedness of human souls to share secrets which she herself could share only with God.

Amy's thoughts were on these experiences as she crossed the sandbar edging the muck of Sabbathday Cove then clambered over the ruins of the old boathouse. Sabbathday Brook held mysteries for Amy no longer, so she peered up its narrow gully only briefly.

Before her, now, was a slender beach strewn with stones of white quartz, red marble, shell fossils, and volcanic rock ranging from pebble size to boulders, stretching in a long arc which Amy had never explored. On the several occasions when she, her brothers, and girls from the village had gone to the cove to swim, the tide had been high and this beach, just across the mouth of Sabbathday Brook, was blanketed in salty waves. Only twice before had Amy ventured down the cliff at low tide, and on these occasions she had been otherwise distracted.

Amy now rolled her denim pants above her knees and waded across the shallow brook. Picking sandy pockets for her bare feet, she made straight for a point at the end of a sloping beach which dropped off so steeply that even at low tide only a narrow strip lay exposed. How utterly like human nature, Amy pondered, to hug to itself as much protection as possible and shrink from exposing its inmost soul even to those in whose loving concern it should confide.

A man in a broad-brimmed felt hat far down the beach beyond the bend caught Amy's eye as she reached the point. She knew this tall figure in bib overalls, lightly bearded in red, limping as he moved toward her. To some villagers, he was thought to be the ghost of Redbeard the Pirate, hanged from his own mast in Portugal Harbor nearly two centuries earlier. More sensible folks merely passed him off as "The Captain's crazy great-grandson."

To Amy, however, Orin Trask was sane and intelligent. She had even found him witty and charming company that May day she had climbed the mountain to escape the curious and inquisitive who wanted to gawk at Portugal's newest celebrity.

Amy scrambled atop a boulder and cradled her chin in her knees, watching the man. There are no clams this high on the beach, she knew. Still, he would bend with his clamming fork every moment or so, then limp toward her on his unequal legs.

Embarrassment crept over her as she realized Orin had seen her at last, though he seemed in no hurry to get there. Though Amy had come to know Orin fairly well through the letters they exchanged during the war, there was something about a beach rendezvous which left her ill at ease. Her mind returned to the moment when he had surprised her at dawn in her nightgown, and remarked, "September Morn," as they passed. Though this was an artistic allusion, Amy was both thrilled and frightened at the vulnerability the memory of his quote now awoke in her mind. Why would she, who had held dying men on battlefields far away, suddenly fear meeting a neighbor, a fellow church member whom she saw at least weekly, in her own backyard practically? The feeling she found herself now fighting was both fearful and wonderful, and Amy could not decide whether she enjoyed it more than she feared it.

Orin had known for some time she was there, Amy was sure. But he continued to pick things up with his fork until he seemed satisfied he had enough. At last, quickening his limping gait, he strode directly toward her boulder. "So we meet in strange places again." Orin's smile was warm. "I'm sorry there are no angry wild bulls to chase off this time."

"A wild bull walrus or fierce sea lion, maybe? But you're not clamming?" Amy queried, noticing the shells and stones in his basket.

"I seldom dig clams now, unless I want to eat them, of course. Just some of God's handiwork to garnish my artwork," he said, indicating the basket's contents. "I don't lack for money now, thanks to your father and Prince Thurston."

"What will you do now—retire on your riches?" Amy giggled nervously. She found herself amazed at how easily she rattled on about matters which now were really nobody's business but Orin's.

"'Retire' is an odd word to describe a man just starting his career, don't you think?" Orin grinned at her. "I've been wanting to give my painting the professional touch that would enable me to live by my talents and use them to honor the Lord. Though I'm used to having little, the concept of the 'starving artist' fails to fascinate me. And since Grandmother Trask died, I've nothing to hold me to the old place."

"But what will you do?" Amy wondered if the high pitch of her voice communicated more concern than Orin would feel was appropriate.

"I've got just enough money left from the lumber sales to pay for a year at the New England Conservatory of Art, in Boston— now that I've spent most of it putting a new roof on that big ark," he said with a nod toward the mansion's gleaming copper roof which rose above the bluff along the beach.

"It does spruce up our neighborhood," Amy laughed. "Folks in town are saying they're glad that the grandest set of buildings in the valley isn't going to be allowed to fall into ruins."

"The grandest in all eastern Maine," Orin corrected truthfully. "My great-grandfather built the finest place east of Bangor, and I'm saddled with keeping it up," he sadly remarked.

"What . . . what will you do with the place?"

"Close it while I'm gone to school, then perhaps sell it to rich summer people looking for a vacation home. With a nice cabin up on the mountain, I don't need the manse. How'd you like a job as a caretaker this winter?" he added, grinning.

"I . . . I'm going to college."

"Great!" Orin's enthusiasm was sincere. "I was teasing about the caretaker bit," he added.

"I wouldn't know how to keep house in such a monstrous mansion. I've never even been inside," Amy wistfully admitted.

"I . . . I'd like to show you my landscape paintings—they're in my parlor. Perhaps someday . . ." Orin's voice trailed off, hesitant, embarrassed at his suggestion that she come with him to the manse.

"Really, I can't," Amy tried to smooth over the awkward moment. "It's past seven. I should go right home and start breakfast."

"You'll not go back by the way you came, nor will I," Orin observed. He pointed to where the point of land she'd passed on her way to the rock-strewn beach was already being lapped by the waves of the incoming tide.

"I hope we're not stranded until the next low tide." Amy viewed the clay-and-rock banks behind them which seemed to rise nearly straight up to the highway shoulder above.

"No problem," Orin answered. "There's a good spot by that big spruce growing out of the bank, with plenty of exposed roots for handholds. And I see you're wearing your climbing shoes," he chuckled, noticing Amy's bare feet.

Atop the cliff, Amy paused with Orin as they caught their breath. The parsonage beckoned just beyond the bridge over the ravine through which flowed Sabbathday Brook. But the Trask Mansion rose stately above two flights of wooden stairs leading up from a roadside mailbox with "O. TRASK" on it in neat letters. The old house was glorious now, every pane of glass aflame with reflections of the sun rising from the sea. It seemed to Amy that Elijah himself could not have had a more impelling desire to visit heaven when bidden to enter the flaming chariot drawn by horses of fire.

Hesitant to break the wonderful spell of the morning, Amy finally turned to her neighbor ... her friend ... and said, "Orin, have you had breakfast?"

"No ... no, I haven't," he admitted.

"Come on," she urged. "Join my family this morning." She gently tugged on his sleeve. "I'm sure Mama would love to see your landscapes after we eat. And so would I."

❦ ❦ ❦

The "Flying Yankee" passenger train barreled along the Sebasticook River Valley from Bangor toward Waterville, Boston, and Pennsylvania to the southwest as Amy watched the late-summer landscape of inland Maine sweep past. But the panorama of her mind swept through her brain with more vivid hues than the blue rivers, white houses, gray-shingled barns, and maples turning to scarlet outside her coach. Behind her in Portugal in the Valley of the Samoset was the little world of Mama, Papa in fragile health, and their struggling church. Wessie now was nearly a young man. Jack was all but an adult. She wept briefly as she remembered the white marble commemorative stone with, "Andrew Andrews, 1926-1945—Until the Last Trumpet Shall Sound," in little Maple Grove Cemetery on the side of Hogback Mountain. Andy *had* been buried at Flanders, to Papa's infinite satisfaction, the family had learned. "At that 'meeting in the air' it will make no difference where our bodies were buried," Papa declared. "What's important is that we are ready to hear the Lord's trumpet when we die."

Then there was Eddie Bessey—good old good-time Eddie, who no doubt would one day be little Portugal's biggest citizen. Amy had feelings for him no more; only with difficulty could she even call to mind the evening when they had said good-bye to the strains of "Maori Melody" on the seaside patio behind Whitcombs Cafe.

Amy unsnapped the leather Bible case she held in her lap and slid forth a new, gilt-edged reference Bible, given her by Papa and Mama as a going-away gift. From inside the cover she pulled forth an ordinary-looking brown envelope, of the type school report cards are sent home in. She had found it tucked into the screen door that morning as Papa was loading the Packard for the trip to the depot in Bangor. Her first name only was on the outside, and something within her heart had constrained her to wait for a special occasion to open it.

Amy slit the envelope open with a bobby pin. She drew forth a stiff sheet of drawing paper, neatly folded in half. She held her breath as she studied the India-ink artwork on the page: It was a drawing of their Cape Cod parsonage with its porches, front and back, the garden, even to the weeds, the Packard in the drive— every detail down to the outhouse and Wessie's bike carelessly dropped in the backyard. It showed a seagull resting on a clothes-line post, exactly as Amy had seen many a morning before breakfast. This bird's-eye view, obviously drawn from the verandah of the Trask Mansion, showed Sabbathday Cove and Portugal Harbor at low tide, the stranded boats, the breakwater and lighthouse, and the Bay of Fundy islands beyond.

But what fascinated Amy most was the silhouette of a disheveled man in boots and bib overalls bending over a clamming fork far out from shore beside a seaweed-shrouded boulder.

The sketch was signed, "Orin Trask."

Amy turned the paper over to find a two-word note: "Please write." The note was likewise signed, "Orin," followed by an address, "New England Conservatory of Art, 17 Tremont St., Boston, Massachusetts," in neat calligraphy.

About the Author

Eric Wiggin is a full-time writer who has also been a pastor, schoolteacher, and journalist. His latest books include a series based on Rebecca of Sunnybrook Farm and *The Heart of a Grandparent*. He and his wife, Dot, make their home in rural Michigan with their youngest son, Brad.

Harvest House Publishers

For the Best
in Inspirational Fiction

RUTH LIVINGSTON HILL CLASSICS
    Bright Conquest
    The Homecoming (mass paper)
    The Jeweled Sword
    The South Wind Blew Softly (mass paper)

June Masters Bacher
PIONEER ROMANCE NOVELS

Series 1
1 Love Is a Gentle
   Stranger
2 Love's Silent Song
3 Diary of a Loving Heart

4 Love Leads Home
5 Love Follows the Heart
6 Love's Enduring Hope

Series 2
1 Journey to Love
2 Dreams Beyond
   Tomorrow
3 Seasons of Love

4 My Heart's Desire
5 The Heart Remembers
6 From This Time Forth

Series 3
1 Love's Soft Whisper
2 Love's Beautiful Dream
3 When Hearts Awaken

4 Another Spring
5 When Morning Comes Again
6 Gently Love Beckons

HEARTLAND HERITAGE SERIES
    No Time for Tears
    Songs in the Whirlwind
    Where Lies Our Hope
    Return to the Heartland

Brenda Wilbee
SWEETBRIAR SERIES
Sweetbriar
The Sweetbriar Bride
Sweetbriar Spring

CLASSIC WOMEN OF FAITH SERIES
Shipwreck!
Lady Rebel (coming 1994)

Lori Wick
THE CAMERON ANNALS
A Place Called Home
A Song for Silas
The Long Road Home
A Gathering of Memories

THE CALIFORNIANS
Whatever Tomorrow Brings
As Time Goes By
Sean Donovan

THE KENSINGTON CHRONICLES
The Hawk and the Jewel

MaryAnn Minatra
THE ALCOTT LEGACY
The Tapestry
The Masterpiece (coming Winter 1994)

Ellen Traylor
BIBLICAL NOVELS
Esther
Joseph (mass paper)
Moses
Joshua

Other Romance Novels
The Hills of God, *Wiggin*

Dear Reader:

We would appreciate hearing from you regarding this Harvest House fiction book. It will enable us to continue to give you the best in Christian publishing.

1. What most influenced you to purchase *The Hills of God*?
   ☐ Author   ☐ Recommendations
   ☐ Subject matter   ☐ Cover/Title
   ☐ Backcover copy   ☐ _____

2. Where did you purchase this book?
   ☐ Christian bookstore   ☐ Grocery store
   ☐ General bookstore   ☐ Other
   ☐ Department store

3. Your overall rating of this book:
   ☐ Excellent   ☐ Very good   ☐ Good   ☐ Fair   ☐ Poor

4. How likely would you be to purchase other books by this author?
   ☐ Very likely   ☐ Not very likely
   ☐ Somewhat likely   ☐ Not at all

5. What types of books most interest you? (Check all that apply.)
   ☐ Women's Books   ☐ Fiction
   ☐ Marriage Books   ☐ Biographies
   ☐ Current Issues   ☐ Children's Books
   ☐ Self Help/Psychology   ☐ Youth Books
   ☐ Bible Studies   ☐ Other _____

6. Please check the box next to your age group.
   ☐ Under 18   ☐ 25-34   ☐ 45-54
   ☐ 18-24   ☐ 35-44   ☐ 55 and over

Mail to: Editorial Director
Harvest House Publishers
1075 Arrowsmith
Eugene, OR 97402

Name _____

Address _____

City _____ State _____ Zip _____

**Thank you for helping us
to help you in future publications!**